PAVEMENT

"I will encounter darkness as a bride,
and hug it in mine arms."

Measure for Measure. Act III, scene 1.

PAVEMENT

Richard Butchins

Cutting
Edge
Press

Acknowledgements:

Dr F: Without you – this would not exist.

I should like to thank my editor Dan Berlinka: "Thank you" and my publisher Martin Hay.

I extend my love and deepest regret to Cate. I also express my gratitude to everyone who has helped me in one way or another, either intentionally or otherwise.

"Death as the destruction of all things no longer had meaning when life was revealed to be a fatuous sequence of empty words, the hollow jingle of a jester's cap and bells." Michel Foucault

A Cutting Edge Press Paperback Original

Published in 2014 by Cutting Edge Press

www.cuttingedgepress.co.uk

Copyright © Richard Butchins

Printed and bound in Great Britain by Biddles

ISBN: 978-1-908122-65-0
E-PUB ISBN: 978-1-908122-66-7

Somewhere in London

Chapter 1: **Broken Bond**

There are one thousand two hundred and sixty seven paving slabs between my room and the Essex Road. The large three foot by two foot paving slabs. Yorkstone, diamond-sawn, is the preferred paving slab for this borough. There is one painted zebra crossing; the other roads have between twelve and sixteen terracotta blister-paving slabs at the point where the road joins the pavement. I have not counted the half-size slabs or the occasional section of smaller fifteen inch by fifteen inch slabs as double, they are all counted as the same size. I tread these streets every day. I am familiar with the pavements, alleyways and subways. I am on intimate terms with the zebra crossings. I am a long-time associate of many public buildings: I can tell you which of them are warmest in winter and the coolest in summer, where you can get a free cup of tea, which of the bookshops you can steal from, and where the security guards are most unfriendly. I also have a sound grasp of the construction techniques and materials used in the making of pavements.

In short, I walk.

Often I will stroll to London Bridge. The views from London's bridges are one of the highpoints of my day, particularly early in the morning with little traffic, the distant sounds of the city and the lights reflecting on the water. I watch my life reflected in this grey water rushing out to sea, being carried away like so much flotsam on the tide; perhaps I'm that plastic bottle or that nondescript piece of wood. By noticing these bits of floating rubbish, I'm paying them more attention than anyone or anything in the world pays me. I'm becoming less visible as every day goes by. Yesterday, as I was walking to the National Gallery in Trafalgar Square, my reflection disappeared in the window of a Starbucks. I stopped and searched for it but it was nowhere to be seen.

Perhaps it's an optical illusion, but nobody reacted to me staring at the window either. Then it happened again while I was loitering by a bus stop at the top of Whitehall, the south end of Trafalgar square. I don't catch a bus often because I never have to be anywhere, except the Job Centre to sign on, or the doctor's. But I'm at the bus stop and a gaggle of American students walk past. They're in their early teens, all teeth braces and puppy fat, they look straight at me, that is, they stare through me – I don't register in their eyes in any way. I am invisible.

I walk down Whitehall past the Cenotaph and the outsize statue of Field Marshal Montgomery to a section of pavement that's being re-laid. It being Whitehall they are using Portland Stone, from the Isle of Portland in Dorset. Vast slabs of limestone laid on a bed of builder's sand and supplied by Stone Firms Ltd, upmarket as far as the world of paving goes. It's the stone used in the Cenotaph and St Paul's Cathedral; even the Tower of London was built with it. It's regal and royal – the paving slab of kings – well, of civil servants at least. It's attractive and gives an enjoyable walking experience. By the time I arrive at Westminster Bridge road, it's back to regular concrete aggregate slabs. I decide not to cross the river at Westminster Bridge but walk further to Lambeth Bridge. I prefer the view of the Palace of Westminster from there and there's less to be seen of the appalling Millennium Wheel. It's not the usual view, the one from Waterloo Bridge, the one on the postcards the tourists buy.

After crossing Lambeth Bridge and passing Lambeth Palace I cut back to my left, parallel to the river, past blocks of red brick local authority housing until I reach Kennington Road. Across the wide street is the domed and distressing Imperial War Museum, which, once upon a time, was a Victorian lunatic asylum that gave its name to a noun – Bedlam. I've walked past it many times, though I never venture inside. With its twin fifteen inch naval guns outside poised and ready to bombard the City of London, it does not attract me and there are always large noisy parties of schoolchildren visiting; they are tiresome to the Invisible as they jostle and stamp and shove. It seems a strange place to take children, this building which venerates the act of war whilst dancing on the ghosts of the insane and demented. I continue walking along Lambeth Road towards the roundabout with a miniature obelisk in the middle. The column has "... erected in the XI year of the reign of George the Third" etched into one side of the column; on the other three sides is engraved the useful information about how far the column is from "... Fleet Street, one mile CCCV feet; Palace Yard, Westminster, one mile; London Bridge, one mile XXXX feet". The derelict Duke of Clarence pub and a row of houses stand on the corner. The houses have boards along the front on which are painted brightly coloured murals depicting the same houses as if they were being joyously occupied, which they are most definitely not; they belong to South Bank University which is going to knock them down to redevelop some additional student accommodation. Its only recent resident had been a tall imposing man called Jason, an ex-RAF engineer. He'd squatted the buildings, installed power and opened them up to young artists who had 'pop-up' art exhibitions until he was evicted. It was the haunt of many young and oh-so-clever radical art students. I visited it once and was visible by virtue of the fact that, as a middle aged man, I might be someone important in the art world. Of course, when they realised I wasn't, my visibility faded.

I turn left and walk north on Waterloo Road towards Waterloo Bridge. The pavements in SE1 have a mix of paving slabs, small square ones measuring fifteen inches and larger ones, varying from two foot eleven inches by one foot eleven inches, a rather odd size, to the largest at four feet by two feet. In fact, if you bother to examine the ground beneath your feet you will find the pavements of the city to be a complex and varied set of structures that link and discriminate between different boroughs and social strata. The paving of Whitehall differs in quality, style, construction, ingredients and demeanour from that of, for example, Tower Hamlets.

I walk along Waterloo Road, past Webber Row, Barons Place, and Gray Street on my right. Just past Gray Street is a stone frieze on a boarded up building. It reads: Go forth to every part of the world and proclaim the good news to the whole Creation. There's no context for this statement so I choose to feel that it describes the pavements along which it stands, and the need to proclaim the good news of their creation. I walk along the road, nobody noticing or seeing me – as usual. A tall young black man, wearing his hurry and impatience as badly as his ill-fitting suit, collides with me and stumbles on without looking, muttering something about being sorry that he didn't see me. Of course he didn't see me. I pass the Old Vic Theatre on the other side of the road; I have never been inside. I cross Bayliss Road and on the corner is a cheap bookshop called Book Warehouse. It contains many fascinating books at 'low low prices'. I sometimes go in and buy a £2.99 book, or steal one if I can't afford £2.99. I have no money, I survive on welfare, on government handouts, and I'm a scrounger in the eyes of many, a most undeserving case indeed. I contest this and argue I am incapable of working in most environments either through physical and social disability or lack of appropriate education.

I don't go into the bookshop. I carry on walking toward the huge Imax cinema just before the Bridge. This used to be the location of Cardboard City – I lived there once for four months, in a construction made from Fortnum and Mason cardboard boxes and old blankets, a kind of homeless hamper. Now they have constructed a giant temple to fantasy, and crushed a cardboard community in the process. I haven't been inside the cinema.

I head onto Waterloo Bridge, passing the grey concrete bunker that's the Hayward Gallery and the South Bank complex. If Hitler had designed the South Bank this is what it would look like, a series of sea defences in Normandy moved to London.

On the bridge a cold and a bitter wind whips along the Thames lifting small pieces of litter, paper, plastic bags, and fancy recycled paper cups from coffee chains. All this trash is blown at speed across the Bridge, getting trapped on the fencing that stops pedestrians using the pathway due to repairs. They're re-laying the paving slabs. Copies of the free paper, Metro, flap against the fences and a paper cup hits me on the head on its way to Kingston-on-Thames.

I pull my hat further down on my head. I lose at least 4 hats a year. Black woolly beanie hats like those used by gang members and robbers. I like them, they keep me warm, and with the cheap waxed black jacket / coat that I wear I never get harassed – guess I look like a tramp or a mugger. The hats gloves and scarves keep getting lost, I lose them all. Often you can see me – or rather, if I was visible you could – wearing mismatched gloves, which I find outside subway stations, and unusual scarves which I often find tied to lampposts.

I cross Waterloo Bridge; the pavement is three large and two small paving stones wide with a pretty gully of eight-inch bricks between the two foot square and fifteen inch square slabs. On my left are the Houses of Parliament – the Palace of Westminster to give it its proper name. In front of them is Charing Cross Railway Bridge with its new footbridge alongside it. I have always thought Charing Cross Bridge is the most romantic of London's bridges. I used to love the old soot-stained, blackened footbridge running alongside the railway bridge, and the way that you could watch the trains as they drifted in and out of the station, through the struts of the bridge they flow like an old movie, stuttering and jittering in and out of Charing Cross. I remember, as a child, watching them at dusk with the lights inside the carriages flickering past. In those days I was highly visible, a small child glued to the railings staring at the trains snaking past, oblivious of the drop to the dark rushing waters below. Passers-by would stop and check to see if I was accompanied by an adult or that I was not lost, or any number of worthwhile things.

Charing Cross.

A monochrome bridge. A black and white movie. A steam-wreathed symbol of love. Now, however, the white masts of improvement that signify the new footbridge – out with the old and in with the new – they've dissipated the bridge's romantic mystery. The soot and smoke washed away by New Labour, replacing the work of the past with the fury of the future. The steam has evaporated and the scene is in a beautiful nouveau colour, all romance denuded by a downpour of modernity with a massive full stop at the end of the bridge: the Millennium Wheel, like some child's Meccano construction with its pods of tourists slowly rising and tumbling through the sky like flies in test tubes.

I look away and, on the other side, I see Blackfriars Bridge choking in the grip of the never-ending Thameslink rail development, promising bigger and better. Beyond that, the dome of St Paul's Cathedral – all that Portland stone – and then the Gherkin. I have no idea what that building is for but I suspect it's the top half of a rocket-ship for the Gods of Finance to recline in as they blast off into the stratosphere to their palaces in the sky, high up beyond the likes of me. We cannot reach, nor even gaze upon their glory. Were it to be visible to people like me, it would cause unending pain and our souls would be rent from our bodies and thrown down into hell.

I flick my head back, the cold wind piercing my skin with stinging needles of cold water. It complements the pain I feel inside: a pain that isn't physical, a pain I've felt all my life, a pain that's continued to grow as relentlessly as my toenails and is as impervious to pruning as they are.

I come off the bridge onto Lancaster Place. As I walk into the lee of the buildings, the wind drops and the pain in my face lessens. There is the Strand underpass: I have never been through it, you cannot walk through it, so I head to the Strand and round the Aldwych, avoiding being mown down by cyclists, those sanctimonious parasites of the highway. I walk up Kingsway, which just may be the most dreary road in London, certainly in central London, a tree-lined testament to boredom in stone and glass. Taxis jam the road and the lights are beginning to come on. Past Keely Street and Great Queen Street with a Starbucks on the corner, again no reflection.. Onwards through crowds of commuters, I have to weave and swerve to avoid them, their eyes failing to register me. Eventually I stand still, and am rammed into by two fat ladies, one wearing an enormous pink tracksuit and puffa jacket, the other in a suit and raincoat. Both are carrying briefcases, my leg is gashed.

"Fuck off, you fat fucking cows!"

The one in Pink ignores me. The other looks round perhaps seeking the source of the words, but shrugs and walks on. I limp over and sit on the steps of some building built in a pseudo ancient Greek style, my legs bleeding, the right leg of my jeans turning reddish black.

"Invisible. Fuck, it's not all it's cracked up to be."

I stem the bleeding and limp on my way along Southampton Row. I'm about thirty minutes or so from my room, maybe forty-five if the leg does not improve. I limp past the window of RG Lewis, the Camera shop with its display of Leica and other cameras. They sit, black and squat in the window, like self-satisfied insects. I used to be a photographer once, a long, long time ago. I would like to have a camera, one of the new digital ones – no need for film or expensive chemicals and darkrooms – just a card and a laptop. How amazing. People don't recognise the fantastic nature of this because they have yet to have it removed. I will not try to pretend life was better years ago when I was younger. It looks much better now – if you're visible that is. I'm not, so it's worse. I carry on limping, though it hurts less and I can walk faster now. I head towards Russell Square. Russell Square always seems to promise more than it can deliver: with the rump of the British Museum in one corner and the arse of London University in the other, it always feels full to the brim with intellectual excreta. The gardens are dull and bleak, the railings keep nothing in and let nothing out. I trudge past them into Bedford Way, a boring concrete street not worthy of remark. The pavement here echoes the dismal nature of the buildings, concrete slabs two foot by two foot laid all the way along the street, interspersed by lacklustre plane trees. The saving grace of this street comes on the right, just at the very end of the road. A place called Bloomsbury Lanes, a subterranean bowling alley. The place is encased in the 1950s; to walk inside is to travel back in time to a world of bowling, baggy trousers and bad hair, though every period in the past always has worse hair than the current one. The basement building has seedy sofas and dirty bowling lanes, eight in number. I rarely go there now but I have been – it's a testament to people always wanting to be in the past that this recreation of a non-existent reality has been built, and it is used to extract money from people living in a disaffected present. It's under the Tavistock Hotel and next to an underground car park. The entrance is painted a sickly cream and has two atrocious paintings, one either side of the door, showing a man and a woman in bowling poses; it has a decrepit charm. I turn right, my limp has lessened and it's easier to walk. I trundle out of Tavistock Square onto Tavistock Road and past the beautiful Mary Ward House, a fascinating building built in the late nineteenth century by the wealthy philanthropist Passmore Edwards. Mary Ward, the novelist and social reformer, was the inspiration behind an attempt to provide training, care and entertainment for the less fortunate in society. Now such unfortunates as Microsoft, Marks and Spencer, Nokia and the BBC use it. The building brightens my darkening mood, which matches the darkening clouds overhead as they start to spew out spiteful rain into my face. The walk through Bloomsbury toward King's Cross and up the hill to the Angel is uneventful, as are pretty much all my walks. Being invisible makes for uneventful walking, unless the pavements are crowded. Of course, there are landmarks: Clerkenwell Magistrates Court is now a hostel for foreign students learning English. The building where

I received my first criminal conviction is now given over to the construction of sentences of a different nature, many of them, I suspect, also in the past. I bypass the Angel to get to Colebroke Row and the Regent's Canal tunnel. The tunnel is not so much a landmark as an invisible wound a half a mile long under the hill of affluence that comprises Angel Islington. The Regent's Canal is now desirable, the rich and affluent rush to pay a premium for a touch of designer poverty-chic in their apartments, some cracked plaster, a bare stone wall or floor, a hatch in the wall, or something that smacks of Dickensian London, but without the smell or the shit that went with it. Even today's poor don't smell, so things are getting better. I walk down Colebroke Row, so desirable and well-paved. I cut down Noel Road and swing left past the Zenith bar, and then the now boarded up Packington Estate. This used to be the unpleasant part of the Angel, if an angel has any unpleasant parts. Divinity, in the form of the Council, decided to knock it down and replace it with a more desirable set of buildings. Those council bureaucrats must be the only people on earth unaware of the irony of trying to redesign an angel. A few more twists and turns, and I'm in sight of the battered door with the peeling green paint that marks my home. I'm back; it engenders only a feeling of bleakness.

Chapter 2: **Home is Where a Heart Beats**

This is where I live. I have lived here for more years than I'd like to count although as a matter of fact it is twelve. Twelve years.

"Is this home?"

It is where I live, I suppose in that sense it's my home, but not in the common perception of home as somewhere that involves roots, happiness, congeniality, or at least comfort and a refuge from the world. In that respect this is no home, it provides no emotional solace, nor does it bear any trace of tenderness. It does provide shelter from the elements. I include people as one of those undesirable elements; they assault my senses with all the shock of a winter storm.

I have one room in the basement of a four-story Victorian terraced house. The house is divided into bedsits. Mine is about twelve feet by nine feet. It has a small wet-room attached with a toilet and shower inside. There is a two-ring electric stove on top of a cupboard in the corner; a small bed and a chair, table and chest of drawers, a rail in the alcove that serves as a wardrobe. The room is dark, the basement and hallway are dark, painted white years ago and now dirty grey, drifting into brown along the architrave and across the ceiling. A single bare light bulb hangs from a twisted cord; the illumination it provides is fitful. The floor is carpeted with a stained beige rag of a carpet, threadbare in more places than it retains its weave. The wall has a host of disjointed letterboxes nailed to it. I don't check mine, there is no point, there's rarely anything inside. The hallway is not dirty; it's just worn out and tired. The stairs are the same; they are in the winter of their years and have seen better days and happier feet. I walk down the twisting staircase to the basement and the short hallway at the end of which is the door to my room, the room next door, and the adjacent door to the yard outside. The yard always feels dark even when the sun is shining. There's something about this house that hoards the dark and cold, even on the sunniest, brightest, warmest August day. It's as if the house were invisible and impermeable to any kind of future. It's the perfect place for me.

I unlock the door to my room. It's a heavy brown fire door with a closer on the inside. All the rooms have them, they help keep the noise out and fire, if we have one, which would be surprising considering how damp the house is. There are 13 rooms in the four-storey house, a rabbit warren of lost hope and denial. I sometimes hear people arguing or the sound of their TVs. There is a room next to mine with its door facing the bottom of the stairs. I have never heard any sound from it, perhaps it's empty – I don't know and I don't care. I push open my door. As I walk inside, I flick the light switch, the light stutters and then, as if with a sigh, sheds a grey light on my world. I close the door to the rest of it – this is my true world, this small room.

Inside, the window shutters are closed, they're always closed, and a red velvet curtain embossed with a fleur-de-lys pattern hangs across the shutters like a damp lettuce leaf. It's warmer with the shutters closed and the curtain hung up; the trade-off is that the room is always dark. I like the dark at night when not even a smidgen of light can penetrate, though it can be wearing in the day. Sometimes I forget that there is any daylight and if I leave for a walk the sunlight can be a shock to me. Perhaps spending so much time in an unlit basement is adding to my visibility problems in the outside world.

I sit on my chair. It's a foldout white plastic chair with a chromed tubular metal frame purchased from IKEA. All the furniture in the room is from IKEA. The white chest of drawers with semi-transparent corrugated plastic, the table, the bed: all IKEA. Cheap and cheerless.

My possessions are scattered around. I have:

Seventeen DVDs and no DVD player. A Chinese wind-up clock (broken).

Lots of books from the Book Warehouse. Seventy three, to be precise, many of them classic works of fiction because they are £1.99 each. Jane Austen and Wilkie Collins lying on top of Conrad and Dickens.

Five old pornography magazines that I use for masturbation.

One pair of cowboy boots.

One pair of baseball boots – Onitsuka Tiger high tops.

Two second-hand pairs of brogues by Church's of Northampton.

A large rucksack, black, kept under the bed along with a shoulder bag and a checked plastic laundry bag.

A membership card to the Wellcome Institute library – I like it there and it's free and warm and full of interesting books.

An old broken laptop from years ago – a Toshiba Satellite – it still works. I can write on it but that's all, there's no access to the internet from here – I have to go to the local library for that; they let you have an hour free in the mornings but it's very busy. There should be somewhere you can get free internet – it's a very useful resource and I would like to be able use it more. I am not a technophobe, I don't hate it, I just cannot afford to access it. Can't have it if you can't pay for it.

I have:

3 pairs of blue jeans, patched. I do my own sewing.

10 black t-shirts.

7 pairs of socks.

6 pairs of underpants.

1 old suit.

2 shirts and 2 sweaters.

This comprises most of my possessions. I also have a passport and a birth certificate, a driving license and a national insurance number, so I am not an invisible person in the official sense, at least not yet.

There is a white door set in the wall: behind it is my wet-room. It is six foot long and about three foot wide. It has a porcelain toilet and a chrome shower, a small white sink and a metal bathroom cabinet with a mirror on the front. There are two lights recessed into the ceiling and I think that's where the extractor fan is hidden, there is no window. The shower is powerful and hot, perhaps because I am in the basement. I like the shower and use it every day, it's a high point. I wake up, I masturbate, I stretch and then I shower. In the cabinet are my few toiletries. My shaving brush, the only remnant of my father – he bought it in 1952 when he joined the Air Force – it's all that is left of him. I think about him on his deathbed and the moment just before he kicked the bucket, when he spat in my face and hissed at me to "Fuck Off"

There's my toothpaste. A block of shaving soap. My toothbrush. Some dental floss, unused. My razor. A condom. Two strips of Propananol 40mg, some aspirin and a soggy box of Elastoplasts.

The wet-room floor is covered in small grey mosaic tiles, each one is two inches square, the wall with larger grey tiles, thirteen inches by ten, and placed in the same traverse broken bond style as paving slabs are laid; perhaps the pattern soaked into my subconscious over the years and has resulted in my fascination with paving. The pattern dripped into my mind which absorbed it like a sponge and there it is, lodged forever. If this is the case I'm not unhappy about it, an obsession with paving is, at least, not harmful, and is easily satisfied given the ubiquitous nature of the stuff. The toilet is an old Armitage Shanks, a 'Tiffany' with the cistern perched just above the toilet. The seat is white plastic, which is convenient, as the shower is next to it on the wall, so every time I take a shower the toilet seat gets a soaking. There's a small metal drain set in the floor, it is five inches square. The ceiling is painted white, the paint is flaking, and there's black mould growing in the corners which is spreading with slow but insistent stealth down the walls along the grouting between the tiles.

I look at myself in the mirror on the front of the cheap metal bathroom cabinet that sits above the small white sink with its teardrop green stain where the water from the dripping tap has worn away the enamel. I can see the lines radiating out from the corners of my eyes and the furrows across my forehead. My chin is covered in grey and black bristles. I shave only when necessary to avoid a beard. As I stare, the image in the mirror becomes indistinct and wavers. I shake my head, close my eyes and open them. The reflection stares back sharp and true. I blink. The reflection blinks. I blink again. The reflection does not. Or was it me that didn't blink and the reflection that did? I'm confused. The reflection smiles, or is it me? The reflection wavers and the light goes out.

Darkness.

"Shit"

No money in the meter. I teeter to the door – I know so well where everything is I avoid knocking anything over. I open the door and go to the meter across the hall, insert the key and turn. Light is back in my room. I return and, shutting the door, I lie on the bed. Thoughts tumble through my brain and out onto the flat grey duvet. None of these thoughts are useful, I sweep them off the bed with a deft brush of my hand, they make a dull thump as they hit the dumb weft of the brown carpet on the floor. From the bed I stare at the shelf with the Belling two-ring stove on it and the food cupboard and mini refrigerator below. On the corner shelf above the stove are stacked two dinner plates, one side plate and dessert bowl, one china mug and two saucepans, and a small nine inch frying pan. A knife, fork, two soup spoons, a paring knife and a meat cleaver that I found in a skip just by Smithfield market. In the food cupboard there is:

A tin of broccoli.
3 tins of corned beef.
A tin of chicken soup.
4 tins of sardines in tomato sauce and a 6-pack of tins of tuna.

There is also a bottle of Blair's Death sauce and a contingent of 'value' foods from the local *Express* branch of a giant supermarket chain. I am not sure who these products represent value for: it's meant to be the poverty-stricken consumer such as myself, but I suspect they are far better value to the mammoth supermarket chain that will be making 400% mark-up on every tin of value beans. I have in my store the following 'value' products:

2 tins of spaghetti at 19p each.
4 tins of baked beans at 29p each.
1 tin of value marrowfat peas and a tin of mushy peas 12p each.
1 large pack of Bourbon creams 45p (these I despise also).
1 litre of soya milk 60p.
A pack of 80 teabags 28p.
1 kilo of porridge oats 58p.
3 tins of vegetable soup 17p each and a kilo of long grain rice for 73p.

It's not the most healthy or tasty diet in the world.

I don't eat bread, sugar, drink alcohol, take drugs, or smoke cigarettes. I try to stay away from processed foods as much as possible, but on my income it's hard. I collect waste food from the markets and the back of restaurants, though it's become much more difficult of late due to our caring Council's waste and health policies.

Lying on my bed reviewing my foodstuff and my increasing lack of substance I cannot arrive at any conclusion apart from that I am not hungry and that I am not yet fully invisible. A feeling of helplessness washes over me like cold sour water. I turn off the light and let sleep come to me; it does so reluctantly and with a sneer.

"Where's the way out?"
    "Which door is the right one?"

"*FUCK…*"

The staircase goes up into the backstage area of an antiquated theatre. There is some kind of performance taking place. On the stage are beautiful women dressed in sharp coloured carnival clothes dancing with boys of equal beauty, also wearing circus costumes. They are watched by hawk-eyed ancient men and women sitting in a darkened auditorium. I cannot see them but I know they're there; I can feel their fetid stares caressing the dancers. I crouch in the wings and leer at the beautiful ones dancing beside me.

"*Take the knives and cut them to the bone.*"

"*Remove the beauty.*"

"*Clothe yourself in it.*"

These are voices from the auditorium – they know I am hiding here, I don't want to cut the beautiful ones, but there is no other way out. It's the only way to leave. As one of the boys swirls close to me I pick up a sword from the floor, grab his foot and pull him off the stage, he is as light as balsa wood. I cut his throat and he smiles two smiles at me as his blood pours over my hands and arms and onto the floor which is tiled with small grey tiles. Another dancer comes close, this time, a girl. I step up and slash her down the front of her face and body. She parts in two separate directions, blood sprays out and coats the floor. A round of appreciative murmuring and applause from the audience.

Still the dancers whirl and sway as I hack my way through their lithe young bodies, forging towards the auditorium and the aged ones sitting there, the creatures who are making me turn beauty into butchery. The young ones seem oblivious to my actions, but not the aged ones: they are almost lapping up the blood. I am near the edge of the stage, a few more feet and I will be able to turn my cleaver on the true villains – the ones making us all perform to their pied pipe. I can see them looking at me in a mockery of fear – they are amused and disinterested. One of them looks at me, he is tall and gaunt and very old. He wears a red velvet coat and a battered top hat. He waves and gestures at me with a dismissive flick of the hand.

The stage trapdoor opens and I fall, fall, and fall. Turning to dust, I hit the ground and look around. Nothing to see but darkness and the smell of my own sweat. I am awake.

I lie in bed after the dream, disturbed. I have an erection, it annoys me. I stroke it and try to bend it into submission but it demands attention so I masturbate to a dirty fantasy, and after a few minutes I come. It's not a pleasant orgasm, more a function of relief than of pleasure. The bed is damp from sweat and the room dark and cold. I try to return to sleep and almost succeed, but as soon as I doze the dream starts to creep in through the corners of my consciousness. I give up and snap on the light.

The tins of soup and sardines gaze at me in fear. The cleaver hangs on its hook over the sink and, as I rise to take a piss, the floor of the wet room is not covered in blood – I am relieved, though I fear one day it might be. A hesitant stream of dark yellow urine arcs into the Armitage Shanks toilet bowl: dehydrated. I finish and turn on the tap in the sink and drink deeply. I flush the toilet and walk back to bed. I am naked, I always sleep naked, I cannot sleep in clothes or any kind of pyjama, it constricts me and seems pointless: why go to bed in clothes? I sleep naked and I sleep alone.

Climbing back into bed I pull the duvet around my head and try to get back to sleep. Why is it that when we are asleep we don't know we are asleep, and yet we do know when we are awake? Or do we? I'm fidgety and restless. The curtain has moved and a slice of daylight has fallen onto the bed and across the floor. The dream fades but I can remember parts of it and I know I have had this dream, or similar dreams, before. I may as well get dressed and have breakfast, I am not going to sleep any more today. I check the time on my mobile phone, it's really a clock as I never put credit on it, nobody rings me on it, and I have no intention of ringing anyone, but these days you have to have a number for the welfare people or they will claim you are not actively seeking employment and stop giving me the pittance that the government decides I need to live on. They give me an unemployment allowance, a disability allowance, they pay my rent direct to the landlady. In return I have to go and 'sign on' every two weeks on a Monday at 9.00am. This is to say that I am available and looking for work. I have to show them that I have done three things to look for work each time I go and 'sign' but it's been going on so long they don't usually bother to ask me. It's an unsatisfactory system for both parties. Today is Monday.

I'm not dead, starving or sleeping on the streets. So I suppose they must, in some way, be right.

It's 6am.

I think it's porridge made with soya milk for breakfast. It's not so bad but, after the first year, it starts to taste of defeat. All my food tastes of defeat.

I take the smaller of my two saucepans – six inch diameter, two point five inch deep stainless steel with a black plastic handle, – comes in a set of three from IKEA. I have two. I have no idea where the third is, perhaps in the silence of the next-door room. This saucepan is the definition of ordinary, it is so completely average and unremarkable. I turn on the ring on the cooker; after a minute or so it glows orange, it looks like one of the mosquito coils we used to burn in Africa when I was a child, to keep from being bitten by the mosquitoes. They didn't work; at ten years old I caught malaria.

I pop the pan onto the ring and pour in some soya milk and add porridge oats.

Stir.

Eat.

Wash the pan, the bowl and spoon in the sink in the wet-room.

In this small room I have learned to clean and tidy as I go. If I don't, it becomes impossible to live in this small space. I have so few possessions, so few I have effectively listed them all, except for the titles of the books and DVDs, which would be boring beyond belief.

Today I must 'sign'. I shall walk to the Job Centre on Barnsbury Road. After that I will take an amble along the Regent's Canal to Camden and back.

After my bowl of porridge I stretch out, a two minute groin stretch which is basically the splits while leaning my weight on my right arm. Then glutes, and then touching my toes. It loosens the tension in my body that builds up overnight. I always wake up tense and stiff, sometimes I wake in the night with a spasm of sharp pain in my calf muscles from cramp and have to jump out of the bed and walk around until it subsides.

It is unfair that sleep – that relaxing, rejuvenating presence for other people – causes me distress and pain. The doctor is unsympathetic, as they always are. Perhaps they read my medical history and just write me off as a no-hoper. I find the medical profession to be arrogant, judgemental and superior. This makes me angry in a powerless way; one would expect all that intelligence and education to produce a better result, though I am not surprised. I have long since realised that wisdom and intelligence are not reliant upon, nor even related to, each other. The end result of that visit to the doctor was the advice to drink a cup of warm milk and add more salt to my food.

"My fucking grandmother could have told me that and she worked in a jigsaw puzzle factory."

It's 7am and I get dressed, I always eat my breakfast and stretch naked. The last thing I do before leaving the house is to get dressed, if I keep on losing visibility at this rate perhaps I won't even bother to do that. I pull on fresh black underpants and black socks. I only have black, it makes life simpler, and I'm always for the simple life – that's why I'm living this way – and am becoming invisible, although the invisibility was not my idea. I drop a black t-shirt over my body and tug on my blue jeans, patched over ten years of wear and tear. I grab a grey sweater, wriggle into it and pull on my black Onitsuka high-tops. Just the coat, and I'm prepared for the outside world. Once the coat is on I check that I have my required pocket items:

Wallet.
Clock/phone.
Keys.
Money.
Signing Book.
I am ready.

I open my door, turn off the light and step into the dull grey light of another morning, no different to thousands of other mornings. Daylight loiters shame-faced in the small basement corridor, like a dog that's soiled a carpet. I notice the door to the silent room next to mine is open just a crack. I take note.

I breathe in and out several times, perhaps I should take a Propananol – there's the faintest tickle of a panic attack in the back of my head. I back into my room, turn on the light. I go into the wet-room, open the cabinet, two white plastic blister packs of Propananol stare blindly at me. I fill my mouth with water from the tap and, holding in, I pop a tablet from the pack and slip it into my mouth between my closed lips and swallow it with the water. I have always taken medication this way, – if I try to swallow without water in my mouth the tablet will always stick on my throat and cause me to gag and cough it back up. It terrifies me.

If I place the tablet in my mouth and then try and drink water and swallow, I can't, it just spurts out of my mouth like a demented fountain, along with the tablet. So I developed this way of taking tablets and it reduces the fear by a considerable amount, although I still worry after I have swallowed it, whatever it may be, that I am going to die, because I have no idea what is really in the tablet that I've just taken. The feeling and the process is always the same even though I have been taking these beta-blockers for years. One day one of them may not be what it is supposed to be and then bingo! I'm dead. This tablet, however, is not the one marked for my death. I place the strip of tablets back in the cabinet and shut the door.

There I am in the mirror, stern faced and hazy. That could be due to the grime on the mirror. I turn out the lights again and step back into the corridor. A sliver of sunlight makes an audacious play for attention before being ejected by the greyness from the hallway. I shut and lock my door. It has a Chubb deadlock that I put on myself, about four years ago, after being burgled by an upstairs junkie. There wasn't much to steal so he took a shit in my bed instead. He doesn't live here anymore. I tread my way up the flight of stairs to the landing and walk down the hall to the front door. I find myself trying to work out if the house has become this way because of the residents, or if the residents are the way they are because of the house, or whether both are attracted to each other in the first place, because of a symbiosis – one feeding the other.

I don't often see the landlady anymore, she's a short black woman who parades a lot of gold jewellery and wears bright African print sari type affairs. She has a purple Afro hairdo and a lemon yellow BMW car. She possesses a voice that sounds far too large to fit inside her body. She used to yell in a cheery way about getting the rent; every month she would stand outside my door and bellow and holler and bawl. In between shouting she would shell peanuts and eat them. By the time she left after half an hour of shouting, the floor would be covered in a small sea of nutshells which she would have trodden into the carpet with her worn out gold Crocs. I arranged for the rent to be paid direct to her bank account and that stopped the shouting, at least outside my door. I sometimes hear her shouting outside other tenants' doors and there's often a trail of nutshells along the floor from the front door to the stairs leading up to the other rooms. But I never see her anymore or have to deal with the roaring and the sea of nutshells.

I open the front door walking on the piles of junk mail as I do so. The street is bright with sunshine, it plays along the far side of the street like happy children on a seaside trip. The air is cold and sharp but not unpleasant. I drop down the four steps that lead from the front door to the street and head off at a diagonal, toward the

Job Centre and the labyrinth of nonsense thought up by one set of people and applied to another. The Job Centre staff are like a far distant and alien race that neither cares about nor understands the people they have to deal with.

Chapter 3: **Wealth, Health and Unwisdom**

Making my way along the streets: past the former social housing now being redeveloped for the chattering media monkeys and financial services workers who love to live in a formerly run down area. I pass the Leftover Café, which does a breakfast for £3.50. Eggs, bacon, sausage, toast, mushrooms and fried tomato, along with tea or coffee. I occasionally treat myself to a breakfast there. The owner is an old Italian man. He knows his onions. He's kind to his regular pensioner customers and treats them well. This morning is not one for me but I glance in through the window to look at the usual mix of people: there are some old folk; there are some building workers, East European and British, wearing yellow vests. Each of the vest-wearers has a number on their back: 1509, 4501, 1204. I don't know what the numbers denote, perhaps one day I will ask, but for now I prefer to think it represents the number of bricks they have laid or pipes welded or something to do with productivity. I am almost certainly wrong about that, most likely it's just the number of the vest.

I slide past the antique shops and print galleries, and coffee shops selling 'eco fair trade', never-hurt-no-one everybody's-happy coffee. Towards the Job Centre, past a supermarket with a 'free' – as long as you spend £10 – car park.

Bus-stops and taxis with no passengers.

The Job Centre is near the police station.

I walk along a tarmac pavement, its flat featureless surface a welcome relief from the continuous broken bond of the slab pavements. The tarmac surface has little rises and cracks in its surface, they're from the tree roots that have pushed and distorted the flat pavement. It is like the view of the Carpathian Mountains from the air. I've never seen the Carpathian Mountains but my imagination likes the comparison and so now in a way I have seen them. To my left are some bushes in a brick enclosure – they have orange berries and unpleasant thorns, not the most community-friendly plants but they are probably theft proof, and that's what matters in this area. Beyond them is a small municipal park with a children's playground containing brightly coloured climbing equipment, and strange flat beast shapes on wobbling springs that children sit on and tame whilst conquering the world. I stand looking at the playground through the municipal regulation railings. I don't stand long – it will be viewed as suspect, as if I was planning to sexually predate the children, rather than as a wistful longing for lost childhood and the possibilities that lay ahead in life. There is only one woman and three children in the playground. The children run around and two of them fight over who's going to drive the giant red tractor that waits in the middle of black rubberised flooring. The children ignore me. The woman ignores me. I sneeze.

The woman shoots me a dirty look.

She sees me, well not me, but a man shape by the railings.

I move on.

The brick cube of the police station looms up on the left. The building is unappetising: its gold-mirrored windows, CCTV cameras and spikes on the walls, rows of police vans, and two flagpoles. A tatty Metropolitan Police flag flying from one and a grubby Union Jack on the other, not flying as it's entangled in the forest of radio masts that jut out of the roof. In front of the police station, behind pale blue railings, in an alcove made by two parts of the building, are sculptures – a weird tableau of primary colour sculpture and bold shapes meant to represent the sound nature of community relations between the police and the residents. The first is of a couple, a person of indeterminate gender and a policeman who is either holding the other one's hand or leading him / her away under arrest, it's impossible to know. Neither character has a face. Next to that is a shape that seems to me to be a bright blue squashed elephant with an Eskimo child escaping from its head. Behind this is a giant eye and a giant hand, then a huge set of chains attached to a blue post.

A woman being consumed in flames.

An enormous flat blue football with a white stripe and 'POLICE' painted across the middle.

The last sculpture is of an explosion. A large flat comic book "Zap" shape in yellow and orange with sharp grey shards all through it.

Then comes the entrance to the police station. The doorway is festooned with CCTV cameras; this is not a door through which anyone wants to pass. After the door there are more railings, through which are more unsettling sculptures: a police Dalek and a Lego-like Police helicopter. These sculptures are like some nightmare vision of a two dimensional Lego future where everyone has to follow exact instructions or risk being burned, blown up, squashed or imprisoned. There is nothing reassuring about the police station and its bizarre statues.

The only reassuring thing about the modern Police force is its ineptness. Well, reassuring for criminals that is.

I am not a criminal.

I turn the corner and over the road is the 'Job Centre Plus'. I wonder about the plus. Plus what? It's an embarrassed building, only sporting a small green sign with the legend 'Job Centre Plus' in white and yellow writing. It looks like this:

job (white letters)
centre (yellow letters)
plus (white letters)

All in lower case writing, as if emphasising its disgrace about existing at all. The arched windows are covered in metal caging whose struts form a giant X across the window. It's the only building in the street with this metal caging on the windows and I wonder why it is felt necessary. Is it to keep people in? Surely no one is going to want to break into the place, desperate as they may be to get a job. Perhaps it's part of the new way of dealing with poverty, by disguising it as opportunity. Round the corner of the building is the entrance. A dour smoked plastic eye gazes down at the doors.

Inside, the automatic doors slide open, and two security guards stand either side of them. The staff inside these places are given special training to be able to see the invisibles who populate their building in the daytime. Now I am visible, now I can be seen, I am totally opaque. The internal cameras mounted in the walls scan me. The facial recognition cameras were introduced by the new government to reduce fraud. They scan you and match your face to the photograph they take of you every year and store on the computers.

I hand my little booklet to the lady standing next to a lectern and sit on one of the bright blue seats.

"Place your left thumb on the scanner please."

I lift my left hand on to the biometric scanner with my right one, and push my thumb down on the glass plate. The woman looks at the screen. She taps a key. I am on time.

The place has the feeling of a nursery about it, a place where none of the clients can be trusted to behave properly. There are plenty of grey 'job points' standing like sentinels, waist-high altars. These computerised job boards replaced the old metal boards that had cards with jobs on some time ago. You tap the buttons and it takes you to the available jobs via a cascade of green and yellow screens. I always check them but there's never anything suitable. One has to arrive on time although one is never called to the appointment with the job adviser on time, they run 20-30 minutes late. I suppose they figure that the unemployed have nothing better to do than wait around to be patronised by a bored, self-righteous job advisor quizzing them about looking for non-existent work.

Eventually my name is called and I walk, cap in hand, to the desk and sit on the grey metal frame chair. The woman is called Anna, at least, according to her name tag. She clicks at her keyboard in a desultory way, tapping in my national insurance number one finger at a time. In this system, it's your number, not your name, that's the key to your existence; in fact, your identity has already been removed by the very act of enumerating you. I am no longer visible as a discrete entity with feelings, thoughts, and actions. I have become a set of numbers in a computer. Statistics. Ones and Zeros and that's it, literally the sum total of my existence. Anna glances over at me, she's looking for my 'job search' booklet, the grey paper pamphlet you have to fill out with details of your 'job search'. Three actions a week need to be entered. These advisors get ten minutes to interview a client and enter the details into the computer. It's their target to interview and process so many people a day – that's their priority – the target. It can be helpful for people like me. I know she doesn't care and just wants to get onto the next person. Play the game:

"How's your job search going, Mr Smith?"

"Badly, or I wouldn't be sitting here."

She flicks the booklet pages.

"Anything I can do to assist you?"

It's at this point you have to be careful. Never say yes. She doesn't want you to say yes, but don't say no either.

"Thank you but I think I will just keep looking, something's sure to come up soon."

"OK, Mr Smith. Thank you for coming in."

She clicks the keyboard and hands me a paper slip which has columns of my signatures, each one where I have signed for a previous fortnight.

"Have you done any work, paid or unpaid, in the last two weeks?"

I think about how much work it is to merely be alive.

"No."

"Sign here."

I make my mark at which point I fade from view.

"Thank you. See you in a fortnight."

I say this as I rise from the chair. There is no answer from Anna.

I am invisible again.

I make my way out of the building. It's only a short walk through the housing estate to the canal path at the point where the canal emerges from the Islington tunnel, like the River Styx emerging from the mouth of Hades.

I cut through the houses and past the blocks of apartments, past the metal phone box with the garish cards advertising prostitutes plastered over the inside. A5 postcards with photos of enticing and beautiful girls, taken from magazines or the internet, with details like 'Yuko Japanese Model' and a list of services: A&O, Lesbo Actions, VIP massage, uniforms, spanking, watersports, toys. She's local and does hotel visits; her number is 07733 788443 There's 'Tia Black Student' and 'Hot Latino' and a woman with enormous breasts. There is 'ROSI BUM in town', with a pencil and crayon picture of a young girl kneeling down in school uniform with her buttocks exposed, each one sporting bright red patches from a spanking session. The girl in the picture is smiling. There are even a couple of handwritten cards, one for 'Honey 18 Years Old English Brunette'. I wonder about these girls. I would like to visit them to see what they look like and who they really are.

They are also invisible, even to the men that fuck them – the men don't see the real person, just the image in their brain that they fuck. They are not as invisible as me but, in their own way, they are just as unseen; they have always interested me. I pick a couple of the better cards from the phone booth. I collect them. I have collected them for over ten years, ever since I first saw them. Each card has a story attached; I doubt they are happy. I would like to know those stories, all of them in their way, as pathetic, sad and vicious as mine.

I leave the phone booth and wander down through the Half Moon Crescent Tenants' Co-operative. These used to be social housing but, years ago, the residents bought their homes and formed a co-op. There's an alley that cuts alongside the well-kept brick 1970s houses, with neat communal gardens, past a caged-in basketball court and out on to the street. Across the road are the stairs at the side of the canal, there's a choice of access to the towpath, a ramp that leads straight down to the towpath used by cyclists, or a pointless stainless steel and wood spiral staircase and observation platform; I always use the stairs. I like the walk along the canal, water is soothing for some reason; even the fetid liquid that squats in the Regent's Canal is soothing, despite its empty beer cans, tyres and trash. Why is that? The peace offered by bodies of water – perhaps it's the idea of another world, silent, dark and cold, containing life totally different from us – the strange nature of its substance, both solid and liquid, life giving and life removing. Sometimes, on the rare occasions I get to be by the sea, I feel a powerful urge to walk into it and drown, to let it close over my body and remove me from the world. I have heard that drowning is a peaceful way to die.

The towpath has been well restored and is used by large numbers of people these days. I can remember when walking along this canal was a dangerous thing to do: gang-rape, murder, and robbery were frequent events. I used to use it as a safe way to carry drugs from one place to another. Now, of course, walking the towpath is just another delightful thing to do on a warm weekend day. There are even coffee stands along the sides of the path. It's busy today, even for a Monday morning. Cyclists use it, which is unfortunate. I long to push one of the arrogant cunts into the canal as they ding their bells, expecting the walkers to avoid them. The path is made mainly from concrete blocks; sometimes there are gaps between them and water bubbles through. There are ten bridges and four locks between the tunnel and Camden. The bridge that carries Caledonian Road over the canal has little box-like holes along the top of the supports. In each hole sits a pigeon. One pigeon one hole, their gentle cooing echoes across the water and their shit stains the walls. If you ever wondered where pigeons go at night, it's under bridges with the homeless.

The old path was dirty and dangerous and mostly deserted, I preferred it that way. There are so many people in London that solitude is impossible, though invisibility is easier to achieve. The economic crisis caused by the ending of air travel for a year due to the volcanic eruption in Iceland did put a stop to the crazed influx of people. But not that you'd notice. The eruption covered the country in various levels of grey ash and took ages to clean up. It was another excuse to introduce more control. They finally managed to make ID cards compulsory. I never carry mine – I am invisible, so what's the point? I'm convinced that there's such a thing as information overload: they gather too much and now there's so much information it has become impossible to sift it all. It's humans that do the noticing and humans like to have cups of coffee and go for a shit or a wank, or flirt, or read the paper. Over sixty-seven million people with a file of information on each and every one of them.

It's easy to slip through the cracks. The cracks the government says don't exist. Perhaps the system has no cracks, but people do. People are full of cracks and holes and if people invented the system, then so is the system. The machines can see me but the people don't.

The sun glints off the dirty green water. It's not deep, maybe five or six feet at best, perhaps less. It had been cleared of most of its underwater junk in the 1980s and it's usable. There are basins where narrowboats are permanently parked up with people living on them, a fantasy of a bohemian travelling life complete with broadband and satellite communications, never far from the upmarket restaurants, bars and clubs of the city. The grimy warehouses of the past have been removed and replaced by luxury new-build apartments or reconditioned into slick, feel poor, lo-fi, live rich, hi-tech, media villages. Nothing is left of the industry that caused the canal to come into existence in the first place. The tall new white buildings alongside the canal are topped with penthouse apartments that gaze down at the old canal. Through the floor-to-ceiling glass windows, I can see little people, like figures on a wedding cake.

I snake along the path, nobody noticing me. I hug the walls and dart under the bridges. I am not in a hurry. It's just the way I walk: fast, urgent and with purpose, even though I have none.

Today, though, I will end up at the Wellcome Institute library. I will walk from Camden to Euston to the Institute on Euston Road, and spend the day reading.

It's free and contains a lot of fascinating texts. One of these days I will put some of the information I have learned to good use.

I dart along the crowded towpath passing the Constitution pub now taken over by loud, young, drunk Australians. I wonder why people travel thousands of miles from their homes to hang out entirely with people from their own culture.

On the far bank is a row of aluminium houses built in the 1980s. They've always fascinated me. They were designed by Nicholas Grimshaw and called the Grand Union Walk Housing Units, completed in December 1988. They look like upended airstream trailers and, although they show signs of wear and tear, they still grab the eye. I would love to live there. I want to go inside and look around; I wish to know the people who live in them, hoping they are as individual as the buildings in which they live.

As it winds toward the Market, the towpath bustles with activity. Camden Lock: the place is a Dante-esque carnival of mass-produced individualism, a lesson in how to be different and yet stay the same. A homogenous mass all bellowing "I'm different". One million ways to be the same, a plethora of choice that will cause no mental consternation to anyone involved. It represents no choice at all.

The canal side fills up with people as I approach Chalk Farm Road. They are young adolescents and young adults, all garish hair and big boots, all slightly drunk or slightly high, all enraptured by the assortment of garish and low quality goods for sale. It's the modern equivalent of a medieval fair, minus a dancing bear or two. It's busy for a Monday but, then again, it's busy every day, unbearable on weekends. I despise these people and their mindless consumption of baubles, bangles and assorted crap. Why do they have to work so hard at not thinking, not feeling, and always having to live life as if it's a non-stop thirty-second advert on the TV? None of them want to feel the torture of thought or the pain of awareness, the agony of an emotion truly felt. I can remember when I, too, spent most of my time avoiding myself and running around like a jackdaw accumulating, thinking things would make me mean something.

On the bridge over the Regent's Canal I look around and see the huge CAMDEN LOCK painted on the green railway bridge that spans Chalk Farm Road. I came here many years ago when it was just a small market. I had my tarot cards read. It was something you do at seventeen years old. I still recall that reading: I picked the Devil card; the reader told me I would always undermine my achievements and be my own mortal enemy.

I turn to my right and look at the trails of people shopping their way along both sides of the road. The pavements are newly-paved with small bricks, they've been widened to accommodate more people. And now I have to navigate all these shoppers. Cockroaches are more useful than these consumers; at least cockroaches can't think, they have no choice about their actions. People do have choices, although watching and listening to them, one could be forgiven for thinking they are as mindless as the insects. They infest this place in the same way as cockroaches might infest the back of your sink or under your floor. They are disgusting. To get to Camden High Street, I will have to pass through them, these insect people, and they won't even see me. I feel a cold murderous rage in my chest, it tenses all my muscles and I want to kill all of them, and I mean all of them. I wonder how many I could get with a razor-sharp samurai sword before my arm tired out and I had to stop. A good few, I reckon. I see the face recognition cameras on the walls, they're all over London, but particularly in places were the authorities feel dissent is likely or high numbers of felons may hang around. The cameras match faces to records and alert authorities if the name is tagged. At least, that's the rumour. So, no killing here. I weave my way toward Camden High Street deep in thought and entirely unseen by other people.

"If I am invisible then surely I can kill without being noticed."

I have often wondered what it would feel like to take another human's life. Not one I know but one that is random and with whom I have no connection, one about whom I know nothing and care not a jot.

Chapter 4: **Anatomy for Beginners**

The theatre is full, I can't see the audience but I know they are there. I can hear them in my mind and they are old, so very old, and they are pleased with my performance. All around me on the stage are limbs and bits of beautiful young bodies. The stage floor is slick with blood. I try to walk off but I slide and fall, landing face to face with the head of a young woman, maybe 23 years old, her perfect features distorted by the pain in which she died. I clamber to my feet, the audience hissing inside my brain. I have cut the dancers to pieces.

Every single one.

The limbs on the stage are strong and smooth and dead. I let the sword drop from my hand and carefully step to the wings.

An old man with no teeth and a cadaverous grin, like a drain, hands me a towel. I wipe down the sweat from my face, only to find that the moisture is blood and it's not mine.

I look at my body, I am naked and covered in blood.

A marvellous performance sir, let's hope tomorrow's is as good.

I walk into a dressing room and find myself in an ornamental garden. There are neatly trimmed privet hedges in box shapes surrounding conifer trees, and topiary in the shape of animals; there's a rabbit and there, a giraffe. The pathways are gravel, two centimetre round gravel, I notice. I am wearing a long fur coat and my breath steams in the cold air; it is morning and there has been a light smattering of snow in the night.

The garden is enclosed by high fir trees. The light filtering from the sky is grey and dull. The pathways lead in all directions: away past the hedges and topiary. I feel pulled to the path on my left. Starting the walk, I look down and I see I am wearing Crocs. Unusual. I never would wear such footwear but I am now, one green and one gold. My feet are not cold. I walk down the pathway towards a gate. It is getting colder and darker. I reach the gate, it is old, metal and rusty, but it opens easily enough. I pass through into a tunnel that is rose-coloured, translucent. It is rounded and the walls feel smooth and seem to pulse slightly. It is warm. The tunnel curves and ends. I step out into a room which seems to be the inside of a ship's hold. In front of me is a table, above it a woman is suspended, tied, bound, gagged. She spins slowly, her legs are parted and her vagina shaved. A smear of deep red blood covers her labia. On the table, there are three small tumblers; in each one there's a liquid: dark red, light green, black. On the table is a knife, a pencil and a book.

I am puzzled.

"What do I do?" I ask the woman, because she is the only other person present.

She does not answer. How can she, she is gagged.

"Drink"

I cannot see the source of the voice.

"Which?"

"Any or all."

I look at the table and then notice the dog, a large dog lying under the table, a kind of Doberman, greyhound cross. Its jaws drip saliva.

"Drink," it says.

I step up and look at the drinks. Which? And what do they do? I look at each:

The green one. It glows, resembles mucus. No.

The red one, thick and specked with white flecks. The woman's menstrual blood? I feel it is. No.

The black drink looks like a liquid toffee and smells of cardamom. Yes.

I drink and the room melts away.

Circus music.

The sound of metal being sharpened.

I am in the theatre again. It's time for another performance. I am tired I want to sleep, but there's no time for sleep. I have to work again. I walk up the steps, toward the stage, sword in hand, the voice in my head, the ancient audience telling me to cut and slice, teach the young ones a lesson that they will be incapable of remembering.

I hear the music and the laughter of the young beautiful dancers.

I tremble as I approach the side of the stage.

Now I can see the bright costumes and hear their feet and breathing, heavy from exertion.

I am naked and I have an erection. I grip the sword and step out, slashing at the nearest dancer, who loses an arm and catapults screaming into the scenery.

I wake with a start, it's dark and I am covered in sweat. I lie in my bed trying to rid my head of the images of blood and slaughter. My hand slides to my penis, it's rock hard. I don't want to masturbate. I try to force my penis into flaccid submission but it's useless. My penis commands me to masturbate. I cannot leave the bed until I have come. Reluctantly I grasp my cock. I hate it for making me do this but I have no choice.

I come. It's a relief.

I snap on the light and am glad to see that everything in my room is as I left it the night before, though why wouldn't it be – nobody comes in here but me.

I throw the bed cover back and get up, stretch and shower. The usual routine.

As I stand, head back, eyes shut under the hot jets of water in the steam-filled wet-room, visions of me hacking the legs off a young girl dancer fill my mind, a scene from my dream. I stagger and flick open my eyes. For a moment, the girl's pain-drenched face and the music from the dance is still there – it always drowns out the screams – then everything vanishes as swiftly as it arrived. I shake my head and rub my face under the hot water, removing the traces of the dream from my mind. I turn the water to cold, it streams over me jolting me to reality. I slam the taps off and grab the damp towel from the hook. I dry my goose-bumped body and look at myself. Two muscular legs. On the left thigh, a tattoo: a strand of barbed wire inked onto the flesh, it snakes downward, twining its way around my leg and reappearing under my knee, winding down my calf, stopping at my foot. My penis hangs, shrunken by the cold water, a small, circumcised mushroom of a cock. My torso is lean, not much body fat, a combination of all that walking and no money.

"The poverty diet, it's a winner every time."

I dislike my body, it makes me feel uncomfortable and awkward. I try not to look at it, so I have no mirrors in my room, only the grimy one set into the cabinet door in the wet room, and I only use that for shaving. I am showing signs of ageing, there's a crumpled lack of elasticity to my skin which adds weariness to my gloom.

I dress as normal: blue jeans, black t-shirt, grey sweater, the black-waxed jacket. I pick up a notebook and pencil. Today I have to visit the doctor at the local health centre. You can't see the same doctor twice. The old system of having a local doctor in his practice that got to know his patients, their idiosyncrasies and foibles, who would know that some patients needed a chat and a handshake and others needed medication, and what worked best for whom, that has gone. It has been replaced by an industrial system. You get to the medical centre and they allocate you a doctor – that's if the diagnostic terminals can't help. These are computers where you sit and tap in your symptoms and number. It scans your retina to confirm your identity and then tells you to attach an oversize 'crocodile' clip made from reassuring plastic onto your finger. The machine checks your temperature and pulse, tells you what's wrong with you, and either prints out a prescription or refers you to a human doctor who is invariably about twenty five and totally uninterested in who you are or anything about you as a person, and just doles out whatever the latest policy directive is along with some ineffective tablets. These 'health points', or 'docbots' were introduced as a way to improve the service and to allocate doctors' time to more important cases. They are notorious for telling people with cancer that they have a cold and similar nightmares; there's a theory that they are deliberately programmed to misdiagnose to save money on treatment. I suspect it's just incompetence. There are quotas and targets and, at the moment, they are hot on diabetes, and candida in kids.

I get to see the doctor because I have a chronic and socially proscribed disease. The new government put certain disorders on a list of socially undesirable conditions and Hepatitis C is one of them. As I have it and am disabled, I have to go to the medical centre every six months to be examined and tested, and if I miss the appointment I will have my welfare payments removed. So here I am sitting in a grey metal-frame chair, waiting for the bored youth who's today's doctor to pronounce something or another. He taps the keyboard, presumably looking at my records. He does not look at me.

Tap Tap Tap, goes the keyboard. "Mmm," the doctor mutters. I notice that Hewlett Packard manufactures the doctor's computer. The doctor himself is wearing a white Calvin Klein shirt, grey slacks and black scuffed slip-on shoes; he's not a man to notice the pavement on which he walks. He has the air of an incompetent and mendacious estate agent with tousled black hair into which he has ladled some kind of product which makes it stand out at obscure angles, like a cartoon cat with its tail in an electric socket. I loathe him. He taps the keyboard again, still not looking at me. He prints something out and still does not see me, he actually hands the slip of paper over without looking at me. I don't take it, his hand stays outstretched. He looks over as if puzzled as to why his hand is sticking out holding a green piece of official paper. His gaze travels along his own arm to his hand and then up to me.

"I have been having terrible nightmares." I say.

The doctor 'thing' blinks. He is only focused on the one thing. Getting me out of his office.

"Can you see me?" I say.

The doctor 'thing' blinks again.

"Take this and see the nurse for your tests," the doctor thing says.

"So you can see me, you do know I am here, that I actually fucking exist and am not just a cunting number in your machine?" I say, quite reasonably.

The doctor 'thing' sits up straight, alarmed by aggressive words delivered in a sing-song reasonable voice. Now he can see me, I have jumped into sharp relief. I have ticked one of his policy response boxes. The sign on the wall tells me abuse of staff will not be tolerated in anyway or at any time. No mention is made of abuse of the patients, or clients, as we are known.

"No need for that kind of language Mr … er Mr…er..."

"SMITH." I emphasise.

I stand and snatch the slip of paper. I leave and slam the door behind me; as it shuts I can see that the doctor 'thing' is back to his computer, using a joystick to play some kind of computer game.

I make my way along the corridor, its walls full of public health posters and messages, towards the nurses' station to have my blood tests: liver function, AST and ALT tests, cholesterol, diabetes and whatever else they may decide I need to be screened for. They don't have to tell you anymore; since the public health act they can test anyone for anything at anytime without telling them what it is they test for, or the results.

It's all justified in the name of public health, order and the personal freedom to be free from the possibility of being infected.

The nurse takes the slip and she taps at a keyboard, at least she looks at me. "Take a seat over there and we'll call you, shouldn't be long." She smiles.

She hands back the green slip and I look at her, I can't process the smile. She smiles more widely, then stands.

"Hi Claudia," she says past my shoulder. Ah, the smile wasn't for me at all, but for Claudia, over my shoulder. For a moment, I had the ridiculous idea that it might have been for me.

I sit in the grey metal-frame chair by the door of the treatment room, waiting my turn. I can never remember any of the other people waiting at the same time as me. Perhaps it is because I am so self-absorbed or perhaps they, like me, are invisible. The nurse and Claudia are in an animated conversation about Claudia's boyfriend, – apparently he has a new job in local government, supervising the installation of litter bins and recycling centres, apparently he's changing the emptying routines to twice a week on Wednesdays and Mondays. Their conversation is carried on in voices that are just a bit too loud, as if to tell everyone else that you should hear what we have to say, but you shouldn't be listening. I shut my eyes and my mind blanks everything out. Someone tugs at my shoulder. It's the nurse.

"Mr Smith, wake up it's your turn."

"I'm not asleep."

I stand and enter the room.

"You will need to use a butterfly on my hand, the veins in my arm are too difficult." The Nurse looked at me and then at my file on her screen. It must have confirmed what I said as she goes to the metal cabinet and pulls out a sterile pack.

"Sit down."

I sit and she takes the blood. I leave with a band-aid over the back of my hand and a bruise ripening like a plum underneath. I want to rip that doctor's and nurse's fucking heads off.

I walk.

Heading toward the Wellcome Library, I pass Angel. They are replacing the old concrete paving stones with attractive new stone now they have cleared the streets of rough sleepers and refugees. Crates of large, pristine 650mm by 450 mm by 75mm Fielden Regal Collection Tarndale sawn paving slabs are stacked along the edge of the road, and the area to be paved has a smooth flat layer of builders' sand across it. Two men are manoeuvring slabs into place using a Probst Vacuum Power Handy VPH lifting machine. It's a vacuum pad attached to a rod with a vacuum pump powered by a 12v battery and has two sets of handles jutting out at right angles. The workman places the pad in the middle of a slab weighing up to one hundred and fifty kilos although your average precast concrete slab weighs around thirty to sixty kilos depending on size and what it's made from. When the pump is turned on, the men can lift the slab quite easily and with less risk of injury. These devices are standard now as the Health and Safety act 'manual operation and handling regulations (1994)', as amended in 2004 forbids the manual handling of large paving slabs. The successful construction of a concrete flag-paved area depends of five main operations:

Preparation
Detailing
Compaction of sub layers
Bedding of flags
Jointing

The work at the Angel is going well, and the old stained and broken slabs are piled up on the corner, like a stack of old newspapers awaiting collection and recycling. But I have no time to admire the paving kings at work: I have to get to the library. The encounter with the doctor has made me more determined to consider murder as a possible way of regaining some kind of visibility. At the Wellcome I am reading up on the structure of the human body so I can reverse engineer one and take it apart effectively. I find the books very interesting, but then I always have had a thirst for understanding. As I trundle down Pentonville Road, the sun is out. I feel less dark and gloomy out in the street with the traffic and the sunshine and the noise. Was it twelve years ago that I came to London? I left my family, such as it was. I was once married to a normal woman and had a career of sorts, as a civil engineer. A son. A little house, nothing majestic and nothing out of the ordinary, a small family car. There was the terrible recession that hit so many people. So I just upped and left. I haven't seen them since. I never concern myself with their whereabouts or what they might be doing. My son Sam was a selfish shit at the best of times: he was eight when I left, all sandy hair and sunny smiles, always happy, never gave a thought about anyone else. Parasites, that's what children are: they contribute nothing to society, they just take and take, yet everyone thinks they are so great and that children are the future; they are nothing more than the broken condoms of the past.

My mood darkens. The last time I had sex was about two years ago, I save up a little money each week and, every two years or so, I have sex with a prostitute. It serves a need and I like the conversation, I get so little of it apart from the continual monologue inside my head.

The wife, what was her name again, Joyce, Jane... No, it was less mundane than that. I can't think of her name.

She was a cunt anyway, a nameless cunt.

Jamillia, that was it. Jamillia the Cunt.

I stop, I need to sit down. I find myself crying, big fat salty tears are rolling down my face.

This is not good. I crouch on a step and wipe away the drops of the past. More just spring up in their place, I can't stop them. They dribble all over my face and snot drips from my nose. I wipe it on my sleeve.

Every so often, it sneaks up on me, makes me feel. Behind the anger and the rage, a sadness squats and waits.

Well it can fuck off. As I sit weeping on the step, people pass. A constant stream of them in all shapes and sizes and colours.

A cacophony of people.

No-one looks at me or stops or asks, or even throws a coin my way.

A grown shabby man sitting on a doorstep in King's Cross, sobbing and nobody can see him.

I know the sadness will pass and the anger and bitter rage will return. But for now I am exposed and my red thumping heart is on display. It is at these moments I should be visible, that someone should show a penny's worth of concern. Lives can turn on that, a little *Are you alright?* or a *Can I help?* That could revitalise an invisible person. It does not come and I pull myself together.

I stand, feeling a little shaky and shuddering as I walk to the corner of York Way. I decide to treat myself and head into the shiny clean interior of the early morning McDonald's to buy a coffee and a burger. The outside is a drab olive green with only a discreet hanging sign, the golden arches set against the olive drab. Inside it's filled with bright dayglo orange workmen on a break. The walls are covered with abstract murals in green and red and orange, set against the granite grey of the walls and tables and floors. It's not an altogether unrelaxing environment. I get a breakfast: egg McMuffin and a latte at £2.89 and £1.54 respectively. Expensive. The tall blonde manager with her five gold stars and too-tight blue-and-white-striped blouse constantly scans the customers and workforce, marching up and down adjusting that and moving this and giving customers a slap-on smile as synthetic as the food they are pretending to eat. This is not something I would usually do, but this feels like an unusual day. I head upstairs and find a quiet corner, the food tastes bland and chewy there's no distinct flavour and the coffee is hot and frothy and milky. It's inoffensive and by the time I have finished it, I want more. I trek downstairs, past a couple of young staff too busy flirting to see me.

I am, however, visible in the Wellcome Institute library, which is one of its attractions. That and the books, or rather, what's in the books. Of course the irony is – if it is irony – that in there I can't have a conversation with anyone because you have to be silent. The other thing I like about the library is that they don't have face recognition cameras, or any CCTV, in fact. The books are implanted so that if you try to leave with one, it will set off an alarm. That's all – they only care about the books and making sure they are safe – they don't mind or care who's reading them. Nor do they record who reads what; you come in and read and leave and, as long as the books are safe, they don't bother you in any way.

People have to be busy, they have to be doing something to organise their time. One of the worst things about being invisible and a social reject is the amount of time it gives you, coupled with the absolute lack of money. It's a vile combination. The human being needs organisation: poor women have children, children keep them busy and give them a sense of purpose, the same with drink or drugs, they keep you focused and numb the sense of purposelessness and failure that people in my position feel. I am not in favour of that solution. I have always been organised. When I left, I was purposeful about it. I searched out the best location although, to be fair, I didn't realise that there would be the eruption and all the social and economic chaos that went with that. I didn't know that I would be workless for this long. I found a place. I got rid of my cellphone and opened another bank account and closed the old one. Sold the car and left. Nobody knows where I am, I didn't tell anyone especially Jamillia the Cunt. I left on a Tuesday afternoon and never turned my head back.

The block of yellow bricks that is King's Cross sits in front of me, and the ornate red brick tower of St Pancras station can be seen poking up behind. It smirks its superiority over the more workaday appearance of King's Cross, trumpeting in a sly way about how it was chosen for the Eurostar and King's Cross was passed over, left to deliver people to the grimy north, not the joys of Paris and the sunny south.

I make my way through the hordes of people entering and leaving the station by bus or subway or mainline train, past groups of foreign children chattering excitedly to each other. There are confused looking families, all suitcases, buggies and crying kids, and the ubiquitous commuters, grim faced and determined. I pass through and around them all. My moment of weakness and fear has gone. I will head to the library and complete my plan. In the library I have an existence and a reason to be there. In the library people can see me, even occasionally talk to me, if I request a book or ask for help looking something up, they are polite and helpful. I like that.

It's not far along the Euston Road to Euston station. Opposite, at number 183 Euston Road, is the Wellcome Institute library where everything is harmonious, egalitarian, sensible. I head towards the twin grey metal lamps that mark either side of the doors. The upright metal lamps are in the shape of flaming torches; twisted around them are two snakes, perhaps poisonous, perhaps not. I wonder if the lampmaker was making a subtle point having the bright flame of knowledge entwined with the poisonous snakes of the pharmaceutical industry. Probably not, I tend to read too much into things. The double glass doors slide open. I pass through, into the open hall, up the marble steps, past the expensive café and bookshop, to the elevators. The library is on the first floor.

The double doors are already propped open. I swing through, sliding my card through the reader and clicking the turnstile leg. I have been here many times and know exactly where my books are located. I turn left and head towards the main reading room. It's a beautiful space with a mezzanine running around it on the first floor. I am going up to the medical collection: rows QS4 for dissection; ED for pathology. The wide stone staircase at the far end of the room sweeps upstairs. An arrogance of white stone, it branches right and left at the top. On either side are ten foot high paintings of a man: the left side is the front view and the right side is the rear view, in anatomical cross section, skin flayed off and muscles exposed; from the mezzanine you can see down into the large reading room. The mezzanine has names embossed in gold gilt letters against a white background all around the bottom edge. Jenner, Hunter, Pavlov, Darwin, Roentgen and others. It's a roll call of medical fascists, men who had the arrogance possessed only by those with the power over life and death: doctors, dictators, executioners.

The place is light, airy, filled with industrious students of all colours and ages. The sounds of gentle keyboard-tapping and the occasional rustle of pages turned are the only noises to filter through; the bliss brought about by quiet in our noise-infested world is not to be underestimated. The pleasure I gained from the year without aeroplanes was immense: the background noise level dropped and the air was clearer; apart from the clouds of ash, the sky was pure. Most people were too busy panicking about economic collapse to notice, but I had nothing to panic about: no money, no job, no house. Nothing. I just enjoyed the lower noise levels. I enjoyed the discomfort of a society so delicately balanced and neurotic that the absence of exotic fruit from supermarkets nearly led to riots in the streets. The equilibrium was soon restored and strawberries were back on the shelves in January, just like always. The only difference was fewer flights and people taking their holidays on the English Riviera instead of the Spanish, Italian or French ones. The new government took the opportunity to clean up the streets, and not just of volcanic ash: of homeless people, illegal immigrants, troublesome elements of all kinds. The immigrants they placed on ships and sent to the resettlement camps in Iceland.

I fish out the book I'm looking for, *Practical Pathology: A Manual for Students and Practitioners*. Published in 1883, it's a gem. I love the dark brown leather binding with the title engraved in gold, not in a solemn typeface, which you might expect, but in a light-hearted handwriting style. Quite out of character, you might think, considering the contents, but the writing is engaging, and the content fascinating. Admittedly, the author is writing about post mortems: how to examine the deceased and find out the cause of death. I won't need to know this because, with what I'm planning, I will be the cause of death, but the detail and descriptions are useful. I am familiarising myself with the inside of the body, somewhere most people are loathe to go. The writer describes the tools needed for a successful dissection:

1. Instruments required:

Two or three 'section' knives, strong enough to be used as cartilage knives. The handle must be strong and thick, so that it may be grasped firmly in the palm of the hand; the blade stout with the belly curved and sharpened up to the point, which should be well rounded off. With the knives (fig 1.) made for me by Mr Gardener of Edinburgh, there is little or no danger of punctured post mortem wounds.

Now, this knife has a strong resemblance to the long spatula-shaped knives used in Greek and Turkish kebab shops to carve meat from the upright pillar of meat. He continues:

A couple of scalpels, such as are supplied in the ordinary dissecting cases for dividing the costal cartilages, Coats recommends a knife with a triangular blade, the edge being straight, and forming an angle of about 35 degrees from the back, which should be very strong and thick; the handle should be strong, and the blade prolonged through it from end to end (Lindsay Steven).

Two curved bistouries: one probe-pointed, the other sharpened up to the point.

A hollow ground razor (Heifors army razor), or better still a Valentine's knife, for cutting thin sections of fresh tissues.

A long thin bladed knife, about one inch broad and ten or twelve inches long, for making complete sections through the various viscera. This is especially useful for cutting into the brain but one rather shorter, though of similar make is frequently used for cutting into the other organs. For the first incision into the brain a thin narrow knife, about one third to one half inch in breadth, and ten to twelve inches long is also exceedingly useful but by no means necessary.

I like the detail, even if I have no idea what some of the items are. The concept of a Valentine's knife is terrific, I will have to find out what it is and get one. As you can see, he goes into lots of detail and, to be frank, I won't need all these tools. I will be dissecting to dispose, as opposed to investigate, but forewarned is forearmed and all this information will help me prepare for my ordeal. Should I go ahead?

Two pairs of scissors; one pair large having one blade with the point rounded off, the other sharp; the other pair small, one blade probe-pointed the other sharp pointed.

A pair of intestine scissors, with a long curved and blunt pointed blade with a hook turned backward, and a shorter square ended blade which closes behind the curve, so that the curved blade is never cut out of the bowel.

A small bone saw, with a strong movable back and fine teeth, well set and one with long curved handle for sawing through the lamina of the vertebra.

A mallet – or steel hammer with a hook at the end of the handle, this is very useful in laying hold of and lifting the calvarias – and a steel chisel, in the shape of a capital T; the blade and cross piece of the chisel should each be about six inches in length, and the blade, one inch broad may be made with a guard at a distance of about one third of an inch from the point. This guard is of use when the skull cap is being removed, but it interferes with the use of the chisel for other purposes, such as talking out the spinal cord, so that when the guard is adopted a second straight steel chisel should be added to the list of instruments.

The list goes on to add various analytical objects such as scales, litmus paper and magnifying glasses, all things I will not need as I will be well aware of the cause of death. The section on precautionary measures is useful, plenty of running water and bleach seem to be the order of the day, and be careful not to cut myself on splintered bone or when using tools – I could get an infection, although I suppose there's a poetic justice in catching a fatal infection from the body of a person you have just murdered. As to opening them up and removing the viscera, this is what it says:

> *Stand on the right side of the body, and with a strong sharp knife, held in the palm of the hand, make a single incision through the skin and subcutaneous tissue of the neck, commencing at the symphysis of the chin, continuing it down the middle line of the sternum cutting down to the bone, then through the muscular wall of the abdomen, passing round the umbilicus and extending to the pubes.*

I also refer to *Post Mortem Appearances* by Joan M Ross (1925), and to Theodore Shennan's *Post Mortems and Morbid Anatomy* (1935). It's odd that all the books I have found useful are so old, I could not find any modern ones. Perhaps the human body is still the same as it was a hundred years ago and we are not so different as we might like to think, at least not when it comes to viscera and organs.

Joan Ross states succinctly, in the section entitled 'Signs of Death':

> *It may not be amiss to deal here briefly with the so-called 'signs of death', since all or some of them will be present in every case. They are as follows:*
>
> ***Cessation of Respiration and Circulation.*** *– The normal translucent reappearance, seen in a living person, on examining the web of fingers in front of a light gives place at death to a general opacity. No swelling is produced at the end of the finger by tying a ligature tightly around it. A mirror, held before the mouth, is not dimmed if death has taken place.*

Condition of the eyes. – *The Pupils dilate at the time of death and subsequently contract (from one to forty-eight hours after). After ten or twelve hours the eyeballs begin to look sunken and to soften. The cornea becomes hazy and can easily be dented by the fingernail.*

Post Mortem Cooling. – *From fifteen to twenty hours is the usual time taken for the temperature of a body to fall to that of the surrounding atmosphere. This time, of course, can be greatly modified by circumstances, such as the amount of body fat present and the nature of the medium in which the body lies. Again in some cases of death from small pox, cholera, yellow fever, acute rheumatism, and certain injuries to the central nervous system, a post mortem rise in temperature has be observed.*

Post Mortem Stains. – *(syn., Cadaveric Hypostases, Cadaveric Ecchymoses, Post Mortem Lividities, Sugillations). – These begin to appear on the most dependent parts of the body (in the case of a body lying on its back, the buttocks, the lumbar region, the posterior parts of the arms and legs, the shoulders, and the lobes of the ears) from four to twelve hours after death. The staining is most marked in asphyxia and in certain acuter infective conditions.*

Rigor Mortis. – *Ordinarily the muscles begin to show signs of stiffening in from four to ten hours after death. Rigor Mortis begins in the muscles of the jaw and reaches the limbs last. It usually lasts from twenty four to forty eight hours. The sooner it appears, the sooner it will disappear. Cadaveric spasm (instantaneous rigor) may occur in exceptional circumstances, such as sudden death in battle or in death by drowning.*

Putrefaction. – This has been stated to be the only certain sign that death has taken place. The first sign – a greenish discolouration of the abdominal wall usually appears on the second or third day. External conditions of temperature and moisture may modify the course of putrefaction considerably. Discolouration of the abdomen appears very early in cases of suppurative peritonitis.

So I have forty-eight hours to get rid of the body and I'd better not kill a fat person: apart from the extra disposal issues, they are going to stink sooner. I have a no idea who I am going to kill but at least I have valuable information, and you can't go into a venture like this without a plan.

Chapter 5: **Swimming**

I decide to go swimming. Sometimes I do, though not often. I use the public baths at Highbury Fields or, sometimes, the open air lido in London Fields, but that is a fifty-metre pool, and freezing cold, so I have to be feeling particularly flagellant to swim there. The pool at Highbury is twenty-five metre, indoor, heated and therefore busy, especially at this time of year. I pack my pants, goggles and earplugs into a shoulder bag and leave; it takes about fifteen minutes to walk there. I dislike like the pool, it's always busy and the changing rooms are slimy and reek of cheap disinfectant, the toilets are dirty and the sauna is disgusting. I strip off in the too-cold changing room and, grasping my goggles, I go to the poolside. The pool is divided into four lanes, people swimming clockwise in each of them. One lane for slow swimmers – that's me – one lane for medium swimmers, another for fast swimmers, and another lane that's closed. It's always like this: one lane closed, the other three busy, and the slow lane always the busiest, backed up with large ladies paddling and pawing at the water in a slow incompetent breaststroke. I have to use this lane as I can only use the one arm, so swim quite slowly. I swim too fast for the slow lane and too slowly for the medium lane, I have a tendency to swim in a long slow arc to my right unless I concentrate. Which I do. Hard.

I swim thirty-two slow lengths, mainly looking up the arse of a fat woman in a too-small brown swimsuit. After twenty-seven lengths a red mist seeps from between her legs: menstrual blood. Lovely. I swim right through it; the chlorine in the pool will annihilate any unpleasant germs, or at least that's the theory. At the end of her length, she stops swimming and gets out of the pool, looking sheepish. After that, I find myself staring up the legs of some grey swimming shorts. They're wrapped around a scrawny, leathery old white man. Five more lengths, and I can leave.

It is raining and cold so I spend the rest of the day reviewing my notes from the Wellcome Institute. I open a can of soup and heat it on the small hob in my room and write out a list of the tools I would need to achieve the task I had set myself. It doesn't feel real, the idea of killing someone, it feels more like some childish fantasy, a way of keeping myself occupied, of filling up my time so that I can stay out of the madhouse, although if I carry it out I may well end up in exactly that place. There's a second-hand tool shop on Caledonian Road, I can probably get most of what I need there. I look at my list:

BODY DISPOSAL EQUIPMENT
Hacksaw + blades
Large hammer
Large secateurs, or wire/bolt cutters
Sharp knives, large and small
Whetstone or sharpener
Meat grinder
Bleach
Supermarket plastic bags
Length of rubber hose, about four feet long
Plastic cling film
String and duct tape
Rubber gloves

It's a do-it-yourself post mortem kit, body disposal for dummies. I think I will buy the tools a bit at a time from different places over the next few weeks, partly for cost reasons and partly to allay suspicion and avoid questions. It is early evening and I decide to get some air. It has stopped raining so I thought I would walk a circular route, via Euston Road and up to Camden, then along the canal back home.

I don't often walk at night but it makes a change. The

streetlights give out their orange light reflected in the wet streets and off the paint and windows of cars. It lends a pallor of sickness to the world. I don't know what night it is, maybe Thursday. In my world the names of days of the week are not important; they blend one into another without very much to distinguish between them. Only the bi-weekly signing at the Job Centre has to be remembered with any fervour; fucking up there can cause a world of complications. I stride up Packington Street, looking down into the window of number seventy-eight, a 'garden flat' I believe they call them, just flowery words for a basement. There they are, sitting on their sofa, gazing in adoration at the screens of the Apple Macs on their laps. This young couple living in their delightful world, I always see them, always: sitting on the same place on the same sofa, staring at the computer, mug of steaming coffee in hand, like acolytes to some strange god, making offerings and waiting for a response. I hate them, I loathe them, I despise them, and I envy them. I stand and watch as they patter about their lives, looking unseen into the living room, my eyes burning with hot fury and my body chilled from the cold. I walk on, leaving them in blissful ignorance of the pain their environmentally-friendly liberal existence causes me.

Islington Green is busy, I hunch my shoulders and walk on, ignoring the revellers and late-returning workers, the smokers outside pubs, the homeless man pan-handling for money by performing poorly executed card tricks. Down Pentonville Road for the millionth time, past King's Cross along the Euston Road, turn right up Hampstead Road, towards Camden. It's dark and the wind is chill. My cheeks burn as I walk along the precast concrete slabs, past the old hospital, now all boarded up. It was the place where I picked up my prescription, in the days before I stopped relying on external things to provide a way to cope with the distress of living, before I decided to accept the pain of life, to befriend it and use it for strength. The hospital has a melancholy feel: the Victorian building all shut up, the ornate iron balconies rusty, the

French windows grimy, grey net curtains hanging limp behind the glass. It's probably best closed down It will make lovely apartments, I'm sure.

I approach the impressive building on Mornington Crescent, an art deco monstrosity guarded by two giant black metal cats. In the glowering streetlight, the cats look demonic and the building looms. It reminds me of my dreams. It's only an office building, but the pseudo-Egyptian façade and the giant cats, along with the cat face motif along the second floor, gives it an ominous feel. It doesn't look like my dreams but it feels like my dreams or, more to the point, I feel that way when I look at the building and those cats. Originally it was a cigarette factory called Arcadia Works and belonged to the tobacco company which made Black Cat cigarettes. It was called the Arcadia Works after the owner's original shop in the West End and J.M. Barrie smoked a brand of tobacco he made, called Arcadia. It opened in 1928 and was the first factory in Britain to have air conditioning and to be built using pre-stressed concrete. It also had a full welfare programme for its employees and, on the owner's birthday, all the workers were given a cake and two weeks' wages. The two cats are reproductions of the bronze originals which were cast at the Haskins Foundry in London, versions of the Egyptian god Bast. They are eight feet six inches tall. They stood guard over Arcadia Works until 1959 when the originals took off, one to Essex and the other to Spanish Town, Jamaica. The building dominates this end of Camden town. I wish it were still a tobacco factory and I wish London was still smoggy and grey and the buildings black from soot and smoke and every man wore a hat and smoked a pipe.

I walk up Camden High Street, past the Tube station which spews out people in a never-ending stream of multi-coloured hair and clothing. The vomited mob is noisy and excited about going to bars to drink too much so that they, in turn, can vomit. I force my way through a group of drunken men, all shouting about a football match or something, then past a group of dizzy girls, all high heels and short skirts, tottering around grasping cigarettes and bottles of some bright red liquid, the consumption of which seems primarily to affect the legs and vocal chords Perhaps, without knowing it, they are the followers of Bast, also known as Bubastis. The cat god of Egypt and the eight foot high cats in Mornington Crescent are receiving their homage. Herodotus tells us that the festival of Bubastis (Bast) attracted seven hundred thousand people, men and women but not children. The women engaged in song and dance. Prodigious amounts of wine were drunk. Other Egyptian sources prescribe that the feline goddess be appeased with 'feasts of drunkenness'.

Could it be that, without being aware of it, these hordes of drunken fools trampling around are in the thrall to Bast and her earthly representatives, the ones sitting dark, still and demonic outside Greater London House? Could it be these idiots are forced, via divine methods, to become drunk and foolish beyond their normal capacity?

On the bridge at Camden Lock, I dive off the road onto the towpath. Here, people have been robbed at gunpoint and raped and someone was stabbed to death last year. So it's not that popular as a walking route after dark. I don't mind it, I like the deserted feel and the stillness of the canal water. I walk along the path, through the tunnel at the back of the British Transport Police HQ, the tunnel with neon strip along the roof. It turns into a wide pool and I stop to rest, sitting on a block of concrete, gazing at the water as it laps the edge of the canal about two feet below the concrete lip. I sit in silence for a while, then I hear a whooshing, crunching, noise and two cyclists come tearing round the bend out of the tunnel, laughing and chatting to each other, voices loud enough to be heard over the noise of their bicycles. They pass, unaware of me watching, then they are gone. It's quiet once more.

After a long while I decide to continue my trip home, when I hear footsteps. The footfall is uneven and halting. A man appears from round the corner. He is young, maybe twenty-three or twenty-five years old, wearing blue jeans, big black boots, and a large sheepskin coat buttoned up at the front. He looks aggressive and very drunk, he is weaving as he walks, and he spots me. I start to walk away but for some reason best known only to him he speeds up to intercept me.

"Got any money old man?"

He grabs the front of my jacket near the neck.

"Got any cash you old cunt?"

He moves his face close to mine, maybe an inch away. I can smell the sourness of alcohol on his breath. I don't answer. I just look at him in the eye.

"You cunt, I want your cash and your phone or you're fucked, you old cunt."

We're standing face to face, side on to the water.

He grabs the right side of my jacket with his left hand, his right hand held just out of sight behind him. He may have had a knife, or not, I don't care.

I raise my right hand palm out and, twisting my hips to give added power, I jab him in the ribs just below the armpit, hard.

He looks surprised. Letting go of my jacket to keep his balance, he makes a drunken pirouette then topples into the canal with a quiet splash.

He's drunk and it's dark, he has no chance. He doesn't cry out, the impact of the cold water has taken his breath away.

He's trying to swim and find the edge of the canal; he ends up over at the far side where there is just a sheer wall rising out of the water.

He claws at the wall with both hands, trying, in vain, to get a grip on the wet slimy stone.

I watch.

He flails about, sinking under the water because of the weight of his waterlogged clothes and boots. He's now in the middle of the canal, eyes wide with panic, cheeks puffing in and out, hair plastered across his face, which seems pale blue in the sickly neon glow from the strip in the roof of the tunnel. His hand outstretched, he sinks again and then emerges nearer to me on the concrete lip of the canal side. Still clawing, he manages to get one hand over the edge of the concrete. I grasp it and he grips my hand. Once I've lifted it free of the edge, I reverse my pull into a push and shove him back into the water. For good measure, I pick up length of wood which is floating in the water and push it into his back, thrusting him under the water. He kicks like a dying frog and I push harder. Some bubbles break the surface and one of his hands flaps as if beckoning me to join him. And then he's still.

A couple of minutes later, I pull the wood away. He lies in the water face down and sinks out of sight. I put my hand into my pocket and pull out a fistful of loose change, throwing it into the canal after him.

"Here's some money, cunt."

I push my hands into my pockets and walk away down the towpath.

I feel elated.

I feel liberated.

I have struck back at life, at the pointless trivial society that makes me disappear. It's like the feeling I had the first time I fucked a prostitute, guilt-free and empowered.

I was in charge for once.

I was making the decision.

I had the power.

I feel exceptional.

It made me feel happy. It's funny that after all my studying and preparation, all my research, I end up killing some young drunken twat trying to rob me on the side of the canal. I was amused that I pushed him into the water and drowned him, nothing premeditated, prepared or technical. It wasn't the experience I thought I would have. How ridiculous! I guessed the body would resurface in a day or so – the canal isn't deep and he would bloat up quickly, unless he became entangled in some underwater rubbish, an old bike frame or shopping trolley, for example. If so, he might be gone a little longer, but he'd surface at some point. Not that the thought bothered me, there's no way I would ever be linked to the death. No, they would just assume he had fallen into the canal, drunk, and drowned. In a way, he had. No CCTV along the canal. The local environmental group Wild Camden had campaigned against installing cameras and they had won. Heaven knows why. The towpath is a haven for criminals at night. The police do patrol but not often, and they are never where they need to be. They patrol in little rubber boats that look really stupid. So there's nothing to connect me to the dead man, no witnesses and no CCTV. I am safe. And I know I am capable of killing, getting away with murder. I could have walked away after I had pushed him in, he may well have drowned anyway. But I didn't, and I am glad. I have drawn a line between society and myself. The rest of the walk home was uneventful, as always.

I strip off my clothes and clean my teeth. I go to bed but lie awake in the dark for a while, replaying the killing of the drunk in my mind. Had I really killed him? Eventually, I fall asleep, failing as always to locate the exact moment that I pass from the realm of the conscious to that of the unconscious. I doubt if anybody can catch that moment.

I sleep.

Chapter 6: **Life after Death**

The theatre is the only building on a dark road, lit from the inside. An eerie red light crawls out of the windows and doors like blood seeping from the orifices of a body, escaping onto the street, surrounding the building with an odious glow. The main doors are open. They are waiting for me, I know they are. I can feel it. They are quiet this time.

I walk up the grand steps into the foyer of the theatre. It is deserted. I can hear the music sneaking out of the auditorium. I run down the side passage towards the back stage. I am naked but I am carrying the samurai sword again. I know what will happen. I go through a small door and emerge at the side of the stage. The beautiful boys and girls are dancing, as usual, and I am waiting to kill them, as usual. The audience of ancients is silent, and I find this disconcerting. The limelight burns higher and I start to step out on to the stage when the old toothless stage assistant walks in front of me, appearing from nowhere.

"Not tonight, Sir. You cannot perform."

"Why not? I always perform."

"Not always," says the man, and he pushes me down into an armchair with clamps that clasp my hands tight so I am restrained naked in the chair.

"What? Why?"

"It's just the way it is, Sir."

I look at the stage. Another man steps out and starts to slash the dancers. They shriek with agony as they die, but never stop dancing. The killer is also naked and dripping in his victims' blood.

I am afraid. I was not afraid when I was the slaughterer; as a spectator it is terrifying.

I close my eyes.

I am on an alpine hillside. I am no longer in the chair but I am still naked. There is a small wooden cabin to my right. The scene looks like something from The Adventures of Heidi. *I walk toward a chalet. The door is slightly open. I push it and look inside. The same old man from the theatre is there. He has a girl, a young girl with blonde pigtails and a little blue dress. He has bent her over a bench and her dress is up around her waist. Her panties are round her knees. He is sticking his fingers – no, his hand – inside her.*

He looks at me and smiles. He reaches into his pocket and pulls out a knife, holding it in the air. The blade reflects the sunlight that streams through the doorway. The girl whimpers.

"It's my Valentine's knife," he says.

"Happy Valentine," he says to me, and stabs the girl in the neck. Blood jets out and he lets her fall to the ground. He holds the knife out handle first, toward me.

"For you," he smiles.

I cannot touch the knife. I am frozen to the spot. I look down, my feet have grown into the wooden floor and I am sinking down into it.

I am terrified.

The small girl sits up and looks at me, blood still pouring from her neck. Her dress is soaked in the stuff and her face covered by a red sheen. She speaks in a melodic voice, like crystal glass being tapped with a silver spoon.

"Mary Mary quite contrary,
how does your garden grow?
With silver bells and cockleshells
and pretty maids all in a row."

The girl stands up. By now I'm sunken to my hips in the floor and sweat is pouring off me. The girl walks up to me and lifts her blood soaked skirt. I am eye level with her vagina.

"CUNT!" she shouts, sounding like the chimes of an expensive clock. I disappear into the floor. I can't breathe, the ground is filling my lungs. Dirt and dust fall into my mouth and throat, dry and cloying. I feel my lungs straining. I claw at the earth with my hands.

I burst to the surface, but it's the surface of the canal. I can see myself further down the bank, forcing the drunk under the water with a piece of wood. Beyond that, I can see myself staggering back and falling into the canal while the man I have drowned stabs me. I thrash at the water, making my way to the edge of the canal as fast as I can. As I do so, the water seems to warm up between my legs.

I'm awake.

I've pissed the bed.

Light seeps around the edge of the curtain.

I have wet myself before, but not for a long time.

I'm not disturbed by the event. I just get out of bed and strip the sheet off. It could do with a wash, it hasn't seen the inside of a washing machine for at least six months.

I scrub the mattress with a dirty t-shirt and then flip the mattress over. The duvet is not wet so I climb back onto the bare mattress and pull the duvet over my head, trying to get back to sleep. Half sleeping. It's not taking a grip so I lie there, tired and annoyed. Staring at the light as it oozes around the curtain edge. I think about my dreams. They're getting more intense and taking longer to leave me. I find that unsettling. I realise that I can remember more and more detail from them and that I can picture scenes from them for quite a while after I have woken. The feeling they evoke is not so far from the feelings I carry about with me in the waking world. The murder feels like it could be a scene from my dream. I'm not even sure it wasn't. Yes, perhaps it was just a dream. I decide to get out of bed and shower. I don't have an erection this morning, which is a relief. I think I'll visit the local library and use the internet.

Once out of bed, I kick the soiled sheet into the corner by the chest of drawers with my other dirty washing. I wash clothes about every three weeks. I use the Laundromat at the end of the road. There's a nice middle aged woman who works there. If I talk to her pleasantly, she folds my clothes and matches my socks, not that it's hard. I have very few clothes and all my socks are black. I shower and eat a little tuna straight from the can, spooning it into my mouth. I have not been hungry much lately. I look around my room as I thrust the food into my mouth haphazardly. Bits of the beige fish meat fall from the spoon and land on my naked thighs. Lumps of flaky oily flesh. I pick them off with my fingers and pop them into my mouth. Oil runs down my legs. I rub it in, fishy olive oil. I don't care. I dump the empty can into the trash and pull on my underwear and jeans. I slide into another black t-shirt, grab my usual stuff, and leave my room. In the hallway, I can hear the landlady upstairs, outside someone else's room, bellowing for the rent. Peanut shells rain down the stairs, bouncing off the walls and stairs. Dodging the hail of nutshells and opening the front door I leave behind the noise of the roaring proprietor and her detritus.

The library, the municipal library, is open to all, and it's the only place that someone poor can get onto the internet. They allow you one hour a day and have a row of five old computers perched next to each other on brightly coloured Formica tables. The sort of tables you get in primary school classrooms. There is no screening between computers, so there is no privacy. Anyone can see what you are accessing and, of course, they have a key logger on each computer so they can see exactly what was entered and where you went and they can get the passwords to your email accounts if you have them.

I don't.

However; it pays to be circumspect when using the terminals at the library. They have face recognition cameras installed. They don't have to be marked, which means that you're never sure if it's a FC cam or a regular CCTV camera. When the government announced with a great flourish of trumpets that they were abolishing ID cards, they neglected to mention the fact that pretty much everybody's photo was already on record and the new generation FC cameras made ID cards redundant. Fortunately or unfortunately, depending on your point of view, the FC cameras are regularly vandalised, presumably by exactly the kind of person they are designed to observe. At any rate, you have to be careful what you look at in the library. The terminals are always busy, mostly with people looking up welfare information on government websites. It's ironic that the resource for finding out about what benefit you can claim is to be found on the Internet, a resource most poor people don't have access to. I was not looking up benefits, I was just checking the local and national news to see if the fuckwit's body had turned up. There was no indication that it had. I wasn't worried, just curious. I browsed some random stuff about the council's pavement repair schedule and, at the last moment, I punched in 'missing persons'. Up came a site with details about people who were missing and there he was, the fuckwit. Brian Harris, aged twenty-four, male, five feet nine inches, blond hair, athletic build, last seen in the Camden Arms 3 days ago... and so on, his parents say he's a lovely man, very friendly and would always stop to help someone in distress. I don't click on his picture to get more information, just scroll down the page and click through to some other links and scroll around those pages, then log off. The terminal tells me my hour is up and then promptly locks me out. I leave.

I wander up the Essex Road in an aimless way. For once it's a warm sunny day, blue sky marred in places by discoloured white clouds, floating like grey cotton wool balls in a pond. Good weather is unusual these days, or perhaps I just haven't noticed any. I decide to go to Demeter's tool shop up on the Balls Pond Road. It's a ramshackle place full of old second hand tools and plastic buckets full of light switches or thermostats and piles of toilet seats and wire, an Aladdin's cave of D.I.Y. elements. There are hand-cut, hand-written brown cardboard stars taped to the windows bearing statements like 'All Yale and Chubb locks half price' or, 'All screws and copper fittings bargain prices'. The tools are just piled up in the window. Chisels nestle up to planes and screwdrivers compete with claw hammers and plasterers' trowels for room to be noticed. Bunches of yellow and red plastic handles splay out like bouquets of flowers; clusters of assorted tools, set squares, hacksaws, mole grips and other, more esoteric, items hang from hooks like sausages in a Spanish delicatessen. More chisels and planes sit on the benches, their old wooden handles aged with a patina of time, sharp and dull. In one corner of the window leans an old bookcase, the shelves filled with a jumble of unidentifiable objects to do with plumbing or electrics or some other arcane construction art. To enter, you have to ring the grubby doorbell and Demeter will shuffle to the door and let you inside his lair. It resembles a cave, a Moroccan souk and a delicatessen, all at once. The shop extends back far further than you would expect, back into the depths of the building, endless shelves and buckets and tubs of building materials and equipment for allied trades. It's a strange mixture of second-hand and new bits and bobs. Demeter himself is an ancient man: bald, small, wizened, and wearing a bright purple hearing aid that never quite seems to work. He lets me in and I rummage through a few tubs of tools until I find what I need. I leave the store half an hour later, a large five pound lump hammer in my hand, and head back toward my room.

I will dump the hammer and take off to Camden. I want to see what's going on along the canal. They say a murderer always returns to the scene of the crime. I drop down the hill at Angel to get to the canal at the exit – or is it the entrance? – to the Islington tunnel. It's about a twenty-minute walk to Camden Lock and I'm in jovial mood as I stride along the towpath. Soon, I am at the spot where Brian had his mishap. The canal surface is smooth and unbroken, apart from a coot paddling around, searching for food. I peer into the murky water. There's nothing to be seen. I notice the water goes under a concrete ledge that juts out on the other bank. It overlaps the canal where the water takes a bend next to the old tea warehouse. A body could get stuck under there.

I wonder when he will surface, and where? I suppose it will be around here; there's little to no current in the canal. It's a strange feeling, being drawn to a place you'd think you'd want to avoid at all costs. I'm sort of excited by the thought that he's lying under the water because of me. The fact that nobody will ever link me to the event gives me a kind of ownership over my invisibility. I am using it to my advantage now, not just being invisible because nobody cares. This is the price of them not caring: me, an invisible killer in their midst.

I stroll along to Camden Lock and up onto Chalk Farm Road. It's busy, but I don't care. All the people just look like potential victims to me now, and I'm feeling well disposed toward them, so I let them live.

As I approach the station, I see a woman handing out leaflets. She is about fifty and has grey hair tied back in a ponytail with straggles of loose hair sticking to her face. She's wearing baggy blue jeans and a woollen green sweater. The sweater's tight over her large breasts. She has a careworn expression and is pressing leaflets on passers-by, her eyes tired, darting back and forth across the crowds. Back and forth. Back and forth. I wonder if this woman is looking for Fuckwit. I change my trajectory to walk closer to her.

"Please take one of these. Perhaps you have seen my son, Brian."

I smile inside. I stop and give her a serious, concerned look.

"What's the matter? What has happened to your son?"

"He is missing, disappeared the other night after watching a football match in a pub."

She pauses.

I wait.

"He's a lovely lad and wouldn't stay out without calling."

"Perhaps he's lost his phone," I suggest. I recall him demanding my phone along with my money.

"No, he would have borrowed someone's and called. I am so worried."

"Well I'm sure he'll surface soon enough."

I take one of the leaflets and wish her all the best before heading home. I'm feeling great. Not about her misery, not about her impending sorrow – I feel for her in that regard, really I do – but I'm celebrating the fact that I'm in control of something, even if it's just information about a terrible deed that I have committed. I'll take a bus home in celebration. I needed to do something big. As big as taking on society's biggest taboo, breaking it and not attempting to justify it. Now, where's that bus-stop?

The number two seven four winds round the back streets of Camden to the Angel.

I clamber on the bus but don't pay.

The drivers are shut inside a little cubicle. If you don't bother to swipe your travel card or pay a fare, generally they don't bother to get out of their box and challenge you, especially if the bus is busy as this one is. Mostly they leave you alone. The worst they can do is make you get off the bus, in which case you just wait for the next one.

I work my way past the tangle of people and find a seat next to a woman in her mid-forties, slim, and dressed in a fetching 1940s style with modern flourishes. I sit, she stares straight ahead, I glare at the rag tag collection of passengers. One of the reasons I avoid public transport is the pick and mix of humanity that crush themselves into these dirty and uncomfortable moving vehicles, usually poor and mostly foreign. The bus is a multicultural freak show, a circus containing the discarded flotsam from a thousand cultures and countries. This can be entertaining and funny for a short journey but any longer than ten minutes and it starts to become irritating.

"I'd have to kill a lot of people to make this city liveable in…"

"Pardon?" says the woman next to me.

I spoke aloud when I had only meant to think.

She must have thought I was talking to her.

What to do – apologise, or engage her in conversation? Perhaps I could lure her off the bus, kill her. No, there's CCTV here and, anyway, she does not have the feel of a victim about her.

"I said I'd have to kill a lot of people to make this city liveable in."

She laughs, a nervous tinkle of a laugh, like china shattering.

"Too true."

She thinks I'm joking. I'm not, but still, it's a way in, to let people think you are joking when you say things too awful or uncomfortable for them.

"Trouble is, who would I start with, almost spoilt for choice." I said this with a smile.

"Oh, any of them would do."

"Including you?" I enquire politely.

"Obviously not me."

"Why not you?" Still smiling.

She's nervous, the china-smashing laugh starts up again.

"Well, I rather think I have something to live for."

"Yes. Yes, you do. And I like your outfit, by the way." I smile again, time to change the subject.

"Oh, thank you. I bought it at a vintage store…"

She blathers on about her clothes. I pretend to listen but do not. I am thinking about my cock in her mouth. That's what I am thinking about but then, when I look at any woman's mouth, that's what I think about. That's what all men think about, and don't believe them if they say different. Gay men think the same, only about other men. She finishes chatting and looks expectant. I snap out of my lewd fantasy.

"Oh yes, I agree. Where are you getting off by the way?"

"Finsbury Park."

"Get off at Highbury and let's grab a coffee."

Murder does amazing things for your confidence. She could see me, was having a conversation with me. I couldn't have imagined that two weeks ago.

"Why not, I am a bit early anyway."

"Great."

We jump off the bus at Highbury Corner and head into Starbucks for a coffee. I would never normally spend the money but this was a special occasion. We chat. Well, mainly I listen and pretend to be interested in whatever it is she's saying. We sit for an hour or so, until she announces that she has to leave. I lean toward her and kiss her, much to my surprise, she responds by kissing me back. *Remarkable*, I thought. *Why on earth would she do this?*

We finish the kiss and leave the coffee shop. She seems in good spirits.

"I have to go and meet someone, but let's meet later in the week. Give me your mobile number and let's arrange something."

My mobile phone number, what was it? I never use it. Then I remember I have written it down on a slip of card and stored it in my wallet. I fish it out. She's hovering, holding a shiny mobile device. Waiting.

"Sorry, I can never remember the damn thing."

I reel off the number to her, she dabs the screen of her device with her fingers. She looks over my shoulder.

"My bus." She smiles a genuine smile, places a small kiss on my cheek, and leaves.

I'm bemused. This woman, what's her name – Martha, yes that was it – had engaged in a conversation that was entirely about her. I revealed practically nothing about myself, and most of what I did reveal was made up. And then, at the end, she had allowed me to kiss her, and taken my number and…

My phone beeped. This was the first time it had ever made a sound apart from when I use it as an alarm clock. I hooked it out of my pocket and looked at the screen:

01777567432 …Martha's number see u soon x.

There was no way I could kill her now, which was a shame because, towards the end of her talking at length about her troubles at work, I was beginning to think that she would be better off dead and I was just the man to help her. Should I text her back?

Later, I'll think about what to say. I make my way back to the house. I'm hungry and tired. This event has made me feel disjointed and defocused. That was more personal interaction than I have had in ages. It is tiring having to listen to people bang on about themselves. People love talking about themselves; why don't they shut the fuck up? The puny pathetic lives that they live are hardly worth a sentence, let alone a conversation.

I tramp down the street toward the house. The broken flagstones groan under my feet. People walk past. I catch sight of my reflection in a shop window. No, it was not mine, it was someone else's. I reach my door and enter.

The nutshells have been swept up and the post has been piled against the wall. I go downstairs to my room and heat a tin of beans, and place the hammer with my small but increasing pile of dismemberment tools. I sit and eat the beans. What to say to Martha? I ponder, and then retrieve my phone and reply to her text: *great to meat u – look fwd to seeing you soon.* I go to press send and stop. I can see the word meat and should change it to meet, but then again, I am a murderer. No, I'll change it. I press send and it's gone, words flying through the air and ending up in a little box in someone's pocket, I wonder how many millions of words a minute are spinning around the earth from one person to another?

I pick up a book and lie back on my bed to read. This one is stolen from Islington Libraries: Pema Chodron's *The Places That Scare You: A Guide to Fearlessness in Modern Times.* It's a book of Buddhist platitudes and mawkish sentiment about how to live life. I suppose I have, in my own way, turned terror and pain into joy. I am merely a beginner, but I look forward to becoming better.

Chapter 7: **Sleepwalking**

I'm standing on a flat deserted seashore. There are large cube-like blocks of black stone that appear to have been frozen in mid-tumble to the water's edge. They're heaped up and strewn around like children's building blocks. The ocean is metallic grey, oily and flat, like the surface of an ice rink. I might have thought it was solid but I know it's not, small waves lapping at the rocks along the edge show me this. I am aware of things under the surface of the water, things terrifying and deadly. The shoreline disappears into the distance in either direction, a straight line, as far as I can see. It vanishes into the murky sky, a sky that is dark grey and boiling with clouds that burst with silent sheet lightning. The horizon is a mixture of blood red and a sickly green light filtered through the angry clouds. There is complete silence, as if all noise has been removed from the universe. I am standing on a narrow pathway set back from the shore and made, I notice, from Portland stone slabs. The surface is new and the slabs perfectly set. This path has never been walked, of that I am sure. It leads off in both directions. I am alone. I turn to look behind me, inland there is nothing to be seen, just a wall of blackness. A dark so tangible you can grasp it in your hand like clay. I have to go somewhere, so I walk, and as I walk the scenery stays the same. I can see tiny movements in my peripheral vision. In the tangible dark something is moving. I walk for hours and as I walk, the dark recedes to reveal a landscape of huge stone slabs and shards, piled up high into the sky, they look as if they should collapse at any moment. Giant paving slabs piled up to the sky by an autistic ogre. These piles of rocks pay only lip service to gravity. The pavement under my feet is warm and comfortable, a fantastic walking experience. I look at my feet and they are glowing and perfect, no shoes, in fact, I am naked. I continue to walk, the perfect path caressing my feet, mountains of slabs to my left, and always the static, endless and menacing ocean to my right. Where am I going? My feet are happy on the path and there is no change to the landscape visible ahead. I wonder where I am: it's familiar and yet unknown. I walk and walk, the light stays the same, there is still no sound. I see a small boat sitting next to a jetty that slinks out into the water. I know I have to go to the boat and let it take me to wherever it's going. I clamber over the black rocks and down to the jetty – the boat is a few feet lower than the jetty. It's a wooden row-boat with an antiquated outboard motor on the back. Inside is a bench but no oars. I sit on the edge of the jetty and give the boat's hull a tentative push; the boat rocks and sways but appears seaworthy. I lurch down into it and sit, twisting my body; I see the motor is a Neptune Mighty Mite, an iconic 2hp engine made from 1938 to 1987 by the Muncie Corp of Muncie Indiana. Though this looks like the 1960s engine made in Cordele Georgia, judging by the gold colour and the squared-off fuel tank. Rumour had it that after the company moved to Lehigh Acres Florida all the engines were assembled by senior citizens. It's a strange little portion of detail in an otherwise featureless environment. I give the outboard's starting cord a yank, it does not start; another, the engine coughs and turns over, but still doesn't engage, another, it splutters into life, clouds of blue smoke belch from the motor and it idles. I adjust my seating position so I can look ahead and control the motor and throttle with my right hand. I am comfortable, although my feet yearn for the feel of the perfect path. I twist the throttle and the boat zips forward cutting a wide V-shape through the still surface of the sea. I head randomly away from the shore, random in the sense that I have no conscious idea where I am going but then this is not the world of the conscious and the boat or my hand or something else knows where to go. The water turns to a less oily consistency and the stillness leaves it as I head away from the shore, taking on the more natural attributes of water. There is a swell, and waves and wind, although still no sound.

The clouds heave above me and rain starts to fall. I am wet and somewhat troubled, but I have no choice and press onward. The rain drives almost horizontal and the waves tower above me, yet no water comes into the boat. Ahead I can see the outline of an Island. High cliffs and storm-battered headlands. The boat continues towards an inlet, a rocky fiord; as the boat heads into the inlet the storm stops. The boat cuts along the narrow canyon, high intimidating cliffs on either side, for miles and miles it glides along, and then around a bend is a house set into the cliff side. The house is unusual. I can see that the boat can motor straight into a water garage built under the house. The house itself climbs up several stories, it's hard to make out how many, and it's made from the same stone as the cliff. It looks as if the cliff-face has been extruded to form the front and side walls of the house and then sheared flat and burnished to a high sheen. The windows are all smoked glass; there appears to be no external entrance. I suppose I must enter the house from the water level. I pilot the boat into the entrance in the side of the cliff and on into the cavern. It's lit by a blue glow; I can't see the source of the illumination. There's a small stone jetty with steps and a ramp.

I pull the boat alongside and as I do the motor cuts out. It's only after it has stopped running that I realise I could hear it, it's audible only by its absence. I step out of the boat and walk up the ramp to the door at the top. The door is a frosted glass such as you might find in an expensive hotel or penthouse apartment. It has a brass metal handle.

I pull.

It opens.

Beyond are stone steps leading up.

I climb.

At the top is a large room with full-length glass windows overlooking the fiord. Standing to one side against the wall and staring out of the windows at the storm is a beautiful redheaded woman.

She is very tall.

I stare at her.

She does not move or notice me. I look around and behind me against the wall is a portable butcher's block on a wheeled stand and a rack of sharp knives. I know what I have to do next.

The woman turns to face me. She has long elegant fingers, much longer than is anatomically possible. In fact although her arms and legs are too long by a fair amount, this adds to her beauty and grace. Her hair is long and tumbles over her white shoulders and frames her face, which is chiselled and fine, her grey eyes look directly into mine. She moves sideways to stand in front of the windows, her long limbs crablike against the light. She waits.

I select a long bladed knife with a heavy black handle. I walk towards her; as I reach her she smiles and looks at me.
She links her eyes to mine.

Silence.

I plunge the knife into her abdomen just above the pubic bone and pull the blade upwards, opening her belly. Intestines and blood cascade out, but she stays standing, her eyes locked to mine, a smile welded to her face. The blade slides easily up her torso reaching her breastbone, slicing through it like a scythe, opening her chest. I cut through her throat and up to her lower jaw. The smile is gone but she is still looking at me. One last upward heave and I slice her head in half. It's like cutting a slice of cake. Her body opens up like a flower and crumples to the floor in a slow delicate arc, landing in a vast pool of blood and organs.

I am covered in her warm sticky fluids. My hand hangs limply by my side holding the knife. My cock stands hard and proud covered in her blood.

As I stare at her eviscerated body I see a movement inside the chest cavity and a small silver beast, like a cat mixed with an armadillo. There is something of her face and look about the thing as it clambers out of her body. It sits on what remains of her and licks the goo off its body, and then it jumps toward the window and runs through it. The glass does not break and the window is not open – it has just passed through the glass, if there is any glass? I step over her body and walk to the window: glass, hard, cold, solid. Well, I should not be surprised by anything here. What was that creature? Do we all have one inside us?

I turn and she has gone, the floor is clean, it's as if she was never there, which, of course, she never was. I find it strange that I have moments of lucidity when I'm aware of the dream and then longer moments when I am immersed and everything is real, which, of course it is. What happens if I have an accident or hurt myself? I look at the knife in my hand: the blade is sparkling clean. I pull the edge across the back of my left hand, – Ouch!– it hurts and blood immediately wells up from a long thin cut. I put the knife back on the block and lift my hand to my mouth to lick the wound. My left arm and hand is free of the sticky congealing mess that covers the rest of me. I need to wash. I head to a door on the far side of the room and open it. A wet-room. I turn the tap and hot water fires out of the showerhead, I can hear the noise, it is as welcome as sunshine, all that silence was oppressive.

I shower and clean the dead woman from my body. There are no towels. I will have to drip dry. I walk out of the wet-room to find myself on another floor, or at least not in the same place as before, or perhaps another part of the same place, things do not work the same here. I'm in a long hallway with black wooden floorboards and a purple runner on the floor; there are doors off the hallway on either side, and at the far end a large door which is ajar. I am pulled to the room with the half open door. Light spills out and inside is a small bedroom similar to my own but lighter and without the kitchen part. There is a bed and a wardrobe and in the middle of the room, a lectern on which is laid a large book. The book is closed. I shiver and then notice the clothes laid out on the bed. I walk to them and put them on, black t-shirt, blue jeans, black socks, underwear, and a grey sweater.

I go to the lectern and stare at the book, it's large like an old bible and the cover is black inlaid with red and blue leather in a complicated intertwined abstract design. There are no words on the outside of the book. It sits waiting for me to open it, so I do, I open it at random about half way through. It is a photograph album, I open it on a page of old photographs of dead children laid out in Victorian finery surrounded by relatives both adult and child also dressed in their Sunday best. The picture I look at shows a dead boy of around ten lying on a couch; behind him lined up in order of height are his brothers and sisters. There are six of them, three girls and three boys. On either side of the couch are four adults all dressed in black, two men in mourning suits and two women in widow's weeds. The boy lies on the couch and for some reason is wearing a miniature, military uniform, his expression is peaceful and his face is mine.

I'm shocked and turn the page to look at the next photograph, there are two pictures on this page, a portrait of a mother sitting on a chair, hair in a bonnet, baby on her knee wrapped in a swaddling cloth. The woman looks grim, then I realise her baby is dead and the baby's face? Mine. The next photograph, a full length picture of a little girl laid out on a couch wearing a full-length white dress, her tiny feet crossed over each other enclosed in white boots, her hair neat and tied back, her head tilted to one side, eyes closed, she looks as if she's sleeping. One arm lays on the couch the other on her chest grasping a rose. She is unbearably beautiful. Her face is mine. I turn the pages – there are more and more photographs of dead Victorian children, all of them look like me.

I slam the book shut.

I am afraid and anxious.

There is a dragging and bumping sound outside in the corridor. I don't want to open the door to find out what it is; instead I slide the bolt closed on the back of the door and climb into the bed. I am overcome by tiredness and drag the blankets up my body. I can hear the storm outside in the fiord and the dragging sound out in the corridor.

I close my eyes and sleep.

Nothing…

My eyes open, it is dark, so dark I can see nothing and there's no sound. I lie very still wondering where am I? Am I still in the room with the photographs next to the fiord? Am I in my room in Islington? Of course I am, the fiord was a dream right? I reach out to my left and feel the table. Walking my fingers along it I find the light and the switch. I snap it on. My eyes pulsate with the sudden brightness and my room leaps into view. No lectern, no book containing a thousand photographs of a dead me.

"Good."

I throw back the duvet. The back of my left hand is cut, it hurts, and I can see the long red weal on the back. I must have scraped it along the edge of the table in my sleep. I sit up and swing my legs over the edge of the bed onto the floor. My left foot feels something cold under my toes. I look down and see a knife on the floor by the bed. It's long and with a black handle. The knife I bought last week for my project. How did that get there? I pick it up and examine it. It seems fine and I put it back over by the wardrobe with the other project tools.

The dream is still darting around in my head. I shake my head and rub my eyes, a shower will wash the remnants out of my mind. As I walk to the shower, grabbing the towel, I wonder if anything ever leaves your mind, or is it all in there, somewhere, everything we ever think, see, hear, feel, all stored inside our brains somewhere? I shudder and twist the taps, the shower bursts on.

Hot water.

Under the water I scrub my hair and body. My muscles ache and my shoulders are tense as if I had expended extra effort – more than usual – which I haven't. I think about the woman in the dream, the silver beast, and the photographs of dead children. It felt, still feels, so real, so vivid. I remember that someone, maybe Jamillia the cunt, told me that the Kabala says that the soul leaves the body while we sleep and visits its heavenly source to replenish its energy, leaving a part of the soul in the body to keep it alive. That's when the soul is free to experience visions and encounters that are usually off-limits to beings of this world. Sounds like a load of ancient mystical claptrap to me. What sort of a heaven was that place?

I let the water pour over me.

I feel better by the end of the shower and the images and feelings from the dream have receded. Still, I make a point of noting them down on a piece of paper.

I make soymilk porridge for breakfast,. it's disgusting.

Later in the day I pick up a copy of the Camden Journal. It leads with a story about local council rubbish collections being increased to two a week for both domestic collections and the street trash-cans after local residents' groups withheld tax payments because of the amount of trash spilling out of the bins and onto the street. Underneath that is a photo of the Fuckwit. There he is, smiling from a photograph taken in some other part of the world, surrounded by grinning urchins. The story is headlined "Sad death of much loved charity worker". I read on, – apparently Brian Harris, 23, was a man who had returned from working with street children in Bolivia, helping to set up an orphanage, called "The House of the Future". He was due to get married in July. Could this story get anymore cloying? It continues:

"His body was found yesterday in the Regent's Canal by the Royal College St Bridge, it had been trapped under a concrete plinth and it seems he had drowned several days before being found. It appears to be an unfortunate accident as when last seen Mr Harris had been drinking at the Camden Arms. The police do not suspect foul play. A coroner's inquest will take place on Tuesday at St Pancreas Coroners Court."

That's tomorrow; I think about going, how do I do that? His mother was quoted as saying that he'd be much missed by his family and the children at the "Children create our future" project. I start to feel sick. No mention of his propensity to try and rob defenceless disabled people. Still, foul play was not suspected. I will go to the inquest; it'll be fun to watch myself get away with murder.

I walk along Upper Street thinking about the difference in the person I read about and the person I drowned on the Regent's Canal not five days previously. This discrepancy is odd. Perhaps he was one of those people that didn't cope well with booze. I can relate to that, it's why I gave up drinking all those years ago. I was a terrible drunk and behaved appallingly, fighting people and driving my car when really smashed. Once I crashed it into seven parked cars, another time I climbed into a tree and fell asleep and woke up in the morning, and promptly fell out – that hurt. I have woken up in hospitals and police stations and on strangers' floors. Perhaps the fact that he was drunk accounts for it, but then again, maybe the real person is let out by the relaxing capacity of alcohol. I mean, I'm sober and I murdered him. On a scale of badness this ranks way higher than him trying to rob me when he was drunk, and yet I feel that I am definitely a better person for my actions. So I suppose he didn't die in vain.

I walk to the library and sit at an internet terminal. For some reason the library is empty, maybe the good weather means all the poor people like me, that use the library as a warm place to sit around, are out and about. I don't know and it doesn't matter. Out of curiosity aroused by the apparent dichotomy of Fuckwit's behaviour I decide to punch in Fuckwit's charity. I entered "the House of the Future + Bolivia" into Google and it returns about ten pages of results, including the home's own website. These are never to be trusted – any organisation's website is riddled with lies and deceit. I think about it this way: if you were going to put up a web page about yourself, you would lie about some things and omit plenty of others, well, businesses and especially charities do the same in order to present the best possible picture of themselves. I scan down the page looking for something, I don't know what. There's a listing on WeKnoAboutU.com, the headline is << Snow orphans in Bolivia>> I click on it and it takes me to a site that carries news of an investigation into "House of the Future" which claims that it's a front for child sex trafficking and cocaine manufacture. It appears that several local workers at the home were arrested, as was the director, after allegations of abuse and drug taking were made by ex-residents. The authorities in Santa Cruz de la Sierra are interested in talking to a Mr Brian Harris.

It would seem our fantastic charity worker's halo could be tarnished.

I smile.

Chapter 8: **Cut and Thrust**

My phone rings.

I stare at it, shocked, it has never rung, not once.

Never.

It sits on my bedside table lit up and chirruping at me, flashing a number.

I don't know what to do, so I just stare at it until it stops. I'm relieved, but continue to scrutinise the phone. It lights up again and beeps. I stare at it some more, sitting stock still, unsure about what to do. After a few minutes I pick up the phone from the table and press the menu button; the phone tells me there is a voicemail waiting and do I want to call to hear it? I do and I do. The message service answers telling me I have one new message and to press three to hear it, I press three on the keypad.

"Hello, it's Martha. I was wondering if you were free tonight?" I'm free every night.

" I was thinking it would be nice to meet up." Nice, nice for who?

"Maybe we could meet in a pub." I hate pubs, the smell, the noise and the stupid stink of drunken words.

"And perhaps go for a drink" I don't drink.

"er…well, anyway give me a call back if you want." Do I want to call back?

"see you later bye." Assumption.

Do I want to see her and go to a pub? It's not something I ever think of doing, drinking turns me into someone else. I am not good at it, or maybe I am too good at it, either way two pints of Stella and I am fit to murder someone. As I think this I realise that I have, in fact, murdered someone. So I might as well go out for a drink as alcohol may not have been the reason I felt like murdering people.

Perhaps the booze just let that part of me get closer to the surface. The logic seems impregnable so I find the missed call log on the phone and hit redial. I have a slight churning in my stomach, what if she says no? Wait – she invited me, of course she won't say no, in fact, she'll be chuffed that I called back so quickly and accepted her invite, – she will see it as a sigh of positive interest and then, in that way females have, she will misinterpret my interest and make it whatever she wants it to be.

The phone rang, after five rings it stopped and her voice popped into my head.

"Hello, thanks for calling back, how are you?"

"I'm good thanks, about that drink."

"Oh yes, would you like…"

"Yes, where and when?"

"The Wenlock Arms about 8pm?"

"Ok where's the Wenlock Arms?"

"Wenlock Street, surprisingly," she let out a little nervous laugh.

"Of course it is, I'm a bit of a dummy." She laughs more.

"I'll see you there at 8pm then." I say.

We say our goodbyes and I rang off. I have a date, remarkable, this is almost a first. A first in about 10 years. I have a few hours to kill, so I return to what I was doing before the phone rang, which was preparing to sharpen my knives on a whetstone.

An Ardennes Couticle, a natural yellow whetstone mined in Belgium. This is an irregular shaped stone called a "bout"; I found it along with an couple of smaller stones around the back of an old butcher's shop being stripped down and converted into a new media creative node. In the bins with the old counters, wood and plaster was this lovely little whetstone. They're expensive and this is a beauty. Probably the workmen didn't know what it was and threw it out as junk. These stones contain 40% garnet, and when the cutting edge is drawn across the smooth wet surface of the stone the garnet crystals are released with particles of stone to produce, in combination with the water, a very fine slurry. The garnet crystals cut lightly into the metal taking very fine shavings. The hardness of the garnet allows for a very quick removal of metal, but the roundness of the stone allows for a very exact polish of the honed edge. It's a procedure requiring concentration and skill, it's not to be rushed. I enjoy this – it keeps me focused.

I have set the stones and knives out on the table top, they are lying on some newspaper. Standing next to the stones is the small saucepan with some water in it. I have my cleaver, a long carving knife, a small boning knife and a pair of long metal scissors. All of which require sharpening, or at the very least, stropping. I wet the larger stone and take the smaller blue stone out of the saucepan of water and with a gentle circular motion I rub it across the surface of the larger yellow stone. I choose my boning knife as the first recipient of my love. The trick is to have the back and edge of the blade flat on the stone; it is not like using a steel or a cinderblock. This is the 'Art of Sharpening' as opposed to your father at the table waving a carving knife and steel about, or some dozy chef in a restaurant sharpening one to cut up a turkey.

This is ritual.

I slowly push the blade along the stone away from me, and at the far end of the stone I gently turn it over and pull it back towards me. It makes a gentle metallic scraping sound, softened by the slurry.

I find it soothing, I repeat the movements until I think the blade is sharp and then lift the blade to 45 degrees and sharpen the cutting edge only. When it's sharp I wipe the blade and put the knife on the left side of the table. I repeat the process with the three knives and my meat cleaver. To check the blades' sharpness I carry out the hanging hair test, designed for old style straight razors – it's simple – I pluck out a head hair, a single head hair and see if my knife blades are sharp enough to cut through it when it's held up in the air. You bring the hair slowly down on the blade and it should pass through the hair with no sound or resistance. It's a controversial test in straight razor circles due to the fact that hairs can vary in thickness and oiliness and so on, – there is a lot of passion amongst the aficionados of honing. But for me it's fine; after all it's not as if I am going to be shaving any facial hair, just dismembering a body. I suppose I could just use an axe, a hammer and a saw, but I prefer to be efficient and precise – besides, I want to cut the body up into small, difficult to identify pieces, and do it quickly, so I need very sharp tools.

For good measure I also use the thumbnail test. An Orthodox Jewish slaughter-man in an abattoir in Ireland showed me this test years ago. Jewish slaughter-men kill cattle by cutting their throats with a long knife. It must be extremely sharp and strong. The slaughter-man, an Australian called Daniel, told me that they have two years of training before they are allowed to even pick up a knife and a further year before they can kill their first animal. The knives are kept sharp because the cut has to be quick and effective, no second chances. Daniel's technique was take his thumbnail face up to the blade and at an angle of about 40°, very gently and slowly draw it down the blade, it has to run smoothly all the way along the blade if it catches at any point then you have a chip in the blade and have to hone it more. I carry out this test on my knives and the scissors. They pass both tests.

I asked Danny why the Jews bled meat before eating it and didn't eat any blood products –apparently they believe, and the Sanhedrin tells them – that the soul of a being resides in the blood and by cutting its throat and draining the blood they are allowing the soul to return to 'G-D' before the body gets eaten. I place my new, sharper instruments away and clear up the table.

It's time to go and meet Martha.

I walk to the Wenlock Arms down near the canal. I'm not sure I want to go through with this. It's making me feel nauseous and my hands are sweating. I keep puffing out my cheeks and expelling breath in quick little sighs as I walk toward the pub. It's not easy to find, it's tucked away in a warren of little streets behind the Regent's Canal towards Hackney. The roads aren't busy with people but they're not deserted either. It's in the twilight hours between people finishing work and going out. It takes maybe fifteen minutes, but it's as if the world has gone into slow motion and seems to take hours.

"I shouldn't go.

I have no money.

I don't know her.

I don't want to interact with people.

That's shit, of course I do, I hate being invisible, not existing in the eyes of the world except for officials and machines.

But you have a plan, remember, so what's this got to do with it – you're not going to kill her are you?

It was killing Fuckwit that gave you the confidence to talk to her in the first place and look where that got you – she likes you and it'll be good for you."

The internal dialogue carries on in my head all the way to the pub and then, there it is. An old fashioned pub with live acoustic music, men with beards, bare boards on the floor and lots of real ale. Yellow light spills out of the windows and I hear the discordant chink, chink of a piano, as some unseen hand jabs at it with more enthusiasm than skill. I sidle up to the window and peek in. I see her sitting alone at a table in the back of the pub, tending a pint of beer and reading a paper, nonchalant and relaxed. I'm tensed up like a frog about to snap up a fly. If I go in and it goes well, I could be in trouble. I move too fast emotionally for people, that's why I ended up isolating myself for all these years. If I decide I like someone I am too childish, I end up vulnerable and wanting reassurance and it's always a disaster. I could just look at her as a victim and then I'd feel nothing but disdain and that's wrong, at least rationally. I can see she has done nothing to deserve that, she has shown an interest in me and that's more difficult to deal with than the tidal wave of disinterest shown to me every day by society.

This is personal and it's the personal I can't handle with any certainty. I think about this as I stand outside in the dark watching her reading the paper and looking altogether normal.

The pub door opens and two men reel out, one crashes into me and knocks me off balance into a litterbin, it tips over and I end up on the floor with the litter bin and its contents on top of me.

"Oh sorry mate, didn't see you there, you OK?"

His mate laughs and extends his hand to me to help me get up.

"You must be the fucking invisible man, here let me help you."

I say nothing nor do I take his hand. The other man was standing the bin back up and picking bits of trash off me.

"No harm done, let me buy you a drink."

I don't take the outstretched hand but lift myself to my feet. I stare at the one that knocked me over as he continues trying to pick up the trash, giggling to himself in an inane drunken fashion. I look at his friend – the one who had held out the helping hand that I ignored. He is also watching his mate stagger about.

"He's way too drunk for 8pm," said the man, tucking his hands in his pockets.

"Yeah, he sure is a pissed cunt." I was beginning to find the scenario funny.

"You want that pint then?" said 'hands tucked in pocket man'.

"No, it's okay I don't drink." I watch the drunken man trip on the kerb twisting around and collapsing like a bag full of pies.

"Ok, mate, if you're sure. I'd better get this drunk cunt home, I swear one day he'll get himself killed." The man offers his hand and I shake it.

"He just might, he just might."

The man went and lifted his friend up, and heaved one arm over his shoulder. As he was starting to stagger off carrying his heavy load he shouted.

"Oh and you should do something about that invisible thing."

I wonder what he meant by that. Probably nothing. I have a tendency to read too much into things. At least that was what

Jamillia the Cunt said as she left with my son.

I look back into the pub. The litterbin moment had passed by completely unnoticed. Martha is still reading the paper, her pint not much diminished, all this thinking and litterbin action had only taken a few minutes, felt like a lifetime. I take a deep breath and let it out in a long sigh, push open the door and walk in.

The pub's warm and bright. It's about half full and Martha doesn't look up from the paper. I'm unsure about what attitude to strike, I decide on laid-back and confident as the best approach, though by no means an easy one for me to pull off, at least internally, but then I suppose that doesn't matter as long as it seems real to other people then that's what you are.

I walk to the bar and order a pint of lager shandy with the weakest lager they have in the pub. Once it's poured I grasp the pint and walk over to the table, standing in front of it about five feet away from her. She carries on reading the paper and then looks up and around the pub apparently not seeing me. Am I invisible even to people who actually want to see me?

I cough, she looks round still not seeing me, I step forward.

"Hi." I say, she jumps, startled.

"Hello, for some reason I didn't see you standing there, strange."

"Yeah, I get that a lot." I walk over with a smile and sit on the other stool at the table. She folds the paper and takes a sip of her beer. I sip mine.

"So, how have you been, busy?"

A good opening line: expressing interest in me without being personal.

"Pretty busy, yes, what with one thing and another. How about you?"

Not a bad response – appear to answer whilst giving nothing away and bounce the conversation back to her so she can talk about what she loves to talk about most, herself. I take a sip of my weak beer as she starts off on a monologue about her work and family. I make a mental note of key things, she hates her boss, Barry. Her sister Jane is getting married next month and she doesn't know what to wear, her cat is ill, etcetera. These points I can refer to on occasion and she will be amazed and impressed that I remember, and therefore if I remember I must care. At least in the female mind the two are equated.

I nod a bit here and there and drink my beer, being careful not to drink too fast but encourage her to finish hers.

She does, and offers to buy another. I accept.

"Just a half, I have a lot to do tomorrow." She smiles.

I am so responsible; she likes that.

She walks to the bar, a definite sway to her hips, she's wearing a red patterned knee-length skirt and an ice-blue tight sweater. Sexy. She returns shortly with the two drinks.

"Here you go."

She places the drink on the table and sits opposite me twirling a strand of hair in one hand and playing with her drink in the other. We chat about things of no consequence and the time passes. It's not too unpleasant but there's always this nagging feeling in the back of my brain about what am I supposed to do next. I know that I have already kissed her, so I suppose I should again. I am making her laugh – or she is working on laughing at my stupid jokes.

What the fuck do I do next?

"So what about you? What do you do?"

This caught me by surprise a direct question about me.

I shift in my seat and answer.

"Right now I'm not working, unemployed, but I keep myself busy."

"What do you do when you work then?"

"Engineer but I am on a disability pension."

"Oh how? I haven't noticed"

"Can't use my left arm, industrial accident."

I feel exposed and about six inches tall; this isn't pleasant. Martha doesn't seem fussed about it at all.

"I can see you'd rather not discuss it but all I can say is, it doesn't show and you're a handsome man and funny..."

I'm shocked, complimented and uncomfortable all at the same time. She laughs her nervous laugh, high pitched and hesitant. It doesn't seem to match her demeanour anymore. She is forward, her hand brushing my leg a couple of times as she talks. Perhaps it's because she's older, maybe that makes a woman less inhibited. I catch her eye and she holds contact a bit longer than necessary.

"Shall we go?"

She looks me straight in the eye as she says this.

"I live nearby – you could come and have a coffee."

"*Ok.*"

I'm not in control; perhaps I never had been.

We leave.

We fuck.

I lie in her bed in the dark, she's fast asleep, her breath rattling quietly in her chest. I can't let myself sleep. I'm frightened of having those dreams with her lying there next to me. She had fallen asleep more or less straight after we had finished having sex. I thought it was a very male thing to do. I dozed in fits and starts and somehow I wake myself just as I started to slip into a dream, as if my subconscious is aware that this is not a safe environment in which to descend into that subterranean world. The room is dark, not as dark as mine, it faces the street and an orange glow creeps in past the blinds that hang down in front of the window. She has an entire apartment to herself, luxury compared to my living arrangements. Next to the bedroom is a living room that looks like a photo-shoot from some upmarket interiors magazine, with a shiny black and white kitchen area and a clinical white bathroom off the landing. It's a modern block of apartments. It has CCTV in the corridors and an empty desk sat in the foyer for the concierge service in the daytime. She has a good job, I can't remember what it is, something to do with the government; it seems everyone who has a job works for the government these days. I slide out of the bed and glance at the large red numerals on her big bedside clock 2:48am.

Early.

I gather up my clothes from the floor, grab my shoes and slope off in silence to the living room. I dress, drink a cup of water and leave. It isn't far to my room. I walk along the pavement, the slabs brushed a delicate orange by the streetlights, through the empty streets and back to my room, puzzled by the night's proceedings.

Inside my room I strip off and clamber into bed. I feel physically and emotionally exhausted and I have to be at the coroner's court at 10am for Fuckwit's inquest. I sit up and wonder where my phone is, I remember it's in my trouser pocket. I peel back the duvet and hoist the trousers to my hand with a foot; pulling the phone out I set the alarm: 9.15am, that will be plenty of time, it's only a 20 minute walk away. I dump the trousers back on the floor and toss the phone onto the bedside table. I switch off the light and lie in bed thinking about the evening and Martha and sex. I have always perceived sex as an ordeal to be got through, not a pleasurable fun activity or even an expression of love; it's more a compulsion and if don't ejaculate at least once a day then I get tense and edgy. On the rare occasions I have sex with women there is always a mental wall between them and me: it's as if I am watching them from a distance, watching the whole performance on a screen, like a porn movie. Apparently I am good at it and have a big cock, but it feels as if it's a duty I must perform: make them come, then I must come and then the job is done. I have no idea if this is the way normal men feel about sex. I have never discussed it with anyone, but the empty distant feeling I have conflicts with a mindless feeling of contentment caused by all the chemicals that having sex releases; I suppose it's an evolutionary trick to make us do it more, because masturbation, while giving relief, does not make me feel the same way. There is also a feeling of control: if I make a woman orgasm then she is helpless and under my power. This may be an illusion. All in all, sex and interaction with females is too complicated for me to feel comfortable with.

Sometimes I wonder what I could have achieved if I had used all the energy I've expended on chasing girls, wanking and fucking, on something productive, – perhaps I would have made a full-size replica of the Eiffel tower out of lollipop sticks; at least I would have something to show for all the effort. I'm tired and need to stop this pointless consideration and pull the cover over my head. I have to sleep. I have things to do.

Chapter 9: **Rest in Pieces**

I'm on an aeroplane, a crowded no-frills orange airline. Flying where and why, I have no idea. The sky is slate grey and flat. No up and no down, no indication of where the aircraft is travelling, to, or from. There are people on the flight, hundreds of them, all anonymous. I have an aisle seat, I always have an aisle seat. I look to my left at the old woman sitting next to me, she has a tight grip on the seat rest and is staring fixedly ahead, face drawn and white.

Fear?

The plane hits turbulence and bounces around like a small child on a trampoline, it feels almost playful, bounce first to the right, and then up, and then down and to the left. Items start to fall from the overhead lockers, holiday hats and bottles of duty-free booze bound along the aisle. The plane twists and turns, I can see the stewardess trying to make it to the intercom only to be thrown against the tea trolley, which pours hot water over her upturned face. Her scream of pain starts the passengers off shouting and panicking. Bags, coats and children's toys rain down from the lockers and spring around the floor like popcorn firing from a hot pan. I feel calm and amused. The woman next to me vomits – her eyes wild and her hands trying to rip the armrests from the seat as the plane catapults into a dive.

A voice comes over the intercom.

"Welcome to this flight. We have a selection of fine duty-free items available from our inflight shop…." It snaps off – the recorded voice is replaced by the captain.

"Ladies and gentlemen please remain seated. We are in a spot of intense turbulence but there's nothing, repeat nothing to be worried about."

The announcement is followed by a terrible grinding sound as the side of the plane disappears, and I am sitting all alone in the sky with the old lady next to me, our two seats suspended in the air. Away to my left I can see a flaming hunk of metal falling out of the sky and dotted around other seated people also hurtling downward, why am I not falling? I look at the old woman strapped in next to me her eyes are wide as saucers and her mouth opening and closing like a goldfish, no sound is coming out. I turn to her and unclip her seat belt, she looks at me for a moment – is that gratitude I see as I tip her out of the seat and into the dark grey sky – she is gone. I feel better, the seat remains suspended in the nothingness of the sky, the plane and its inhabitants are gone. Now what?

"Are you comfortable?" says a voice from somewhere close by, but unseen.

"Yes thanks".

There's no response.

I look around and see nothing, just grey blankness everywhere.

Suspended in nothing I decide to leave my seat. I unclip the seat belt and lurch forward. I fall up. I rise as fast as a leaf in a typhoon. The grey gives way to blue and then black, and then I am falling, fast toward the ground, fear grasps me and sweat oozes from every pore. My heart pounds in my ears.

I can see that I'm falling towards a house on the edge of a fiord, the cliffs grey and broken, the water black and swirling. I will die very soon and the thought saddens me, which is a surprise.

"Wait," I say and everything stops. I stop, the fall stops, the water stops swirling, and the wind stops blowing.

I'm inside the house. I recognise the place although it seems different to the last time I was here, subtly changed, it feels warmer and more familiar.

I didn't like the method of my arrival, – I suppose I was not in charge of that aspect of this dream – is this a dream? I walk up the staircase and into the large room with the floor-to-ceiling glass windows. The butcher's block is there – and the knives, but no woman. There is a chair, and in the chair is sitting a small child around 6 years old. The child looks familiar, too familiar.

It should.

It's me.

"What took you so long?" The child asks in a sing-song voice, a voice wrong for the body it's coming from.

"I have been waiting for you."

"Why?"

"You have to complete your tasks to be free and whole again."

What tasks?

"I am you and so you know the answer to that."

Enigma annoys me and I stalk toward the child, intent on extracting an answer, when the chair falls back and the child is running towards the window. He doesn't stop when he reaches the glass, he just runs through it and falls from sight. I chase after him. I catch my foot on the fallen chair, twisting it, and crash into the glass window, bouncing like a rubber ball off the pane and onto the floor, my sight blurred and my head reeling. I can't seem to stand and slide back to the floor. I am going to pass out. Blackness.

My eyes open, it's dark and I'm lying on the floor. I tenderly reach out and feel a cover next to me; as my eyes adjust I can see a slice of dim light cutting down a wall near me and I realise I'm on the floor of my room.

I have fallen out of bed.

I feel battered, my right foot throbs with pain. I'm groggy but I clamber onto my bed and reach for the light. I turn it on. I have twisted and turned, hurt my foot and shuffled off the bed, complete with duvet, onto the floor.

Nothing more than that. As the dream vapour leaves my brain I check the time, it's nearly nine, and I have to be at the Coroner's Court on St Pancras Way behind King's Cross station by ten. It's a half-hour walk away so I clamber into the shower for a speedy wake-up wash and then, still damp, I dress and grab a tin of sardines to eat on the way. I cannot be late for Fuckwit's inquest. I leave my room noticing that the door to the room next to mine, the empty one, is again open a crack. Strange, but I have no time to investigate. I climb the stairs and leave the building, stepping out into an intense sunlit morning. The air is forensic in its brilliance, and the morning shadows are etched into buildings and roads. I set off at a brisk pace past the Packington estate, which is being demolished day-by-day and bit-by-bit.

I make the Coroner's Court by ten minutes to ten. It's a gothic red brick Victorian building, set on the edge of St Pancras Gardens, which are really the grounds to St Pancras Church, an old graveyard that no longer accepts burials, surrounded by local authority housing on three sides in Camden. The arched windows in the side of the Coroner's Court look out over the graveyard. I have time to spare so I walk around the gardens in the bright sunlight. In the middle of the gardens is a large memorial. It's a twenty foot high sundial, a cream and red obelisk topped with typically ornate gothic points, sitting on a set of stepped plinths of red and cream stone, with mosaic tile-work depicting flowers. It is, of course, made out of Portland stone, along with marble, granite and red Mansfield stone. It commemorates a wealthy Victorian woman hailed in her time as "The Queen of the Poor", another of those self-seeking tax-dodging philanthropists, she wanted to rid London of its slums; she failed to do that in the way she wanted, but the poor have been relocated and have hot water and electricity. The slums are gone, converted into desirable residences and new slums now exist. They are more emotional and mental hovels than physical ones, they are slums of the mind, created for the information age.

The memorial squats in the same graveyard that Mary Shelley, the author of Frankenstein, used to play in as a little girl. Her mother is buried here. It seems appropriate that the Coroner's Court is situated in a graveyard, and I think that little Mary would appreciate that I am another kind of monster created by a woman. I go to find the entrance to the court. It turns out I've been wandering the graveyard longer than I thought and the inquest has already started.

I sneak quietly through the dark wooden door and slide onto the last bench at the back against the wall. I like the room with its old fashioned, dark wood panels and deep red wallpaper, it feels reassuring, a mongrel mix between a Victorian classroom and a chapel. There is nothing sinister about this place. All the benches in the room have solid fronts and are just like church pews. At the far end raised up and behind a wooden frontispiece is the Coroner in a high-backed chair with a brass lamp in front of him, and a pile of reports and papers stacked up on either side of the lamp. He has grey hair, pince-nez glasses, a deep grey suit and purple tie, and the air of a kindly doctor. He is twisting a very expensive black Mont Blanc fountain pen between his fingers in a continuous motion while he listens to the witness. The witness is an old man, perhaps seventy years old or more. He has a bald head and a wiry frame and is standing in the witness box, a dark brown pulpit-like affair, leaning on a walking stick. He declines the Coroner's offer for him to sit down. He wears a threadbare blue suit and some kind of regimental tie. He has a proud stance and no doubt was once a strong and forceful man. Now as he struggles to stay standing he is just a useless husk of a person waiting for death, like all old people.

"Could you tell me again how you came to find the body please Mr. Moon?" said the Coroner.

What a ridiculous name

"I was out walking my dog China, I take her out about 6.30am every morning and well, we walk along the canal, "and, we comes to the tunnel and China goes a bit crazy, barking at the water and what not. I thought she's seen a rat, you know, sometimes she'll jump right in after them and kill them, just like that with a snap of her jaws."

Mr Moon stops talking, he is in a momentary trance reliving China's rat-snapping exploits.

"Mr Moon."

"Sorry. Anyways it weren't no rat were it? She jumped in and swam over to the concrete ledge where they used to unload the paper bales back when the printing works used to."

"Mr Moon, Please."

"Sorry your honour. Well, she swims up and goes under, just like when she's after rats and then she surfaces tugging all frantic like and slowly an arm comes out from under the ledge and then the rest of him. All bloated he was."

"What did you do then Mr Moon?"

"Well I was right worried about China so I called the police on my mobile phone and the fire brigade."

"The Fire Brigade?"

"Yes, they always come quicker than the coppers and I was worried 'cos China wouldn't come out of the water. Then they all turn up and there's a right commotion I can tell you."

"Thank you Mr Moon, you may go and sit down."

Mr Moon limps out of the stand and sits on the front bench directly in front of my line of vision. I slide along the bench to get a better view. In front of the Coroner's bench at a table at floor level with their backs to me, Fuckwit's family are sitting. I recognise the mother from giving out leaflets at Camden Town station and next to her is a young woman, maybe her daughter, and an older man, perhaps the father. They are all facing the Coroner and occasionally shuffling papers. The woman gives off an air of tense sorrow, her shoulders hunched and her hair unkempt. I must go and give her my condolences; it would only be proper in the circumstances.

There are several people sat to my left, at the far end of the front bench. A policeman, a fireman, and a man in a suit who I take to be the police surgeon, wait their turn to testify on the sad accident that took Brian Harris' life. There were two rows of empty benches running at right angles to the Coroner's chair, these would be for a jury if one had been thought necessary. The Coroner shuffles his piles of papers and takes a moment to read some of them.

I look around.

The room is lit from above by five lamps, each has five upturned frosted glass lampshades on the end of ornate curved arms attached to a central rod which hangs down from the vaulted ceiling, like large upside down spiders. The ceiling is supported by two sets of iron lattice-work painted white; spider webs of metal with their arachnid architects of brass hanging down from the ceiling, halfway to the floor. Do they come alive at night to continue weaving the web of metal?

The desk at the front has three black rods projecting from it as does the Coroner's bench, the witness stand and the jury benches. These are microphones that resemble dead flies' legs sticking up in the air. The Coroner in his dark Saville Row suit and grey hair is the king spider at the centre of the web.

The image strengthens in my mind: I can't shake it off.

"Sergeant Wolf please take the stand" says the chief spider.

The man in the Police uniform approaches the witness stand and speaks his name and rank into the dead fly-leg in front of him.

"Could you tell us what happened and the circumstances in which you found Mr Harris when you arrived at tunnel number seven on the Regent's Canal please?"

"I arrived after the call from Mr Moon to see a body, apparently that of a young man floating face down in the canal with a dog attached to his arm. Mr Moon," the policeman indicates him with a nod, "was in some distress and calling to the dog to come out of the canal. The dog would not let go of the man's arm, he had him firmly by the wrist. I calmed Mr Moon and called to my colleagues over the radio to inform the fire department to attend the scene so we could recover both the body and the dog. I was told that they were already on their way to the scene."

Wolf I thought, another spider.

"What did you do then?" asks the Coroner.

I am enjoying this very much, but do not allow myself to smile, not outwardly.

"I sat Mr Moon on a bench and ascertained that the dog's

name was China. I used to be a dog handler and I thought I would try to command the dog to drop the man's arm and heel. I shouted firmly at the dog to drop and return and surprisingly he did just that, let go of the man and returned to the bank where I hauled him out of the water by the collar. He returned to Mr Moon and shook himself all over him – turns out China was a retired police dog." The Sergeant looks pleased with himself.

"And then?" says the Coroner.

"Then, the Fire Department arrived and pulled the body to the bank with boat hooks and removed him from the water onto the tow path. The Doctor was also there and he took a quick look and declared the man to be dead."

The mother let out an audible sob, the older man muffled her mouth with his hand and the young woman hugged her tight.

"Have you witnessed many of these kinds of situations Sergeant?"

"Oh yes, we have at least two people drowning a year in the canal – it really should be closed to the public, at least at night-."

"Thank you but we are not here to discuss policy, merely to ascertain the cause of Mr Harris's untimely death. What do you think it was Sergeant Wolf?" The Coroner gives the sergeant a severe look.

"I had the body removed to the Police Mortuary for a post mortem. He hadn't been in the water long I could tell that at the time. I thought it most likely that the gentleman had fallen in the water whilst inebriated – that is the usual cause – or had been pushed as a result of an assault or altercation of some kind."

I perk up my ears at this.

"I could see no obvious bruises or lacerations to the face, and there had been no reports of a fracas of any kind. I knew we would find out more from the post mortem and from scanning the CCTV once the time of death had been set. The Doctor supervised the body's removal and it was transported to the mortuary. I had one of my constables take a statement from Mr Moon and then give him a lift home."

The sergeant stops talking it was as if someone had just hit his off switch. He stands there impassive and still.

"Thank you sergeant Wolf. That will be all for now."

The sergeant sits back down on the bench. The doctor would be next. A nervous shiver passes along my spine – assault, CCTV what will they find out? Nothing, I think, but you can never tell; an overzealous official could find out far too much. We count on our officials being lazy, so we can carry on our lives without them interfering.

The Coroner looks at his papers and twists his pen.

"Would Dr Redback please take the stand?"

Another spider name, the room seems to pulse and I am sure the lamps are a touch lower than before. The doctor walks towards the stand. He is very tall and walks with an awkward gait as if he doesn't have quite enough legs. His head is decorated with a shock of red hair and freckles; he's young, about twenty eight, and clutches a sheaf of papers. He stumbles on the steps into the stand, nearly dropping his notes as he throws out a hand to keep his balance. He speaks his name and occupation – pathologist attached to London Transport Police.

"Dr Redback, would you please tell us the findings of your post mortem?" said the Coroner.

"(coughs) ...Yes, um well, firstly we removed the deceased's clothing and personal effects. In his various pockets we found a wallet with money still inside, a set of keys, a memory stick and a mass transit pass, along with a sealed plastic bag containing an amount of white lumpy powder, which was double bagged. I thought this would probably be illicit drugs of some kind and I passed it to the forensic science team for analysis. I decided, on the strength of this discovery, to carry out a test for toxins and alcohol, took samples, and sent them down to the lab. It was obvious he had died as result of drowning and there were substantial amounts of canal water in his lungs."

"How did you know it was water from the canal?" interrupted the Coroner.

"Oh, we had samples and matched them. It's routine practise. There was no doubt Mr Harris drowned in the Regent's Canal around four or so days prior to his discovery. The temperature of the water and amount of clothing had kept the cadaver reasonably well preserved, although there was some damage from aquatic life. The only thing to establish was why, and how much, if any, alcohol or drugs he may have consumed."

"Were there any signs of a struggle?" asked the Coroner.

The Doctor shuffled his papers but did not refer to them. He just played with them and said

"No, there was a small bruise under the left arm by the 5th rib, another in the small of the back just over L4, but neither of these are indicative of a struggle and either or both could have been received elsewhere as a result of a knock or bump while drunk."

"Was Mr Harris drunk Dr Redback?" Asked the Coroner.

"Yes, most definitely, as the toxicology report confirmed, he had consumed a large amount of alcohol; his BAC was approx 0.021 and had a high level of cocaine. The powder in the bag was found to be high-grade cocaine."

"I see, and no mobile telephone was found on the deceased?"

"No, though you will need to talk to Sergeant Wolf about any other facts regarding the case. All I can say is that he died of drowning and was drunk and under the influence of drugs at the time. I suspect that he fell into the canal and couldn't get out, and subsequently drowned."

The Coroner twists his pen and consults his papers again leaving the other doctor standing, waiting in the box. This goes on for some minutes.

"Thank you Dr Redback that is all for now." Sergeant Wolf would you retake the stand please.

The police officer looks surprised, but goes back into the stand. He taps his fingers against the blue serge of his uniform trousers as he waits, trying to mask his impatience with the Coroner, who is making some notes with his black Mont Blanc pen.

"Sergeant, the deceased had no mobile phone and a quantity of drugs in his pocket. This gives me cause to pause. I find it difficult to believe a man of his age would not possess a phone. Where is it? Did it fall into the canal? And were the drugs more than for personal consumption? While I accept that the deceased drowned in the Regent's Canal what explanation have the police found for the rest of the evidence?"

The sergeant looks pained and clenches and unclenches his fist. It is obvious that this Coroner is well known for going beyond his remit and making everybody waste their time. Or perhaps he is merely doing what he perceived as his duty by the system and the relatives? Either way I am loving it; they have decided that he had fallen into the canal, the rest is icing on the cake for me. The room is illuminated by a sudden shaft of sunlight that bounces off the brass spiders and ripples along the dark wooden fronts of the benches. The beam of sun makes the Coroner wince as it passes over his face and he looks all the more like a startled spider ducking away from the glare.

"Could you let down the blinds please Usher." He says.

The Usher, a middle-aged woman in over-tight black trousers, rolls down the blinds and banishes the sunlight back out into the graveyard, where it can play with time on the Burdett-Coutts memorial sundial.

"Well?" The Coroner peers at the policeman.

"We found that his phone, from the phone records, was last used in a pub 'The Earl of Camden'. Upon further investigation it was found behind the bar of the pub, he had evidently dropped it there. The finding of a bag of drugs on the deceased gave us cause to search the premises where he lives, we found a considerable quantity of cocaine and a computer containing unsettling images of children of an obscene nature. It would appear that the deceased was involved in at least two illegal activities connected with his previous work for charity in Bolivia. However, I do not believe that his death is connected with this and that it was, in fact, the result of him falling into the canal under the influence. The CCTV revealed nobody suspect going onto the towpath, indeed the last person before him entered at least 30 minutes prior." The mother sat shaking at the table, crying?

That would be me. So, Fuckwit was a bad man indeed and it would appear that fate had dealt me the avenging hand. The world was in a tiny way better off without his living breathing presence. I had inadvertently improved mankind's condition, when all I was trying to do was to show myself that my life had purpose. I had achieved more than I could have thought.

"We are conducting an investigation alongside the Bolivian authorities into the charity and it appears a request to interview Mr Harris was issued by the Bolivian Police just prior to his death."

"Do you have any reason to believe his death was in any way connected to his illicit activities Sergeant?" says the Coroner, who is either asking for reiteration, or had not noticed that the sergeant had already said that he did not think the two were connected.

"Er... no, there is no reason to believe there was anything suspicious about Mr Harris' death."

Mrs. Harris' head slumps further into her hands and the man and woman on either side of her have their black-clad arms around her in a protective arc, looking like spiders' legs crawling across her back.

The Coroner dismisses the Policeman and mulls over his reports, twisting his pen first one way and then the other. After a while he taps the thin black fly-leg with the end of the pen. He calls the Fire Officer to the stand. His evidence is much the same and I drift away, distracted by the thin black fly-leg stands pointing up from the various benches and out of the walls. The legs of dead flies used to pile up under the web of a spider that lived in the bedroom that I had as a child. It had a web up in the corner of the sash window in the old Victorian house we lived in. I used to watch the spider, a big fat spider, as it trapped and consumed flies and moths in its web, and the little pile of legs would build up on the windowsill underneath the web. My mother was a slattern and rarely, if ever, cleaned the house, and she never entered my room, preferring to spend much of her time, drunk in front of the TV, or fucking some random man. I even gave the spider a name – Theodore. After a month or so I trapped Theodore in a matchbox. I had an experiment in mind.

I pulled off one of his legs and then returned him to his web to see how he would fare. Seven legs were as good as eight it seemed. I pulled off another one the next day. It was only when Theodore was down to five legs that it really seemed to affect him, by the time he was down to two it was hopeless – he was literally a quarter of the spider he used to be and he couldn't function at all. I had wondered about the possibility of making artificial legs for him but instead I poured lighter fluid over the web and Theodore, and set fire to him.

The Coroner has started to deliver his verdict. A grey-suited Theodore in his web, he speaks softly and with authority:

"After hearing all the evidence, I have decided that a verdict of death by misadventure is to be noted and that the case requires no further investigation. I thank you all for your attendance, and my condolences to the family."

With that, the Coroner stands up and walks out of his spider court via a door in the back wall behind him. As soon as the small door shuts the rest of the room comes to life and the witnesses chat amongst themselves as they leave the room. The mother of Fuckwit stands, her face is drained and grey, and she looks smaller than she had at the tube station. She has the air of a woman from whom everything of value and worth has been stolen. I wait for her and her two escorts to draw level with the bench I am sitting in and then I slip out behind her and tap her on the shoulder. She turns and looks at me, a blank expression in her eyes.

"Excuse me, you won't remember me, I just happen to be one

of the people you handed a leaflet to at Camden Town station." I keep a solemn face, it's difficult, – inside I'm laughing. She looks at me, a small glimmer of recognition quivers in her eyes.

"I'm sure you don't remember, you must have given out so many leaflets."

"No, I remember we talked for a while and you where most kind. But why are you here?"

"Well... Mrs...er?" I look at her with a question mark on my face. "Arachne, my name is Arachne" she says. "It is Greek for spider. My father chose it – he loved spiders." Her eyes flit back to another time, and a reverie passes over her face and just for a moment she looks happy and then it is gone, the sorrow is back, hard, all-consuming sorrow.

"What are you doing here?"

"I happened to see the details in the paper and came to offer my commiserations on your loss. I lost my late wife in the canal many years ago and I don't know – I just felt I should come. I do hope it has not upset you." I'm enjoying this immensely but am the picture of sorrow of that I am sure. Fuckwit had really made a difference to my life and I feel I ought to show some gratitude after all.

"No not at all, thank you Mr ...Mr.." she hesitated.

"Smith." I offered.

"Mr Smith, thank you, if only there were more considerate people like yourself in the world then perhaps dreadful things like this wouldn't happen." Had she completely missed the part about her son being a drug-addled paedophile?

"Quite, quite." I add.

"Well I must be going, I have to arrange Brian's funeral, all a bit difficult considering."

"If I can assist you in any way..." I interrupt.

"Let me give you my number just in case." I said.

"Er...very well. Yes, thank you, thank you Mr Smith."

I write down my mobile number on a slip of paper, and ask for and get hers. I don't know why I want it but I get it anyway. The older man approaches her and quietly tugs her arm.

"Come along Arachne, we should leave." He nods at me and she flicks me a smile and as she turns she says "Forgive my brother he's over protective." She walks away with her brother and the younger woman. I break into a beaming smile and leave the Coroner's Court, the lair of the Doctor, King of Spiders, but it is me spinning a web, why and what to catch I have no idea, but a web it is for sure. I take a piss in the pristine toilets and leave, whistling a merry tune:

" The itsy bitsy spider went up the waterspout.
Down came the rain, and washed the spider out.
Out came the sun, and dried up all the rain,
and the itsy bitsy spider went up the spout again."

Chapter 10: **Water Sports**

I stroll back from the Coroner's Court to my own particular lair via a deserted bleak road that runs along the back of King's Cross station and up to the Regent's Canal. I'm starting to feel the canal is some kind of artery in my destiny, carrying my fate along in its brackish water, all mixed up with diesel oil, tadpoles and dead drug dealers. I had truth in the court. The spiders that weave society's webs are no less real or deadly than the Black Widows of the tropics. Of course, the difference being spiders weave from biological necessity whereas the human spiders in their towers of power weave webs of destitution for fun and profit. They suck us dry as surely as those flies of my childhood were consumed over that summer on the windowsill of my youth.

I think about Fuckwit and my decision to kill him and the fact that Society decided he died from his own misadventure, which I suppose he did in a way, nothing more stupid than drunkenly deciding to rob and assault a sober man at night on a canal's edge, particularly one that happened to be contemplating murder at the time.

That one act of stupidity on his part has unleashed a powerful new me, aware of the fact that I am powerless in the face of the spider-web of oppression in which I am trapped. I, of course, cannot kill those that oppress me, they are invisible and protected. I can only kill other vulnerable and powerless individuals like myself, – why do you think that it's only nursery school children or mothers out shopping that get gunned down in killing sprees? It's never bankers or stockbrokers or politicians, no, they are untouchable. We have to kill ourselves because we are the only ones we can reach and nobody cares about the murder of the powerless and the useless. It makes me sad that I will have to slaughter one of

my own kind to maintain my new found zest for life. Like the spider I survive on your life force. Deep in thought I walk all the way to my room without even noticing. The routes to my room are impressed into my subconscious like the routine of breathing
All pathways lead to my door.

I lie on the bed. It is after midday and I have nothing to do with my time. I close my eyes and allow my mind to drift, to take me where it wants to go. I can see Jamillia the Cunt and my child Sam: they pass by, mocking and contemptuous for a moment, and then they are gone to wherever they are now. I start to fall into a day sleep, images jumbled and threatening. The basement where I was kept, locked in as a young teenager and beaten daily by the owners, my owners with a rod and a belt and thumped repeatedly with a hot saucepan, for what?

I can't remember.

I start to wakefulness.

"Cunts."

The past and everyone in it is a cunt. Disoriented, I stagger to the wet room and wretch into the toilet. I vomit. The saucepan is still crashing into the back of my head – perhaps it will never stop. The owners died after I climbed out of the small basement window they forgot to close one night, and set fire to the house with them inside. I remember watching the flames and the fire engines with the fire crews trying to get to them and listening with sweet joy to their screams as they burned, but the saucepan left with me and they are hitting me with it to this day. Why can't I turn it off? My head hurts. I turn on the light, go to the wet-room and wash my face.

I look in the mirror, I can't see my reflection.

"Fuck you."

I wash my face again and look a second time. There I am, indistinct but visible, drawn, I look as if I am a pencil sketch. I flick the light off and head back to the bed. I will not sleep. I must decide who to kill. I grab my notebook and consult my notes. The decision must be made now and carried out with all haste, then the saucepan will stop hitting me. I search out my box of aspirin and swallow two with water. The pain recedes and I settle back, sitting on the bed with my notes and a pencil.

I have to decide who my victim will be. The ideal candidate would be powerful and rich but there's no chance of luring one of them to my room. I could try to get to one in their location but their houses and social settings are too well protected from the likes of me. I might be able to get to one of them and even kill them but I would definitely be caught and then my actions would be labelled those of a lone lunatic, a madman whose actions were irrational. The press and TV would be full of messages of how wonderful and fantastic the victim was, how they did so much for the poor and I would just be the mad loner who attacked them with sharp knives for some sad deluded reason, and the real reason why they had to die would never come out. No, that is not the way.

I need to pick someone who would visit voluntarily and who won't be missed straight away – when they are missed, people will assume they've just gone off somewhere, – at the very worst they will be listed as a missing person. What about Martha? She would definitely visit and she wouldn't be missed straight away, but she would be eventually and I don't know who she's told about me. I have only slept with her once and she hasn't rung since, but I would be in her phone. Still, even if the police found out she visited, as long as I got rid of her thoroughly they would never suspect me. A lonely old cripple in a dirty basement, hard to imagine me as prime suspect. The problem is that I know her and that makes it personal. In fact, I quite like her, or at least I feel gratitude that she likes me, which isn't quite the same thing. It does seem a touch ungrateful to slaughter the one woman that finds me attractive, not to mention that it might constitute cutting off my nose to spite my face as it were. Martha cannot be the victim, it cannot be a personal murder. It is a cerebral murder. It can't be tainted by personal relationships. Martha cannot be killed, not by me at any rate.

Perhaps I could advertise my services as an English teacher and lure an unsuspecting woman here, but it's obvious there would be too much of a trail. I could grab someone off the street. How? I have no car and my disability would be a handicap in that scenario. Perhaps I should kill a child or several children, – it would be easy to entice the stupid little fuckers to my house and easier yet to butcher them and there would only be a small body to get rid of – but there are problems, children are not responsible and won't understand what is happening to them and they certainly won't understand why. I need a cogent adult that understands the reality of what is happening to them. Perhaps a pregnant woman – that would be a kill-one- get-one-free scenario, – that would have some resonance to today's commercialisation of all things natural and ideal. However, the thought of ripping the dead woman's body open to find the baby was still alive makes me feel nauseous. I would have to kill the baby or maybe I could dispose of the woman's body and keep the baby and raise it as my own.

"What? Don't be fucking stupid. No killing babies or raising them either."

I say this out loud to enforce the thought, because sometimes thoughts seem quite reasonable until you voice them out loud, and that thought didn't sound so great. I take a break, make a cup of tea and look for inspiration. As I place the spoon in the sink I spot the answer. It's staring me in the face, a card lying on the side of the sink:

Yuko Japanese model

A&O, Lesbo Actions, VIP massage, Uniforms, Spanking, Watersports, Toys.

I'm local and can make hotel visits. Call 07902 899Pavement text927.

I pick up the card and sit down with my tea. Of course, the serial killer's old standby – the prostitute, a perfect victim – society hates them and no one cares about them if they disappear. It's just assumed they have moved on, their family ties are weak or non-existent and the media only care if a fair number of them disappear at the same time in a given area, because then people will worry that proper women might become victims by accident. But the hooker, she's expendable and dirty. Society secretly thinks they deserve to die because of the knowledge they carry about what so-called respectable men get up to. I feel ashamed that Yuko will have to be my victim, she feels like a kindred spirit, another invisible person despised by a hypocritical society (albeit far better paid than me). I am also upset that I will be pandering to a cliché in such a blatant way, but it really has to be said that nobody will give a fuck if a hooker vanishes, such is the disposable nature of human concern. Yuko it is. Yuko is as good as dead.

I quite like prostitutes – at least the transaction is honest – in exchange for money they pretend to like you for a moment then you can leave and return to the rest of your life without the worry of any comeback. I don't hold with the argument that it's exploitation of women. Maybe some are exploited but that happens to all kinds of people; the strong will dominate the weak, no matter what. Like the time I was made to lick the toilet bowls at school by large knife- wielding hooded bullies because I was weak and crippled. There is no inherent kindness built into humans – we are designed to nurture our genes and eat, fuck or wear everything else. Women learn the power of the vagina and they use it to control and coerce men, who, in their turn, use physical and social strength to undermine that power. The only reason we have a society, all that social complex outside my room, is all just to protect our offspring. We have to guarantee the survival of others in order to feel secure that our own will mature and reproduce. That's why murder is so frowned upon, not state or institutional murder such as that carried out by armies, no, that's lauded as heroic, but the actions of the lone killer in society, he reminds them that their so called civilisation is gossamer thin. Instead of applauding his creativity and initiative, his bravery in the face of absolute social condemnation, instead of awarding him medals for his dangerous and difficult achievement behind enemy lines, they deride him as mad and lock him up forever in a small inaccessible room, or feed him drugs and electrocute his brain. They call him a killer and a threat to society while the man with the missile launcher that kills two thousand, a hero and protector of civilisation.

I drink my tea in slow deliberate sips. I look at Yuko's card, she will be small, which is going to be helpful, the last thing I'd want to do is kill a fat person. Perhaps the first thing I would teach at murder school is – don't kill a fat person, far too much flesh to get rid of unless you own a rendering plant. Obviously murder is easier the more resources you have. I am at the absolute bottom end of the resource pile and so I take pride in my planning and execution of execution.

I turn the card over in my hand and stare at an incompetent pencil illustration showing a Japanese girl in sexy black lingerie and with breasts that are unreasonably large, a cartoon of a sexy girl with bright pink letters carrying the promise of easy ecstasy in exchange for cash. I place the card in a drawer and lie back on the bed. When am I going to commit this disgusting act? Am I fully prepared? Do I care if I get caught? Do I care, at all, about anything? These, and a thousand other questions crowd into my brain, jostling for attention like a crowd in a dirty bar. I cannot attend to them all. The questions are joined by memories and the bar becomes rowdy, everyone wanting attention at once. I hit myself on my head as if I can shake the thoughts away, as if they are physical things that can be killed or silenced. A groan slips past my lips as the memories multiply, visions of past abuse and distress. Why is it that I have no pleasant memories? Have I forgotten them, or were they never there? Images reel past, none of them good. I focus on the incident with Fuckwit, running through it in detail. This has the effect I want, focusing on the killing of Brian Harris calms my mind, takes away the swirling chaos of the past. I lie in the dark, dull room. I could just lie here until I die and a blessed relief that would be. What is it that stops me from bringing about my own death? That would be perfect murder indeed, perhaps I will murder myself.

But not until after I have killed the little Japanese whore and perhaps one or two others to go with her, a quartet, playing my composition of death. Four killings, each with a very different tempo and tone: first, Fuckwit, male and brash and sudden, then Yuko, female, delicate, deliberate, her death will be sweet and sad. The next two must happen together, they should be related, the two violins to the viola of Yuko and the cello of Fuckwit, chamber murder, instead of chamber music. Maybe I should document the killings in some way? No, that would be a foolish vain act and anyway, I appear to have added another two to my list. Who will they be? I feel a small tingling along my spine at the thought of four. Yes, four is absolutely the right number. I let out an audible chuckle.

"If I didn't know better I'd say I was as mad as a midday moon."

I feel calm now. The hectic bar room of my mind is empty and I can function again. I don't feel like sleeping. I will go for a walk along my beloved pavements down to one of the bridges and watch the grey soiled water of London trying, in vain, to wash away this foul city's sin and ordure into the sea, and I will call Yuko and make an appointment for her to visit tomorrow. I think prostitutes should be far more openly appreciated, they perform a very useful social function, often at great risk to themselves, as I am about to illustrate.

I am walking to London Bridge. The late afternoon light is fecund and bright, as it bounces off the thick glass windows and sheer metal walls of the towers of wealth. I reach the bridge after a forty-minute walk against a tide of workers leaving their offices for home. I stop in a bus shelter and sit down. There are people of all shapes, colours and sizes waiting for the buses to heave them away, the bus is the sole province of the poor of London. They judder along the streets hauling cargos of useless human creatures, like endless families of Joads being transported to some non-existent promised land. The view from London Bridge is its usual magnificent self. I stand and gaze: To the east there is Tower Bridge, a Victorian cake decoration, a marzipan fantasy of a bridge. It's a ridiculous confection set across the river but like all confectionary, pleasing to the eyes. The original walkways high up above the road bridge were haunts for pickpockets and prostitutes after it opened in 1894, and had to be closed in 1910; it's all grist to the tourist mill for the "most famous bridge in the world ". Beyond that I see Canary Wharf blinking in the distance like a giant dumb bird. In front of the toy bridge is HMS Belfast all bristling with guns and bedecked with flags. An aquatic hedgehog of destruction and another museum to the love affair we have with institutional murder. I cross to the west side, the lowering sun glares in my eyes and catches the ripples of dull yellow river water as it flows in reverse into the heart of London. I can see the old Post Office Tower sticking up like a chewed pencil thrust into the ground. As I stare at the water I realise that the river is the perfect place to dispose of the body once I have cut it up into small pieces. I can just scatter them to the water and the fish, crabs and other underwater creepy-crawlies will do the rest. As long as the flesh is small and the bones broken and crushed, no-one will ever find anything. I have walked along the little beach by OXO Wharf and the shingle is covered in bone fragments. I should do it easily on a Saturday morning as there will be no workers, and it will be before the tourists are out, just the invisibles and returning party and club goers, and they are too off their heads to bother some crazy 'homeless guy' with his bags feeding the invisible ducks on the riverside. I will have to kill her on a Friday, book her for her last slot of the day, take her life, then work all night to cut her up and dump her next morning. Excellent – if I am going to break God's laws I may as well break them on the Sabbath to boot. It's the final nail in Yuko's coffin.

Chapter 11: **Till Death Us Do Part**

I am in a theatre, in the round seats surrounding a small stage in the centre, like stands in a circus. The seating tiers rise up high into the roof.

The audience is comprised entirely of pigs, pink snorting pigs, snuffling and sitting, all of them watching the stage.

The theatre becomes dark.

A single spotlight illuminates the round stage.

Placed in the middle of the stage is a small metal podium raised a couple of feet from the floor and about the size of a small writing desk. Two young women walk out into the middle of the stage and stand on either side of the podium. They are naked and oiled, from Mongolia or China perhaps, their small breasts glisten under the light and their vaginas are shaved smooth. Music tinkles from nowhere, an eerie combination of violin and accordion over the top of a piano plinking out of tune. The women dance on either side of the podium, slow and twisting like saplings in a light breeze. They flex from side to side and after a couple of minutes they go into a handstand, feet up in the air, and turn to face away from the podium. They lower their legs so their bodies are in a semi-circle, feet flat on the podium in perfect synchronicity, they flick themselves upright and are standing on the podium. The pigs grunt in appreciation of this remarkable contortion. The girls start to intertwine with each other in a contortionist act of incomprehensible brilliance; they are a human Rubik cube, the pigs make an explosion of appreciative grunts. The two women become interlinked in a series of evermore complicated and obscure anatomical unions. They writhe and slip around and through each other's bodies like snakes in a maze. They appear like one body with too many limbs and like many limbs with no body. Their heads poke through their legs: at one point they have their faces pressed into their vaginas from under their legs, at another, each of their arms seem to dislocate to feed through the other's and their own

120

legs. It is impossible to work out which girl is doing what, as the music reaches a discordant crescendo and the girl with two heads, four legs and arms, freezes on the stage, arched and shaped like a star. One balanced in an arch on top of the other. The women quiver on the podium, muscles trembling under the strain. Then at some signal I am not aware of the pigs in the front tier rush onto the stage and one of them bites into the calf muscle of the woman with her feet on the podium. She screams and blood scatters over the head of the pig. The bite leaves a crescent shape out of her leg, but she doesn't move: the girls remain statue-like on the stage. There is a second of deep silence. The silence that will exist after the universe has ended.

The silence of death.

Then, pandemonium, the pigs hurl themselves at the girls and devour them on the stage. They chomp, rip and tear at the two female bodies, which come apart like rotten cabbages in the jaws of the pigs. The women don't make a sound as the pigs snort, grunt and squeal with pleasure, blood and flesh sprays high in the air. A few minutes later they have eaten every part of the women, the light dims and the pigs mill around, blood dripping from their mouths.

I stand, feeling nauseous and stagger to a door that has appeared in a wall behind me. I walk out of the theatre and instantly throw up. After I have finished vomiting I look around and I am in the formal Versailles garden again, all low hedges and gravel pathways. It is winter, snow coats the path and the tops of the dark green hedges.

"What was that fucking scene in the theatre?"

It was far worse than me having to slaughter the dancers with the sword.

I shiver, not from the cold because it's not cold – even though my breath steams in the air and the snow is fresh – I am not cold.

I notice that I'm naked. At the far end of the garden past the small geometric hedges is a summerhouse or gazebo. It's made of stone and is hexagonal in shape with windows all around, an arched door facing me. I look around, there's nothing else to walk to, just more garden as far as the eye can see. I start a brisk walk towards the gazebo and after only a few steps I am at the door. I try the door handle, it turns and the door opens. I walk through and am in a room not dissimilar to my own, but emptier.

The bed is stripped and the window shuttered. There is a large trunk in the middle of the floor. A tired grey light creeps in, a light too old to impart much illumination to anything it touches. There is no sign of the door that let me into the room. I open a door in front of me and I am in my hallway facing the door to my own room. I have walked out of the door of the room next to mine, the one that had been open a touch when I left this morning. The ancient grey light of day is struggling to keep the hall visible. I feel anxious and confused – am I asleep, but don't feel asleep? I try my door and it is open, I walk into my room, dark and warm. I can see the bed is empty. Thank God for that, the last thing I want to see is myself in that bed. I shut the door and climb into bed. I need to sleep to get far away from this indecipherable unreality. I pull the duvet over my head and will myself to sleep. It arrives like a nurse carrying morphine for the wounded.

I awake to a burst of bright sunlight on my face. The curtain has moved, I have thrashed about in my sleep and allowed the Devil, in sunshine form, into my room. I scrunch my eyes shut and grab the curtain, pulling it back to cover the window. The blessed greyness returns and I sit up startled by the process of waking. Looking around I see that all is normal. I have the picture in my mind of the inside of the next-door room and arriving naked outside my own room. I clamber out of bed and drag my trousers up my body. Opening my door I see that the dull hallway is as reassuringly uninspiring as usual. I walk to the door adjacent to mine. It is shut, and hesitating for a moment I take a deep breath and twist the handle giving it a push. Nothing, the door is locked. I let out my breath in a slow sigh of relief and stagger back to my room and sit on the bed. I cradle my head in my hands.

Turmoil.

I tremble.

I am so tired.

My soul is tired: the years of rejection, disappointment and disillusion pile up inside my mind. My body shakes and streams of tears erupt from my eyes. I shake, fall to the floor and curl up into a quivering ball of middle-aged flesh, crying. I allow myself a moment of indulgence of desperate self-pity. After a small age of weeping and shuddering I feel refreshed, in a strange way clearheaded. If there was some way to add purpose to my life other than the one I have decided upon I would take it.

I sit up and pull myself together. I remove my trousers and take a long shower. I run the water as hot as I can bear and then make it hotter. I let the water burn my scalp and scald away the doubt in my mind, I can have no room for doubt. Martha comes unbidden into my mind. I recall her breasts, the fact that she seemed genuinely interested in what I had to say, and that she enjoyed sucking my cock and the taste of my come. I decide to ring her and arrange to meet on Sunday after I have slaughtered Yuko or whatever her real fucking name might be. The wet-room is swathed in steam and condensation drips from every surface. I hammer the tap to the off position and stand dripping, bright red from the hot water. Cleansed inside and out.

I step out of the shower and search for my mobile phone. What time is it? 6.45 am. Early. Good, I have plenty of time to prepare, or ... to back out ... I am not backing out, this has to be done. I pull a dull yellow towel from the row of hooks on the back of the door and rub the water from my body. Discarding the towel I find clothes and stuff myself into them. I think about breakfast but I know that I won't eat, can't eat, the thought of eating makes me feel nauseous. No breakfast, not today. I stand in the middle of my small world, shifting back and forth from foot to foot, anxiety building inside me but I feel paralysed as if held by chords attached to the walls, tied in such a way as to stop me moving. There's a fist of acid in my throat and my chest is tight, breathing shallow, my head starts to spin. I have to break out of this state. It's as if part of me knows what I plan and wants to stop me. Ridiculous. All of me knows what I am planning – there aren't separate parts of the personality or mind that keep things from each other. I am being dumb,

"STOP IT."

Yelling breaks the grip of whatever was stopping me from moving.

Better, yes better.

I walk to the cupboard and check my knives and tools. I spread them out on the floor and check them. The knives are razor sharp and all the tools are fit for their new purpose. I put them away. How am I going to kill this woman? Strangulation seems the best bet. She'll be small and it's less messy than stabbing her, though not so quick, but I'd never get the blood out of the carpet. I could knock her out and stab her in the wet-room. No, I'll make a garrotte that'll work with one hand. I can use my bad hand as a hook. I'll get wire from Demeter's.

All of a sudden I feel sick, bile rises in my throat and I rush to the toilet and vomit.

I haven't eaten a proper meal for days so there's nothing solid to throw up. I kneel over the toilet bowl, like a supplicant at an altar, retching and heaving. I stop trying to turn my insides out and catch my breath. Shaking my head and unwinding myself from the crouch I stand and move, crablike, to the sink to clean my mouth. I look in the mirror. Who is that man staring back at me? I don't recognise him. It must be me I suppose but it doesn't look like me. His skin is granite and grey-lined with hair-fine cracks, the eyes are of flint and the lips set in a backwards sandstone curl, a snarl almost. The black hair like slate flecked with grey and white.

A face of stone.

A gargoyle.

I thrust the toothbrush into the stone man's mouth and scrub, white foam spews over the lips. His, my, eyes don't move, steam writhes up from the hot tap that I am using to clean the gargoyle's teeth. The steam covers the surface of the glass and the image fades away. I spit out the toothpaste and turn off the tap, washing my mouth with cold water. When I look back to the mirror there's nothing there. I dare not wipe the steam from the glass – I do not want to see the man I have become again. I discard the toothbrush. It clatters into the sink. I slam the door to the wet-room behind me.

The stone man has won and it's time to get stuff done.

I grab my coat, phone and Yuko's card. I'll call her while walking to Demeter's to get bone- snapping bolt cutters and the garrotte wire. I'll call her and arrange for her to come and see me today at six, if she can't make today I'll offer her double rate – that'll get her to my room. Greedy whore.

I look at my phone clock: it's 12 noon. What the fuck happened to the morning? Did I spend all that time lying sobbing like a useless fool on the floor? Perhaps I did, perhaps I needed to kill that part of me, so I could move on. I feel nothing, just a smear of disdain for the side of me that expected any more from life than pain and abuse Hope is the last, most pointless of emotions. When you get to the point of hoping for something then you have lost all possibility of controlling your life. I pull Yuko's card from my pocket. I'll show how useless hope is against a razor sharp will. She's going to end up hoping I don't kill her just before I actually do crack her windpipe. I think a smile crosses my lips although I can't be sure. There's comedy in all this if you can see it, a bitter tear-filled rancid comedy.

I call Yuko's number.

A girl with a distinct London accent answers, not very Japanese I think. I ask if it is she. The voice concurs.

I ask if she will do outcalls.

She says yes.

I ask if she will visit my room.

She asks if it is a hotel, I say no. She says hotel visits only.

I was expecting that.

"I'm disabled. I've saved the money for a girl and hotels are difficult for me to manage and too expensive."

She is silent. I add she could arrive accompanied if she's worried and I'd pay extra.

"No" she says "it's fine, no problem"

"£150 and what's the address?"

I tell her and we agree 6pm today.

Good, I can put an end to all her problems. I knew that the idea of extra money would tempt her away from the normal routine. I smile and walk to Demeter's shop to get my bone cutters and wire. I'll need to get money from my account as well, they always want the money first. Understandable, I mean she's not there because she likes me. I buy my extra equipment at Demeter's and on the way back visit an ATM to withdraw the money.

I also call Martha, she seems happy to hear from me, and chatters on about some crap or another. We arrange to meet on Sunday evening. I tell her I might be tired as I have a lot of work to do on Saturday. She says that's fine, I should come over and chill out at her place.

I accept.

It's 4.00 pm by the time I have run around and done everything. Yuko will be here in two hours and I'm excited at the prospect of her visit, like a teenage boy on his first date. I have to prepare the room. I straighten the bed and wash the dishes and make sure the room is as tidy as possible. I turn the white folding chair around so it faces into the room away from the table and I make sure my knives and tools are in the cupboard. I check them several times for some reason. I take the length of lighting flex I bought at Demeter's and tie a hoop in each end and feed one hooped end through the other to make a primitive noose. If I can slip this over her head and pull it tight with speed, I should be able to render her unconscious in about fifteen seconds, then I can apply pressure on her carotid artery with the handle of the bone cutters and she'll be done for. I would just go for the artery with my hands using a chokehold but with only one working arm, it would be too difficult and give her too much opportunity to fight back. I'd need to turn the head up and to the left to get to the artery. Easier to throttle the bitch into unconsciousness and then kill her. I take the £150 from my wallet and place it in plain view on the table so that she will be able to see it as soon as she walks into the room. I put on a t-shirt and make sure my withered arm is on view. I make myself look as unlike a murderer as I can and as much like a pathetic middle aged cripple as possible. I look around satisfied. The scene is set, everything looks innocuous. She will feel unthreatened by both my room and me. I am sure she has to deal with far more frightening customers than me, except that none of them have killed her.

I sit and await her arrival.

There's an abrupt thudding on my door and a bellowing from the hallway, a loud imperious and inarticulate voice, familiar to me.

"Hey dem ain't paid the rent…yoah yah funny little man, you in der…the council in't paid you rent…you hear?"

I look at the door and then I go and open it. She stands there like a diseased hippo in a filth-encrusted lake. Crushing nutshells in one hand, flicking the peanuts into her mouth and discarding the shells onto the floor all in one deft, well-practised movement.

"I'll sort it out next week Mrs Ferdinand" I say with a deadpan face. As I look at her I know I want to kill her, to remove this fat cockroach from the face of the earth. To extract her from under the kitchen sink of humanity and crush her under my boot heel. This fat parasite that lives off the blood of small broken people – she should be boiled in her own blubber.

"Well make sure you do, little cripple man, make sure you do."

"I will, I will, sorry about that Mrs Ferdinand." I smile and she looks at me down her nose and flicks another nut into her mouth, makes a strange clicking noise, turns and waddles up the stairs nutshells cascading off the walls, floor and banister as she goes.

I shut the door and sit thinking about how I could kill that evil grasping bitch, but there's no way; her tenants would all be prime suspects and anyway that hippo-sized body would be too much to dispose of; but if ever anyone deserved to be slaughtered it was her.

17.45 pm. Fifteen minutes and my doorbell will ring, it hasn't rung for years – not since that policeman turned up to tell me my mother was dead years ago.

Time slows down to a painful crawl.

The bell rings loud and harsh. I lift the intercom handset. It's her. I let her in, waiting for her feet on the stairs and the knock at the door. It comes. I let her in.

She is Japanese-looking and not as young as the card makes out, probably in her early thirties. Her long black hair is pulled back tight from her face, and piled up on top of her scalp in a bun – this is good, it will make throttling her less troublesome and messy. She wears a cheap, faded, black raincoat and carries a patent leather shoulder bag. A pic'n'mix assortment of cheap gold rings are pasted to the fingers of her hands and there are big gold hoops in her ears. All this gold is bright yellow and cheap looking. I can tell that once she had been decoratively pretty but now she has a worn out, pre-fucked, look about her.

"Hello luv, you ain't so bad looking are you?"

I thank her. She dumps her bag on the floor next to the door and sweeps off her raincoat, she throws it and it floats over to the bed. Underneath she's wearing a 'can't bend over in this' short black skirt, black stockings, suspenders, a too-tight white blouse. She's not wearing any panties. Her small tits nestle in a push-up bra forcing the blouse buttons to strain at the buttonholes.

She is a menu of the paraphernalia of male fantasy.

A walking, talking sexual cliché.

Her steel impersonal eyes scan the room like radar taking in every detail of the environment.

She's looking for something.

Her eyes find their target, the money, on the table.

Striding over she grabs the £150, counts it and then pushes it into her bag.

She smiles and starts to remove her blouse. She peels it off slowly, revealing a tattoo on her shoulder of a tarot card.

The Hanged Man.

He sways from an inky branch.

She strips off leaving only her stockings and suspender belt on. The suspender belt is old and frayed with stains along the edges betraying that Yuko is at the tail end of a long whoring career.

She has a lithe slender body, smallish natural breasts with large dark nipples and a neat and tidy labia surrounded by a smooth shaved cunt.

In other days, long gone, I would have fallen in love with this woman.

"Undress honey, c'mon don't be shy." She smiles and walks over to me and starts to lift my t-shirt.

"What's your name darling?" she asks. I tell her it is Brian Harris.

"Well Brian you better get undressed and show me what you've got."

I strip off my clothes removing them at a frantic pace to give the impression of lust and clumsiness, which is real, getting tangled in the legs of my jeans. I ask her to sit in the chair and masturbate in front of me. She does just that and sits on the white fold-out IKEA chair, her legs splayed wide, her left hand dipping in and out of her cunt and her right hand rubbing her clitoris.

She's doing an excellent job of imitating pleasure. I ask her if she has any toys in her bag and she produces a bright red dildo. She returns to the chair licking and sucking the dildo for a few minutes and then spreads her labia with one hand and shoves the dildo into her cunt with the other hand. I watch for a few minutes and then stand up. She lets out a low moan. Fake? I can't tell. She will think I am just watching from different angles, which I am. She's putting on a good show. I move closer to her and kneel between her legs to get a close- up view. I watch as the dildo moves in and out of her cunt; the shaft of the toy glistens slightly and the lips of her labia grip and hold on to the dildo. It looks like death to me.

"Like what you see?" she asks, I don't but I say that I do.

I move behind her to look over her shoulder at the action. She's fucking herself faster now with the dildo, feeling aroused, she's not paying attention to me anymore as I stand behind her peering over her shoulder.

My cock starts to stiffen in anticipation, this surprises me but it makes the moment all the more poignant.

I reach into the drawer and tease out my garrotte. It appears from its lair, silent and black like some lethal snake, and with a swift looping move I swoop it around her long delicate neck and yank hard until it's tight. Her head jerks back and I can see her face, her eyes wide in surprise and fear. Perhaps she hopes it is some sick sex game and not the prelude to her dying, but any such thought must leave her as I twist and tighten the noose.

She lets go of the dildo clutching at the black wire of the garrotte with both hands scraping her lovely painted nails along her slim neck in a desperate attempt to get free, succeeding only in gouging chunks of flesh out of her neck. Deep red blood flows over her hands. I notice it matches the colour of her nail varnish. I love the feel of the garrotte in my hands.

Her nostrils flare and she wildly flings her fist back at me over her head, it connects with my left eye. I pull the garrotte harder. Drool escapes from the corner of my mouth; I am salivating over this. A string of my spit lands in her eye.

She is kicking and jerking her legs like a spastic swimmer.

I hold her on the chair as I twist the garrotte.

The dildo stays firmly planted in her cunt.

Her head rolls to the side and her eyes swivel up into her forehead revealing the whites of her eyes.

My erection is steel-hard as I see and feel her pass out. I relax my grip and tip her from the chair onto the floor. I kneel across her, my shin pressing against her neck and I push down with increasing force, crushing her windpipe cutting of any remaining blood flow to her brain from the carotid artery. She's warm – and dead.

Kneeling over her upper body and sitting back on her small breasts I begin to masturbate. I come in a huge burst of sperm all over her face. I hadn't accounted for the fact that I might get turned on by this event. It wasn't driven by any sexual fantasy that I am aware of.

Strange.

I look at her spunk-covered face and then, bringing my face close to hers, lick my come off it. When I have finished I apologise to her, pointing out it isn't personal – could have been anyone and should have been plenty of other people. I drag her small body into the wet room. It's easily moved, I was right to choose a small woman.

I lay her out on the tiled floor, step over her prone body and leave. I shut the door behind me. That was the easy part.

Chapter 12: **Bits and Pieces**

I lean against the wet room door, ambushed by tiredness. My legs and arms tremble. My eyesight flickers and the colour drains from the room until everything has the look of a 1920's silent film. The upturned chair and Yuko's clothing seem to pulsate in my brain, and her patent plastic handbag is a small nova in the corner of my vision. I close my eyes and slide down the wet room door into a crouch, hooking my hands around my knees, and burying my face in the gap between my arms and my thighs. I breathe in and out in slow deliberate breaths. I do this for what seems like hours, but it must be only ten minutes or so. I start to recover and lift my head opening one eye and see that the room has returned to its drab normality. I open both eyes and look around checking the room. I am no longer trembling. Yuko's bag is leaning against my room door. It occurs to me that she must have seen other punters before me. Unable to stand, I crawl over to her bag and lift it onto my lap, and leaning against my door I open it. There's my £150 and more besides. I see a roll of notes secured by an elastic band. I count it, there's £675 – four and a bit punters. Well, she won't be needing money where she's going so I may as well have it. What else?

A small black cardholder with a travel card and a bankcard in the name of Samantha Chang, I prefer Yuko. There's a pin number on a slip of paper, I'll not be using that.

There's a dozen cocks' worth of condoms.

A small silver box covered in skilful and pretty engraving containing rolling tobacco and papers.

A pack of dog-eared tarot cards; she should have used them this morning, or perhaps she did and hadn't paid attention. There's a rape alarm, a trident triple action, a small aerosol tin that lets off a foul stink and a loud screaming noise, and an indelible UV tracer.

A cellphone, an old model iPhone 6, I'll have to get rid of that, it will have a GPS tracker inside, but for now I turn the power off. Lipstick, 'Hooker Red.'

Unsurprising.

A small moleskin note-pad, some kind of journal and a glass vial of white powder, drugs but no way to know what kind. A small blue box with three blocks of coloured make-up inside, and a foam pad to apply it with, the lid has a mirror inside, so she can see what she's doing, useful to snort the white powder off too. It reminds me of the make-up that Jamillia the Cunt used to have. Wet-wipes and a spare pair of panties and several sets of keys.

I put the money to one side, and stuff the rest of her junk back into the bag. I will have to get rid of it all, shouldn't be too difficult. I think for a moment, open the bag, and extract the travel card, it's an 'oyster' – she might have registered it but I doubt it and I could use the remaining charge on it to travel around disposing of her body parts. I smile at this thought. If she has registered the card it will only seem as if she is travelling on public transport and that would have to mean that she left my house if anyone asks. That's assuming anyone reports her missing at all. I also pull out the bag of white powder; I have no idea about illegal drugs but I reckon it is probably cocaine in which case it will help me stay awake to cut up the body and if it's something else, well, I'd soon find out. I hold the bag in front of my face then open it; the strong smell of acetone greets my nose and I pullback and bang my head on the door. I put the bag down, poke the tip of my index finger into the shiny rocky powder, pull it out, and lick it. It tastes bitter and unpleasant, like sour chalk, a few seconds and my tongue is numb and my gums as well. I am not sure about this at all, reseal the bag, and place it to one side. I dump the bag over by the bed. I have to get to work. I return to the wet-room and move Yuko away from the toilet placing her over by the shower. Her head is propped up against the wall, eyes open staring at me with disapproval.

I ignore her silent complaint, and turn the water on making it as cold as possible to keep the body fresh longer. I need a moment to compose myself and gather my tools. I go to my cupboard and pull out the knives, selecting the long-bladed one, I return to the wet room and switch off the shower. There are droplets of water all over her face hanging off her eyelashes like a row of dainty Christmas decorations and she is still giving me a complaining stare. I place my knife on her chest and step over to the toilet, I need to piss. I stand there and I can't urinate, not with her looking at me like that. I stop and go over to her and twist her head to one side, for some reason I don't want to close her eyes. I want her to watch me cut her up, to see me hack away parts of her being, and hook out her inner organs. I want her to suffer even after death. I wonder as I take a long yellow piss if this is a surrogate killing, the opposite of a surrogate birth but for the same reasons. Did I want to kill Jamillia-the-Cunt or my mother? Maybe I did and never knew it, but obviously I couldn't because I would be suspected straight away, so this stupid innocent woman has had to pay the price for their cruelty to me, – they killed her – I was merely the instrument.

I finish my piss and flush the toilet. Then I pick up the bottle of thin bleach and pour it over her body. I'm still naked and I'm going to stay this way until she has gone. I turn the shower back on, not freezing but cold. I kneel down next to her head. Taking the knife, I slice into her neck to the artery inside; blood escapes but not that much, there's no heart beating to pump it. I am going to have to be the pump that gets the blood out and washed away. I slice open her thighs until I open the big femoral arteries, and then, placing the knife on the toilet seat, I compress her chest performing CPR. The blood actually spurts out of her legs and clogs around the drain. I turn up the shower and pour copious amounts of bleach into the blood and water mixing it all up with my foot. Then I go back to pumping up and down on her ribcage; after twenty minutes I'm tired and my arm aches. The useless one just hangs there witnessing the action. I am not sure how much blood is left in Yuko's body. I have pumped out pints and pints, and the floor is pink with diluted blood and the shower is still running. I stand up and pour more bleach over her. She is pale as a ghost and staring at me with insolence, a slight pout on her blue lips.

"If you're not careful I'll fuck your arse. You should show more respect. I killed you. A cripple killed you. Show some fucking manners."

I wonder what the fuck I am talking about; have I gone fucking mad talking to a dead woman and demanding respect?

I'd be sullen if I'd been murdered.

Next I will have to remove the intestines and internal organs, and wash out the body cavity. The stomach, colon and intestines will need a special trip out to get rid of them before they start to stink. I have the idea I can leave them on the waste ground next to the canal, where the old gas cylinders used to be. There's a family of foxes over there that will make short work of them and what they don't eat the rats and crows will finish by morning; and who's going to investigate a pile of fetid meat amongst the old tyres, broken fridges, human shit and old beer cans that line the edge of the canal?

I'll make the trip out with the viscera about 10 or eleven tonight, when the pubs are kicking out and there're people around, then one man with a rucksack won't make much impact, – best get a move on – not that much time left. I pull Yuko onto her back and push the knife into her body just below the sternum, through the skin, layers of fat and muscle into the thoracic cavity, and slice down towards her pubic bone. My hours of sharpening have paid off, her abdomen opens like a sliding door. I cut a diagonal up from the pubic bone to the side of the ribcage and flip over the skin like folding a tablecloth. Her organs are revealed, exposing to the cold electric light of the wet room a sight that should never be seen by another human being.

The large mass of the liver like a chocolate pudding and the coils and coils of intestines, like a never-ending string of sausages, the spleen and stomach and, of course, the root of the problem, the uterus. The inside of a human being is wet and slippery, even after most of the blood has been removed. I pull out her intestines and pile them up on the tiled floor between her legs cutting them into sections with scissors; believe me when I tell you there is a lot of intestine packed into a person. The smell is beginning to get to me. I need a break, I wash myself down with the shower and step back into my room, closing the door behind me. I towel myself dry, pull on some underwear, and walking across the room I grab a few large black plastic bin liners from the cupboard to put the viscera into.

I sit on the bed and consider the task ahead of me. It feels enormous to dispose of a human being – one that had been living, breathing and talking to me only a couple of hours before – without trace inside 24 hours, and all by hand.

The reality was proving to be altogether tougher and messier than I had calculated for. Still, what's done is done and there's no use crying over spilt guts.

"Have to just get on with it."

I stand and keeping on the black cotton underwear, I re-enter the wet-room.

It's a charnel house.

I gather bits of intestine and colon and squeeze the contents of each section into the toilet bowl, – it's truly disgusting the amount of liquid and effluent inside a human body. I flush the bowl after pouring yet more bleach into the mixture. Then I stuff the rest into the black bag and tie it up putting it to one side, and with the shower running the whole time I kneel between Yuko's legs and hack out her bladder, puncturing it over the toilet to empty it of piss, and then slice out her uterus. I find myself inserting my fingers in the top of her vagina and pushing them until they appear out of the front of her cunt, this makes me chuckle; not often you get to see that. I throw the useless organ into another bag, followed by the liver, spleen and stomach, which I remove carefully so as not to spill the contents. I am more relaxed, getting a rhythm for my work. I cut and slash, removing the kidneys, and reaching inside her ribs, grasp each lung hauling it out, stopping to cut the windpipe. This gave me a thought: I should cut off Yuko's head and place it in the sink so she can watch me at work and sulk about what I was doing to her.

"Good idea."

I take the saw and grind it through her neck, flesh peeling away in chunks. It takes a minute or two to get to the spine. I shear it with my bolt cutters. I pick Yuko's head up by the hair and hold her face close to mine an inch or less away, her lips level with mine, eye to eye.

"I know you can't hear me and I know you are dead, but you are going to watch me and maybe if there's an Afterlife, which I fucking doubt, you can see me at work. I don't hate you. You are just a metaphor that's all. Also you should be careful where you leave your business card."

I place her head in the sink, eyes peeking over the edge watching me with a look of rebuke. It's easier to eviscerate her without her head on, it's more like a lump of meat in a butchers shop.

I relax as I chop up the lungs and liver, I extract her heart and snip it into pieces with the scissors. The body cavity is empty of organs and I spray it out with the hot shower and bleach. I am ready to dump all this offal for the foxes. I turn off the shower and step out of the wetroom lugging the two bin bags of offal – they are heavy considering she was a small girl. I dry myself and dress. Grabbing my rucksack, I stuff the tightly tied bags inside and zip it shut. I'm ready to start spreading Yuko around. I hope she liked animals because they are going to love her.

I walk down to the canal entrance on new North Road. The gates are shut after dark but it's no problem to heave myself over the wall after lobbing the rucksack over first. I drop down onto the towpath and head east. The path is deserted and although lit, many of the nauseous orange lights are not working; this suits me. On the far side of the canal the occasional light twinkles from the small window of a narrow barge; The lights from the old buildings converted into apartments spatter across the dank water. On my side, the towpath side, the buildings are rundown social housing, either derelict, or in a poor state of repair. I walk under several bridges and the surroundings become more and more industrial: once I am past Broadway market there are fewer of the new-build apartments. The disaster that was the Olympic Games led to a lot of planned development being abandoned. I can see the metal framework of the old gas storage tanks rising up above the houses. There's overgrowth and scrub along the edge of the towpath, this part is not well maintained. I decide it would be a good idea to spread out the dumping of Yuko over a wider area, as isolated bits of offal will arise no interest, just disgust should someone find them, but a big pile of guts, – that might cause someone to think twice. I drop the heavy rucksack to the floor and open the top, untying the black plastic sack that I've double-bagged to stop leaks. The smell is offensive. I plunge my arm into the mess inside, grabbing a handful of mixed organs and hurl the mess into the bushes at the back of the path. It's a stupid move, bits of Yuko are now hanging all over the bushes, and I have to go and remove them from the branches. I must place the woman more carefully, the foxes and rats will do the rest. I shoulder the pack and walk on. I stop every fifty metres or so to deposit more of Yuko, out of sight now, along the towpath, rinsing my hand it the canal each time. I come to the bridge opposite the gas towers. I'm on the opposite bank to them and I walk up the steps checking the road. Nothing comes. I clamber over the gate and walk across the bridge to the gates of the closed gas storage centre. The wire gates are bent and twisted and I can just step through. The place has become a rubbish dump and as I walk across the concrete I hear a low bark and growl. I spot two foxes, their mangy red coats and beady eyes shine in the tangerine half-light of the towpath lamps. It makes these seedy creatures look even more feral than usual. They linger and look at me, junkie foxes, always on the make, always looking for a free meal. They aren't wary or frightened; if anything, they're chastising me for trespassing. I drop my backpack and pull out the black bin liners, there's still a fair bit of Yuko left inside, I walk toward the foxes and pour Yuko out of the bag spreading her about. I scrunch up the plastic bag and return it to the rucksack. I shoulder my pack and back away. The foxes who have watched with interest twitch their noses and saunter forward. After a moment of examination they start to eat the offal, tearing at it and taking parts away to stash. Good.

I walk home. It's 11. 28 pm I still have a lot to do and I need more bleach.

I deposit the black plastic bags in a litterbin before I return to my room. I notice the door of the adjacent room is slightly ajar again. I'm too busy to investigate. I enter my room and make a cup of tea. The whole incident feels far away even though I know I have a carcass of a woman in my bathroom; the fact that my room is tidy and I've just been out for a walk along the pavements makes it feel as if the killing of Yuko was a dream. I sit on my bed, mug of tea steaming in my hand, examining my feelings. I don't have any to speak of, I'm detached, I have a job to do and it must be done by morning.

"There's a dead woman in the bathroom you must feel something."

"No."

"Nothing?"

"Nothing."

My conversation with myself is over and my tea is cold. How could such a short talk take so long? I strip to my underpants and walk to the wet room. I open the door.

Inside is a scene of carnage, a slaughterhouse of blood, guts and flesh. It stinks. Yuko's head has somehow turned and faces me from the sink, her eyes stare at me with clouded regret.

"Yuko you are being greatly appreciated at this moment by the local wildlife. I am sure you would approve."

I stop talking, it's not a good sign to be talking to an eviscerated prostitute in your bathroom. No more conversation. I look at the body. I should joint it, two hands, feet, forearms, upper arms, thighs and lower legs. Once I have each of the sections, it will be easier to cut the flesh off.

I grab Yuko's foot and straighten her out. I take the smaller of my very sharp knives and slice through the flesh around her ankle exposing the bone. I place her foot on the floor, take the hammer and smash the ankle joint with three or four well placed blows. I notice that I have cracked a floor tile, – I need a piece of wood to put under the other joints so I can hammer them without damaging the floor – then I twist the foot through 360 degrees. It's like twisting a chicken wing. With a final wrench, the foot comes away from the leg. I'm going to have to do this with every joint. I stand thinking that I may have bitten off more than I can chew. I am sweating but there is no alternative. I turn the shower on and set it to cold to keep the temperature down. I detach Yuko's other foot and then decide to take off her hands next. They are small and delicate and may have once been soft. The fingers have swollen up around the rings on her fingers so I take the bolt cutters and snip each one away. It's like pruning a rose bush. I snip off the tips of each finger to remove any chance of recovering fingerprints and I pull off the rings and put them in the sink with her head; they will have to be thrown away somewhere, along with her other possessions.

I snap forward each stump of her hands until the joint cracks and then I use the bolt cutters again and the hands are free. I am beginning to warm to my work, elbows next, cracked like chestnuts at Christmas. I fetch in the piece of wood that the sharpening stones had been mounted on, from my room and place it on the floor under Yuko's knees, carving away the flesh and muscle until the complicated knee joint is exposed, and then I crunch it with the hammer until it's pulverised and twist off the leg; first the left, then the right. The pile of limbs on the far side of the toilet is growing into a small stockpile. I survey the open torso in front of me with its remnants of arms and legs splayed out like a broken child's toy. I amputate the upper arms, then the upper legs: the hip joints are tough. By the time I've separated both I am sweating and out of breath. It's 2 am. This has taken 3 hours. I must work faster. I look at the torso and decide to leave it until later. First I must fetch more black plastic sacks, cut the flesh off the bones and bag it up as fast as I can without cutting myself. It's the flesh, guts and fat that will stink. The bones, once clean, I can smash up into small pieces and get rid of later. I cut and slice and carve, stopping only to sharpen the blades and drink water. I work fast and in a fever, surrounded by meat, acres of meat and bone. All the while Yuko is watching over me from the sink. I cut flesh into chunks and stuff it into supermarket plastic bags about 2 kilos a bag; it's going to take forty or so bags to portion Yuko up, and then dump into bins around the area.

They empty the litterbins twice a week so she will be gone to the landfill or the incinerator. The bones present more of a problem. I will have to bake them or something to dry them out and then smash them up. By the time 4. am comes around I have more or less bagged Yuko into the supermarket chain plastic bags and tied each one up. I'm covered in sweat and turn on the shower to wash. Yuko's skeleton is dismembered and piled up in the corner of the wet room like white greasy old sticks on a forest floor. I wash and scrub my skin pouring bleach all over the floor and walls of the room. I take a soap bar and scrub my body in a fierce flagellant way. It's not so much killing her that makes me feel discomfort but the dismemberment; it makes me feel dirty in a way I cannot describe, an inner filth, a twisting wrongness inside me like I am no longer human. Steam fills the room and I can see the misty shape of Yuko's head staring from the sink. Eyes looking at me, telling me that I should have known I could not carry this out without feeling this way, denying my humanity is going to cost me my soul even though I don't have one. No one has a soul, the concept is ridiculous, it's just social conditioning. I can beat it. I have been in mortal combat with it since I don't know when and I will win.

I reach over and pull Yuko's eyelids down over her dead cloudy eyes and feel relieved. Why didn't I do that earlier or even straight away? Why did I make her watch me? Why did I make myself suffer? I turn her face to the wall and fall back against the wet room wall, letting the jets of hot water fall on my dog-tired body, breathing in the steam and bleach fumes. I feel sick, a small knot of nausea deep in the pit of my stomach. It turns into a tidal wave, and a tsunami of vomit and bile rises up my innards and out. I reach the toilet in the nick of time and throw up for an age. After, I feel better, less dirty and soiled. I cut off the water and step out into the room past the rucksack stuffed with plastic bags and dry myself, drink water and dress. Time to put the remaining Yuko to rest.

I leave the building, rucksack on my back and a holdall in my hands, just another invisible 'homeless man' tramping the streets in the early hours, and rummaging through the trashcans as he trudges along. I stop and deposit bags in bins again and again in litterbins and wheelie bins and trade disposal bins outside restaurants and sandwich shops. A police car slides along the pavement next to me, the officer in the passenger seat looks me up and down as I walk along, before deciding that I am not worth stopping for and the car accelerates away. They see me but they don't. This part of the task is fast and I am enjoying the cold early morning air after the dank, steamy bleach-filled wet room. There are a few late night club-goers staggering along the roads and sometimes a genuine homeless invisible sleeping under cardboard in a doorway or back alley. I don't see my reflection in any window that I pass. By the time I get to London Bridge I have only a few bags left. I cut down the steps on the far side of the bridge. The streets of London paved with piss and alcohol. At the bottom of the steps I turn right, heading for the Thames Path, past the building that houses the 'Worshipful Company of Launderers'; a plaque on the wall announces this strange organisation, and there are two more for the Worshipful Company of Glaziers and for Instrument Makers. There are 108 of these archaic livery companies, a sort of posh trade union for tradesmen in the City of London, such as

Barbers, Longbow Makers, Cordwainers, and my favourites, the Paviors; perhaps I should petition to add one for murderers –The Worshipful Company of Murderers. I walk past the dock in which Francis Drake's boat The Golden Hind sits. It's a small ship and he must have been invisible indeed on the Atlantic as he sailed into nothing. Now it's there for tourists to gawk and in true modern style it's not the original but a replica. I'm heading toward the little strip of beach by the OXO Tower where I will empty the last remains of Yuko into the river for the fish to eat. Burial at sea, by me, the presiding captain. I walk down the steps to the beach. As the tide races out, the lights of early morning London cascade in rippling salvos off the water. I take the last three bags of Yuko out of the holdall and open them over the grey water of the river, tipping the contents into the stream, and she is gone. Except for the bones and her head that still sit in my wet room.

I pull out the black plastic sacks that I used to line the rucksack, screw them up and release them to the river; in an hour they will be far away. I shoulder the pack and plod back along the little beach to the metal steps that lead up to the beautifully paved walk that sweeps along to the South Bank Centre. I pass the National theatre where people pretend to indulge in dramas that could never match the one I am playing out right now.

I see the hated Charing Cross footbridge ahead. On it, I throw the rucksack into the Thames and walk north towards my room.

I am hungry.

Chapter 13: **A Ripe Harvest**

I celebrate my success with a cup of thick builders' tea and a slap-up breakfast at the mis-named 'Café Bliss' on Dalston Lane. I turn up outside the café and walk towards the open door with its red flaking paint, noticing that I make no reflection in the window. Inside the café is a temple to Formica, steam, shiny soft plastic seat covers, brushed aluminium and the sound of frying. The only customers are a few workmen in their lurid orange waistcoats; with cruel shaved heads they are lounging around a couple of tables in the corner, reading grubby tabloid newspapers. It's early.

The rest of the café is deserted apart from the three bored staff and a tiny elderly woman nursing a cup of tea and two slices of anaemic toast, perched at a table near the counter. She's looking around like a hawk seeking a mouse.

This breakfast is hard earned and I will pay with Yuko's money. I sit down and wait for the server... and wait. After 10 minutes of her walking past me wiping tables and joking with the workmen in their fluorescent orange waistcoats. I march up to the counter.

"Hello, I would like to order some breakfast if you don't mind."

"Sorry love, didn't see you at all."

"Yeah, I get that a lot."

I order set breakfast number three: 2 eggs, 2 bacon, 2 sausage, hash browns, beans, toast and coffee or tea. I ask for the bacon to be well done and the tea to be strong. I take a seat in a two-bench seat booth next to the window. The old woman's head pivots as she watches me walk past; I pay her no heed.

She's invisible.

A few minutes later, my food arrives and so does the old lady. Like a decrepit jack-in-the-box she pops up and sits opposite me, shuffling along the pale blue plastic bench seat until her eyes are level with mine.

"Do you mind?"

She brings with her a cup of tea, loneliness and a manic desire to talk. She is wearing a cheap lilac trouser suit tailored from lost dreams and a life shoddily lived. The cloth of sadness envelops her like a fog.

"You don't mind. I can tell that you don't mind.

I looked at you and you reminded me of my Harry.

He used to work in the box factory, bumped his hip and had to go to the doctor, they told him he'd have to stop.

But he'd had part of his head shot off in the war.

So he liked to work in the Box Factory.

He had 24 carers at home, that's too many isn't it, but you need more for a man there's more to do for a man, do you follow?"

I butter my toast.

"I used to get headaches all the time, you see.

You can understand, I can see by your arm that you understand about headaches.

My friend Sally she told me I should see the psychic down at Bethnal Green.

I used to be the cleaner at the ballroom, 24 years, and then they got a machine and I didn't have a job no more.

Helen got that Xzheimer's disease, you know the one. She died.

Her head fell back and eyes went glassy and her tongue fell out. That's how they go with that Xzheimer's disease you know."

I eat a hash brown.

"Sally and me went to the psychic in the church hall in Bethnal Green, you know the place, next to the Tescos, upstairs. He was very good there was two of him, black fella he was, put his hands on my head. Sally fainted dead away, she did."

I look at her blankly, and place a forkful of bacon and egg into my mouth being careful not to let any drop from the fork. I chew my food slowly and keep my eyes on hers. I swallow.

"Did it work?"

"Did what work?"

"The psychic, did it stop your headaches?"

"Oh yes, completely gone after. It was very satisfying, God is remarkable don't you think and some people can channel him."

"How much did he charge?"

"Who?"

"The psychic."

"Two pounds."

I nod in surprise and give the woman a smile. I'm captivated by her stream of consciousness, her continual shifting between present and past. She is alive and intelligent and yet defunct and useless. All the times she has cleaned up after drunken revellers at the long gone ballroom mean nothing. She would be better off dead, like Yuko; she has no future worth speaking of. Used-up hooker, used-up cleaner, what's the difference?

"What's your name?"

"Me, I am Cathy. You look like a nice man.

See that arm – well my brother had one of those just the same, all withered and ugly and useless. Do you understand?"

I understood.

No-one ever mentions my arm, either out of embarrassment or because I have grown skilful at hiding it. For once it was visible. My shoulder looking like a rat under the cloth of my t-shirt and the upper arm hanging down like a pale sliver of flesh meeting the forearm in a knot of bone and tram-like stitch scars. The small child-sized hand folded back on itself like a broken cat flap.

"I live down the estate now but I had a house up Stoke Newington, 44 years I lived there. I'm 68 now. Me and Harry we live there.

He works in the Box Factory ever since that war, he won a medal you know a shiny one, in the shape of a star."

"I thought he had his head blown off?"

Yes, well not all of it, that's what he won the medal for.

He liked it in the Box Factory, now it's flats it is.

No more work for the likes of us."

"Harry's dead?"

"Who is? Oh...oh yes Harry's dead, been dead for years. Got his head shot off in the war, won a medal. See I don't normally come here but well, it was sunny so thought I would as I am off to see my Harry at the hospital in Homerton"

The Homerton hospital closed years ago just after the disastrous Olympic games. I thought it best not to mention this to the batty old cow.

"Where do you live Cathy"?

"De Beauvoir estate. Er, 16 Cameron House, named it after that Prime Minister fella."

"Do you have kids Cathy?"

"Kids, oh no not children, never did. Harry had some but they died."

I'm growing impatient, where the fuck is this idiot's carer?

"We all used to go to the Lea valley for a picnic. Till they filled it up with all them foreign people. It's so different here now, we used to go dancing over there.

See that arm of yours I knew it would mean you're a nice person.

I don't have no-one to talk to now, not now Harry's gone."

She falls silent. Staring through me, her bright clear blue eyes are alive as she watches some scene from far away. She's no longer in the Café Bliss but in some long distant dancehall with Harry and his half a head. I took this moment to eat the rest of my breakfast. Last year, fifty years or yesterday, are all the same to the imagination. She was back in the dancehalls of her past. I chomp on my sausage and watch her, waiting for the movie in her head to end, as it must. I'm watching for the inevitable jolt. As I finish my sausage it arrives like a freight train full of now. Her hands shake and her eyes move rapidly around. She looks puzzled and frightened. She screws her face up and scrutinises me for about a minute. I wipe my mouth with a napkin and say nothing.

"Oh hello love, do you mind if I sit here, I don't often get out these days."

"No shit !"

"Eh?....well anyway you look like a nice young man, not many like you around here now you know. Do you work in the Box Factory, follow my drift ... I used to have these headaches, terrible headaches. My friend she said the psychic would fix them and he did."

"For two pounds."

"Oh have you been too. I thought you must but he couldn't fix your arm, well sometimes God has a job for people what have to stay cripples."

"Cathy it's been lovely talking to you I have to leave now."

"Oh, ...yes I must go and meet Harry. Bye love, thanks for the tea."

With that she slides along the seat and ups and walks out. Leaving what remains of her life drifting past me like the smell of old coffee. I watch her trot away down the street. She is slim and in good shape, I liked her lined face, once so pretty and smooth. I wonder what she would look like with my cock in her mouth. Do seventy-year-olds give blowjobs?

Maybe I'll pay her a visit.

I finish my tea, pay the woman behind the counter and leave.

On the walk back to my room I see council workmen emptying the litterbins in the street. Yuko is on her last journey to the council incinerator, apart, that is, from her head and bones, they're still in my wet room. I'll dispose of them as soon as I return, though I feel tired. I have been up all night and could do with some sleep before tackling the next part of the task. It again feels unreal to me, as if I've dreamt it all, and considering the vivid nature of my dreams this could well be the case. Maybe when I return to my closet-sized room there will be no trace of any woman, let alone a murder scene with a girl's head staring at me from the bathroom sink. I reach the corner of my road and shuffle along, tired to the core, anxious about what I have or haven't done.

My brain's trying to rewire itself, to erase the facts from my memory, telling me that the events of the last night aren't real ones but created by my imagination. My intellect is having none of this, it is quite unrelenting about the fact that I killed and butchered an innocent woman last night – the internal conflict inside me is maniacal. I stand staring at the shabby front door, my heart racing and my palms sweating. I'm reluctant to move another foot forward for fear of what I will find, but I must. I mount the steps, take a deep breath, walk into the hall and down the dismal stairs to my basement. I stop. The door to the room next to mine is open. I decide to go in, partly to avoid having to enter my room. I push the door to the room, standing back while it swings open.

Slow and silent.

I step inside.

The room is dark. The wooden shutters are closed tight, only a sliver of light slips around their edges.

I flick the light switch.

Nothing.

The light bulb is blown. The room is grey and dusty. There's no furniture just a large wooden trunk in the centre of the floor.

It's closed.

There's a door on the far side of the room that leads out into a small lightwell in a tiny courtyard below street level which gives access to the old coalholes. All the houses have them. I walk over to the shutters and undo them. Light pours in and the room soaks it up like water hitting a dry riverbed. The room is empty apart from the trunk and the door to the outside, which is locked. There's no key that I can see for either the door or the trunk. I notice there's a door at right angles to the entrance door. A wet room – of course, all the rooms have them, apart from at the very top of the house where they share a bathroom. I open the door, it's pitch black. I find the cord for the light and pull, it snaps on. The room is dry as a bone and long unused. In the sink are three keys.

Unusual.

I know without trying that they are the keys to the trunk and the room's two doors. I pick them up and pull the cord, flicking the light off. I open the trunk: it's empty and smells of old antiseptic and newspapers. I try the keys on the door to the lightwell and sure enough one of them opens it. There's nothing; the floor is covered in old leaves and cigarette ends. I shut the door, locking it and leaving the key in the lock. There is nothing of interest in here. I put the other two keys back in the sink and leave closing the door behind me.

I reach for the door handle to my room and open it. There on the bed sits Yuko's handbag. My intellect crows with triumph but my imagination quails in fear.

I feel sick. I really did it? I really killed her. Why?

I stand in the middle of my small room looking at the bag of belongings for a few minutes. I feel unreal as if I am watching some disturbing European art film that has no happy ending. I feel elated at my success; it's less than 24 hours since I liberated Yuko and she's nearly all gone. I feel sad that my life has come to a point where this unspeakable act is the nearest I can get to genuine intimacy. I have to finish the tidying up.

I open the wet room door and look inside. The combination of bleach and meat means the room smells like a public swimming baths meets a butcher's shop. Over in the corner is a pile of bones – some still have shreds of flesh attached, though not many. The rib cage and spine are intact in the opposite corner. The room is clean and there's no sign of all the blood and gore that accompanied my earlier efforts. I shut the door, strip down to my underwear and fetch the bolt cutters. I have to reduce the skeleton to small unrecognisable bits of bone before scattering them around. I return to the wet room. I see Yuko waiting for me, silent and sulking in the sink. I place the bolt cutters on the floor and sit on the toilet; I bring my face to the same level as hers; her eyes are shut and her hair damp. I stroke her cheek; now that she's at peace her face seems smoother, less lined and careworn. I move a strand of hair that has fallen over her sallow face with its recalcitrant beauty. Her lips have taken on a charming blue hue, and as I tell her how successful my mission to feed the foxes and distribute her to the city has been, I notice a tear falling down her cheek. I am startled for a moment. Then I realise it's just water from the wet-room trickling down her face. I pull back one of her eyelids and see that her right blue eye is cloudy and the eyeball has started to collapse. I never realised how blue her eyes were, until now.

I let the eyelid droop back, and I sit back considering Yuko's head for a moment.

"You need a haircut, yes... You do."

I find the scissors and start to hack off her thick back hair. Soon it's gone and there are just untidy clumps jutting out of her skull. I gather the hair and flush it down the toilet. This will make the destruction of her head easier. I turn back to the pile of bones on the floor and pick up the bolt cutters and start to snip. This bit is easy, crack, snip, snap, go the cutters, cutting through bone as if they were air. I have just realised that the next bit – the demolition of Yuko's head is going to be the most difficult thing. For some reason I have saved the worst till last. I am tired.

I snap and snip through the skeleton. It doesn't take long and is far less onerous than chopping up all that fat and flesh was – this is like playing with sticks. That... That was like fighting with trifle. I turn the jets of the shower as hot as I can make them and play them over the bones pouring more bleach over them. I think they should be dry before I spread them across London town. I find a large bath towel and wrap the bones inside it and take them out of the wet room and place them, still wrapped inside the towel, next to the electric radiator and turn it on. I never have the heater on even in the coldest winter; it costs a fortune and why the fuck do I need to be warm? I just wear more clothes or go and find a library or a museum to sit in during the cold days. In the cold nights I just hide under the covers and wait for winter to pass. It always does.

But today I turn it on just to dry Yuko out.

I go back to the wet-room and clean up. Apart from Yuko's bald, sullen head in the sink it's as if she was never there. I gaze at her head in the sink; is she having a nap? The room is her palace or mausoleum. I decide to demolish the head later. First I will scatter the bones.

I make a cup of tea, and then masturbate.

I must be feeling anxious. I only ever masturbate when I am anxious.

I come.

I finish my tea.

I sleep.

I climb out of bed. Naked, I walk out of my room and into the room next door. The trunk is open: Yuko's head is inside. It looks at me and blinks; those collapsed blue eyes follow me across the room to the door in the opposite wall. I open it and leave the room stepping outside onto a dark rocky plateau; it stretches off into the distance, flat, apart from occasional massive cubes of stone dotted across an endless horizontal landscape. The sky is grey and ashen; it looks solid, tangible. I glance behind me and discover the door and house have vanished. I'm alone on this rock desert. I walk. I know it doesn't matter in which direction I travel. It is warm and close. The air seems to stick to my skin making it distasteful to move. It's almost concrete. Then I see it:

A rough chiselled entrance in a block of granite; it's a fair distance away and I know I have to go there. I trudge along through the corporeal air and looking down I can see that my feet are treading through a fine dust, like talcum, black and speckled with tiny bright crystals. As I step through it the tiny bright crystals seem to coalesce into the likeness of faces. These faces move and scream in silence, each face in torment; as I pace through the dust I crush thousands of souls underfoot. The dust feels warm and vital as if it were full of life. The faces distort as they try to avoid my feet. I feel nothing, not even curiosity. The tormented faces do not interest me, my lack of interest does not interest me. I walk on toward the hole in the rock.

I enter the tunnel. It slopes down at a gentle rate. I look at the floor, it is paved, broken bond, the stones so tightly matched that I can barely make out the joins between each flag. The stone is Portland. I am walking on the most perfect and well-made of pavements, quite literally the pavement of my dreams.

The tunnel is bathed with some kind of low level of phosphorescence from the moss on the ceiling. I'm trying to create a rational framework for this place. I laugh, this is the world of the irrational, and logic has no place here. The incline levels out, and in front of me is a wrought-iron gate in the shape of a huge black spider, its fangs at the top of the gate, eyes looking down at me and its legs outstretched on a web of metal. Its fat body is the centre of the gate. There's no handle.

I don't like spiders.

Goosepimples pop up on my skin and I feel the hair on the back of my neck tingle. With a deep breath I touch the body of the spider to push the gate, it gives a little, it's not cold metal, but warm and covered in tiny hairs.

The spider's eyes open one by one. It's alive. It moves upwards into a hole in the roof of the tunnel. It vanishes, leaving the way clear. Inside the gate is a room full of clocks all telling a different time. There are clocks all over the walls and standing on the floor, like a labyrinth made of time. No two clocks are the same. Some are ornate and old, others, brutal and new. I walk through the passageways between the walls of clocks; the ticking and striking noises are deafening, but there is a silence behind the noise. It overpowers the clocks – their clattering seems just a panic in front of an overwhelming assault of silence. The ticking dies and the clocks all stop moving. The upright clocks that stand in the room crumble into dust, the same black sparkling dust that I walked through outside on the rocky plain. The dust pours like liquid across the floor of the room and out through a small hatch set in the floor.

The silence is absolute. I try shouting at the top of my voice. Nothing.

I follow the dust and slip through the hatch, falling in darkness, accompanied by the bright specks that I suppose to be the remnants of people's souls. I try and grasp these specks but they always avoid my outstretched hand. I assume I am falling but there's no way of telling, as there is no sensation of rushing air. I could just as well be hanging in the void surrounded by a million specks of light, like pretty mosquitoes. All sense of time has departed, and I am quite content to hang here in mid-air when it all transforms, and now I am falling toward the rocky plain, hurtling down, headlong and terrified. Just as I think I'm about to hit the ground, I find myself standing on the rocky plain, before me a stone wall behind which I can see the tops of bushes and trees. I walk along the wall to find the way in, there doesn't seem to be one. I have to get inside. I must.

I walk around the perimeter of the wall again, still no entrance. There has to be a way in. I push against the wall. Nothing. The wall is high and smooth. I'll never climb up the sheer surface. How do I get inside? Perhaps I can't. Is there a part of me so fenced off and protected that I can't get at it, is that what this represents? Ridiculous. I look around. About a 100 metres away is a huge lump of rock. I think I will be able to climb it so that I can see over the wall. I walk to the lump of rock and start to climb. It's not too difficult, the rock is like a set of oversize paving slabs, making climbing it like clambering up a set of giant steps. I soon reach the top and stand to look over the wall into the secret garden. I am disappointed. I can only see the tops of the trees, as the entire garden is engulfed in a mist or a fog. I clamber back down the slabs to the ground and walk to the wall. I walk around the perimeter of the wall again and again On my third walk around I notice a rock slab the size and shape of a Portland stone flag leaning against it. It wasn't there the last time I walked round, I am sure of that. I pull it away from the wall and a small hole is revealed; small, but big enough for me to squeeze through. I get down on my hands and knees and edge my shoulders and head into the gap. It's tight but I manage it. I push with my feet and I am through.

I am elated – I am inside a place that didn't want to let me in. I stand, the garden is misty and I can only see a few metres ahead of me. The ground is covered in damp green grass, very fine and soft. I can see *the trunks of trees rising up into the mist ahead of me, and fading into the mist in front. They are like tall grey sentinels fading into the distance. I turn, and behind me the wall has vanished, replaced by more tree trunks and mist. It feels to me that I must walk forward and so I walk between the tree trunks. I can't see up into the boughs of these trees. The mist obscures them. The grass is even and cool under my feet and the mist caresses my body with cool refreshing tendrils. It is silent and delightful. I walk further and the tree trunks give way to smaller more tangled trees, like olive trees, wizened and twisted by time and weather. The mist rises to make a sort of canopy above these smaller trees. I walk on, the trees becoming more twisted and closer together; they are forcing me to take a particular path. I walk along a tunnel of branches and out into a clearing. Ahead of me is a tall black tree with many branches but instead of leaves sprouting out of its boughs there are entrails hanging down, like vines, and I notice the tree is bleeding, deep red blood. As I stand under the tips of the furthermost branches the smell hits me: putrefaction. The stink of death, and I see that hanging from the boughs near the trunk are the fruits of this tree of death. Heads, hanging like apples, weighing down the tree branches. I shiver with fear because each head has its eyes open, blinking at me. Among hundreds of other heads I see Fuckwit's and Yuko's hanging from the branches. All the heads open their mouths and a tortured scream erupts from them simultaneously. It vibrates in my skull. I am not sure it's an audible scream, but the inside of my head shakes with a searing pain. I strike out at the nearest head to me, punching it in the mouth. It spits blood and falls to the ground with a thump. I punch another head and it too falls to the ground and as it detaches, the branch gushes blood. The scream diminishes a touch in my mind. I run from head to head belting each one hard. The pain in my head stops and soon there are only two heads hanging from the tree; as I stand knee-deep in heads, I can feel one or two of them licking my feet. I look down at the head of a young woman; she has her tongue out and is licking my toes. I look back to the heads hanging in front of me. They are Fuckwit and Yuko. I punch Fuckwit and his head flies off the tree with a spurt of blood. Yuko looks at me, her bright blue eyes questioning me. The young woman on the ground has moved on to licking my calf, it tickles. Yuko blinks. Girl's head licks.*

I punch Yuko as hard as I can manage on the right cheek. Her head falls into the pile and I wade out of the pond of heads I have created and look at the disgusting tree dripping blood and entrails. Is there no end to this?

As I watch, large spiders appear and start to spin silk over the heads and the tree; before long the entire scene is a large grey cocoon. I turn and walk away. The wizened old trees have gone, replaced by nothing, just green grass and mist. I am tired and I lie down to sleep.

Chapter 14: **Head and Shoulders**

I open my eyes with a start. Where am I? I look around. I'm in my room on my bed. Yes, I took a nap had another fucking bizarre dream. I sit up.

I stand.

I am not naked but wearing underpants and a t-shirt.

My foot is damp. I look at the towel that contains Yuko's bones. I turn the heater off. They must be dry by now and if they're not it doesn't matter, I have to get rid of her and her stuff as soon as possible. She's having a bad influence on me.

I flick the kettle on and walk to my door. It's unlocked. I step out into the dank grey hall and see the door to the adjacent room is ajar again. I wander over to it, push it open and walk in. The room is shuttered, dark and dim. The trunk is in the middle of the room and the door in the far wall leading out to the old coal store is also open, dusty twilight is peeking around the edge of the door. Weird, it was locked before. I pull it open, there's nothing to see except the empty lightwell. I shut the door. The trunk sitting in the middle of the room is closed. I'd left it open – the door was shut and the trunk was open – how has that been reversed? I open the lid of the trunk. Yuko's head is looking up at me, eyelids open, eyes clouded and glazed. I freeze in shock and fear. I drop the lid closed, and flee back to my room tearing open the wet-room door.

Yuko's head is no longer in the sink; feeling intense relief, I traipse back to the next room and lift the lid of the trunk. There she is, staring at me glum and brooding. I must have sleep-walked and placed her in the trunk. I lift her head and tuck it under my withered arm. It's cold and clammy. I take her back home to the sink.

"No more wandering my dear, I will take you out later."

I place her back in the sink and pat her gently on the skull. I go to the pile of bones wrapped in the towel and take them into the wet-room, which is now dry. I place them on the floor and take the hammer and start smashing the bones through the towel. I pummel and beat them using the piece of wood and placing it on top of the bones, crushing them. I don't want any piece of bone to be longer than four or so inches. I hammer for an hour or so before I am satisfied with my work. Then I transfer the bones to a bin liner and put it in the rucksack. Ready for disposal.

Next the head. I have a cup of tea first. I place the pan on the stove and boil the water.

Her head is not something I will enjoy. I'll have to cut off the lower jaw, remove all her teeth and then hammer the skull and brain to a pulp. I feel a little queasy at the thought of doing this. But it has to be done – there's no doubt. I'll take her head, bones and possessions for a ride on the subway and spread them around London. I look at the clock. It's 6.45pm. Just over 24 hours have passed since I killed her and she is like a fixture in my mind, it feels as if she has been there for years and years. I have to get rid of her.

I make the tea and sip it, looking at her shiny handbag and thinking about a black tree that bleeds, weighed down by heads of the murdered. I wonder what the fuck is going on inside my head, dreams seem real and reality feels like a dream. I seem to be getting the two mixed up. I sip my tea and decide it's Yuko's fault and as soon as she's gone things will revert to normal and I can get on with my life which wasn't so bothersome before she arrived – she should have stayed away – then none of this would be happening.

It's her fault.

I put my teacup down, grab another black rubbish bag and stride into the wet room.

I toss Yuko's head into the bag without ceremony or decorum.

"I'll teach you to fuck with my mind you cunt."

I drop the bag to the floor and kneel down wedging it between my thighs. I bring the hammer down as hard as I can and hear a satisfying crunch. For some minutes I pound away, then I stop. I open the bag.

I see a disgusting shattered mess: bone, teeth, flesh and brains all smashed together in a pulpy mess.

"Oh fuck it – this will do, I am going to bury you somewhere, bitch."

I have given up on her head. I just want her out of my life. I stuff her head inside the rucksack, grab the subway travel card from her bag and get ready to set off. I stop.

I realise I am not dressed. I put on clothes. I go into the wet room and look in the mirror.

Nothing.

FUCK... I smash the mirror with the hammer, and then I see my shattered reflection in the hammered glass, one eye, half a mouth, a smiling ear and drenched hair. I look harder, that's not me I see looking back. *Who is that?*

I shut my eyes and take a deep breath. I turn, eyes still shut and leave the wet room. Once out of the wet room, I open them again, shoulder the rucksack and leave, moving up the stairs two at a time desperate to get out of the house. I stumble out of the door and down the steps onto the pavement, the quiet calming pavement. I sit on the cold flagstones and stroke them. They send a soothing message through my body telling me that everything will be all right. The pavement will look after me.

I must go to the subway station and down into the city's dreadful underbelly, the sewer of society, Civilisation's colon. I walk along the pavement following it like a guide. A pale grey ghost of a path glowing in the dusk, it leads me gently along, the rucksack heavy on my back. I count the paving stones as I walk avoiding the flags that are broken with cracks radiating out from their centre. They feel unclean to me. The path leads me to the Angel where I go underground.

No one gives me a second glance as I wave the travel card over the turnstile and pass through, making my way to the escalator, and down the moving metal stairs – into the bowels of an Angel. It is a long time since I have used the subway. I dislike the anthill-like nature of the place, the feeling of anonymity and the closeness of the people, but both those attributes are now useful to me. The subway is very expensive which is another reason I don't use it;. the invisible have to walk or use the bus. The subway is reserved for worker ants. It's early evening and it is full of these worker ants on their evening off, dressed to kill (or be killed) heading out to indulge in pointless activities. I look upon the multitudes as a horde of decorated mice. I despise them and if they knew what I carried on my back, they would run screaming from me as if I were the aberrant one, as if I was, by virtue of carrying out an unsanctioned act, somehow contagious or dangerous. They are the ones that do not think about their existence, that accept the dictates of the powerful; they are the ants following the programme. They are taught to read and then consume the words. They are fed, like calves suckling at a teat with no discrimination or thought, words designed to anaesthetise reason.

Their lack of thought is far more dangerous than my carefully constructed act of defiance. We all move along the tunnels at the pace of a death march and onto the platform. The noise of chatter interrupted by endless information announcements that convey little information, other than the fact that there is a loudspeaker announcing system in place. We are told that there is a good service on the line. I wonder if this is so unusual that they feel the need to tell us to be ready to reach our destinations without delays. CCTV cameras poke out of the walls and ceilings, some of them move, scanning the faces in the crowds. I wait with the rucksack balanced on the floor gripped between my legs.

Nobody pays me any attention – for once being invisible is a pleasure. The train will be here in one minute. Just four stops to London Bridge and the river. Saturday night: who will care what some old tramp is doing? The train rumbles into the platform. A steel worm collecting the faeces that is humanity and firing it along the intestines of the city. I crush my body into the end of a crowded carriage through a single door dragging the heavy rucksack after me and muttering "*Sorry*" to the people already in the train. Nobody cares.

The doors shut and the train heaves into the tunnel. four stops and I will be at London Bridge. Why didn't I walk?

People stand wedged into the train, too close to each other for comfort, most of them wearing headsets or earphones to provide even more isolation. Nobody looks at anybody else. Nobody wants to attract attention. There is an awful stillness in the moving carriage. It pulls into stations and as the doors open, movement erupts, people push past each other to get in or out, muttered apologies or voices raised in curses always accompanied by the disembodied instructions to "mind the gap, stand clear of the doors" or "move right down inside the carriage". A short time later the train rolls into London Bridge station and a wave of people tumble out of the train. Included in this flood are my cadaverous cargo and me.

I make my way to the surface feeling like a diver that has been too long underwater and who makes the surface just before his lungs burst. I am spewed out onto the pavement with a thousand other souls, except none of them has the demolished head of a prostitute sitting on their backs. I allow a slim smile to slide along my face as I make my way to the OXO Tower beach for the second time. It's dark and the tide is going out. The little beach is partially covered in dirty water but I can get down to the edge. I wedge the rucksack amongst the wooden supports that hold up the walkway above me upon which hundreds of people are walking, all oblivious to me down on the dirty shingle. I rip open the rucksack and remove the plastic bag with Yuko's head inside and place it carefully to one side, then I pull out the bag with the snipped bones inside. I cast her bones to the water like a sowing a harvest, scattering them as far as I can, some kind of exaggerated and macabre feeding of the ducks. It doesn't take long before she has gone. Good. I wash the black bin liner in the water, rip holes in it and let it go with the tide.

Now for her head. I need to get rid of her fucking head. I look in the bag – nothing but a mess of bone and brain, a glutinous mess, a death trifle. I decide to dump her in the food waste bins that serve the OXO Tower Restaurant; these are emptied daily and it amuses me. I walk around to the bins and see a couple of kitchen porters sharing a cigarette. I walk past and sit on a bench waiting for them to finish. The porters return to their pot-washing duties and I sidle up to the large food waste bin, and slide the lid back. Inside it's half full of the debris of part-eaten expensive meals. Who spends that much on food they don't eat? I half-tip, half-pour the sludge of Yuko's head into the slush, it blends well and no one wants to examine the contents of this waste bin.

I walk home.

"What day is it? I killed her on Friday afternoon and stayed up chopping and sawing, it must be Saturday evening, wasn't I going to see Martha? Yes."

I pull my phone out of my pocket and stab her number into the keypad, impressed that I have memorised it. It rings and goes to voicemail. I leave a message apologising for not calling earlier and so on, and say I'll call again later. I want a shower and some food.

I walk along Old Street with its menagerie of painted youth parading like peacocks convinced that they are the first ever peacocks to parade ever, anywhere. It would be endearing if it weren't so arrogant. My phone rings. I answer, it's Martha.

"Hello"

"Hi"

"We are meeting tomorrow, right? Sunday."

"Ah, sorry thought it was tonight. I've been so busy I forgot what day it is."

Her nervous laugh shattered some more crockery.

"What, out killing nightclubbers?"

I start and pull the phone away from my ear then realise that of course she's joking.

"Yes, it's very time-consuming because there's so many of them."

"Well do you want to meet for lunch tomorrow?"

I can't afford to spend money like that and then I remember I have Yuko's fuck money.

"Sure, let's go to the Scolt Head in Islington about one."

"Ok do you want to come by and pick me up?"

"Yes, sure, look forward to it. Bye."

"Bye."

The conversation over. I continue walking to my room, looking forward to taking a shower without the disapproving gaze of that bitch Yuko. Why did she have to come round anyway? The shabby green door welcomes me into the hallway. My room is tidy and cold; for once I notice the temperature. The bag containing Yuko's things is on the bed and her clothes are on the floor. Tomorrow I'll get rid of them. I open a tin of sardines and eat them straight from the tin. They taste of oily death. I discard the tin half-way through and try a tin of pears: they taste of cloying, sweet hatred. I eat a dry cracker and that tastes of dust. I give up and take a hot shower, running the water long enough to fill the wet room with steam: I don't want to see the room in which I have carried out my act of empowerment. I wash for a long time. I wish the searing water could wash off the years, burn away the useless past and let me have a life all over again. I turn off the water and leave the wet-room, I leave the door open and the steam creeps out into my living space. It slinks across the ceiling and wraps itself around the bare light bulb. I decide to stay naked. My wrinkled body taunts me with small indications of a taut past, a muscle ripples here or a joint cracks there, but it's not fooling me – it's had its best days and now it's the, not-so-slow decline into shitting myself and falling down steps to break my hips, – why do the old cling to life so tenaciously? Why do I? I suppose it's because it's all there fucking-well is – after this there's nothing.

I perch on the bed and grab the black patent leather handbag that until recently hung from Yuko's arm. I crack it open and stare at the contents. I should separate them all and throw them away discreetly. A handbag full of stuff would definitely draw attention. I pull out the ragged pack of tarot cards and slip them out of their box. I turn them around in my hands and decide to pull out a couple of cards at random. I spread the pack on the bed face down and hesitate before selecting two cards. I tell myself that this is all rubbish and we have no destiny, nor is there such a thing as fate, but there's a little tiny part of my brain that is niggling me with thoughts to the contrary. I despise this part of me but nonetheless I pinch the corners of three cards and turn them face up on the bed.

The cards have intricate illustrations on them and titles in handwritten letters. They are:

The Magician. This has a drawing of a red-cloaked man, his face covered by some kind of magnifying glass. He is examining a large leather-bound volume in a room with charts and tables pinned to the walls. Two wine goblets are on the table alongside him and he holds a wand. I hold the card close and examine it further. It seems to me that the part of his face that you can see looks a lot like me.

The Tower of Destruction. A picture of a tall medieval tower at the top of a hill, the top half of the building has been struck by lightning and is collapsing in the throes of a great storm. Two figures, skeletons with human faces, can been seen falling from the tower, to be dashed against the rocks below. On closer examination the faces on the card also look like me.

The Wheel of Fortune. In the centre is a large wooden wheel spinning in a clockwise direction. At the top sits a king and on the left of him, a young man climbs the wheel; towards him on his right another young man is falling from the wheel, and in the middle sits a beautiful girl wrapped in a sheet. The faces of all of them look like me.

I rummage through Yuko's bag looking for a book to interpret the meanings, but there's nothing. She knew the cards by heart or they were part of some kinky act she performed for a client, probably the latter. Then I remember the tattoo on her shoulder – it's one of her tarot cards. I turn them all over, searching through until I find it. Yes, the Hanged Man, she had it tattooed on her shoulder, a corpse swinging from an inky branch by one foot, hands tied, gold coins spilling from his pockets and a stupid grin on his already too familiar face. I wish I had taken a closer look at the face on her tattoo. I frown and crumple this card up in my hand and take the rest of the cards, minus my three, and stuff them back in their cardboard box and return them to the bag. I pull out the panties and push my nose into them: they smell of clean cotton. I put them back and close the bag. I'm exhausted, I need to sleep. I clamber into bed, flick off the light and lie down. I like it in the dark under my duvet – it's warm and the mattress is firm.

Chapter 15: **Stationary Movement**

There's a tapping noise in my room, it sounds like the plink, plink of a spoon on a pipe. There's never any noise like this in my room. I wait for it to pass, but it doesn't, it carries on. I will have to turn on the light and track down the sound. For some inexplicable reason I find it hard to lift my arm to get to the light switch. It feels like I am pushing it through thick molasses. I flick the light switch and she's standing in my room. Yuko, or at least a version of her. Her head is mangled and only has one eye, her jaw is crushed, the arms and legs are bleeding and without flesh. One foot is backwards, no, one whole leg is the wrong way round. Blood and some other brown liquid ooze from her joints and drip quietly to the floor. A mockery of the human body. She is tapping one of the water pipes with a knife. One of my knives, which means it's super sharp. I sit bolt upright. "You're not here. This is merely a dream." I say in a quiet voice.

"How do you know?"

"Fuck off. I am not having a philosophical discussion with my subconscious mind in the form of a dead fucking whore."

I have climbed out of the bed. I don't like the deft way she is weaving the knife between her fingers. Mind you, I suppose once you have been jointed, boned and minced you aren't going to be fazed by a few cuts from a knife. I stand naked. The simulacra tilts its head to one side and then with a lightning-fast movement the hand holding the knife snakes out flashing toward my neck. I manage to step back and the point of the blade quivers a few millimetres from my throat. I grab the door handle, heave the door open and leap into the corridor. The door to the adjacent room is open and I dash inside, shutting the door behind me. There is no sign of Yuko. I notice the shower is running in the wet-room. I creep to the door and open it a crack. There she is, Yuko, under the hot jets of water. They mix with blood and brown grunge as the water runs over her body. She is not holding a knife. She seems not to have noticed me.

I shut the door. This is not a good state of affairs. The room is full of fog and I can't see the far wall. I walk into the mist, the floor changes beneath my feet, becoming smooth paving stone. I walk forwards and see a warm yellow light spilling out of some kind of a building in the fog ahead.

As I draw closer it resolves into the theatre. I enter the deserted foyer and look around; the theatre is empty and silent, lights burning, doors open but empty. I walk into the auditorium and am greeted by row after row of vacant seats. The old degenerate creatures that had sat and watched the disembowelling of the young dancers have left. I tread down the aisle and jump up onto the stage, the boards are smooth and dry. I cross into the wings and down the wooden steps to the backstage, also empty. I open the door to a dressing room. On the front of the door is a large red glittering star. The room is empty, the lights are blazing and bouquets of flowers are everywhere. There's no sign of anyone. The smell of lilies fills my nostrils and mixed in with it is the faint background odour of putrefying flesh. I notice a small red door at the back of the dressing room; it is half covered by a dressing table and about four feet high. It draws me. I shift the dressing table and open the little door. It's no more than a hatch. It reveals a long square passageway. If I am going to negotiate it, it will have to be on my hands and knees. Once I am inside, the hatch slams shut. The tunnel floor is smooth, the only sound is the shuffling of my knees and the pat pat pat of my hand on the floor. There are small metal grills placed in the walls of the tunnel. I stop to peer through them and I can see myself in my wet-room. Everyone I look through has me in the wet-room on the other side, but every view is of a different me carrying out different activities. In one I am shaving, in another I am showering, in another I am cutting up Yuko's body, in yet another I am showering and fucking a live Yuko, another grill reveals me eating a small child. I stop looking the tableaux, they make me feel sick. I notice my body is dripping sweat, though I don't feel hot. I stop and look behind me and, of course, there's nothing. No tunnel, no grills no anything, I cannot go back, only forward – if I am going forward? I restart my crawling. It continues for what seems hours. I no longer glance through the metal grates, I hear discomforting noises as I pass them. Grinding and crunching sounds mixed with gasping and the sound of my own cursing and shouting, and always the sound of the water jets from the shower, although the tunnel is in no way wet. I see a junction ahead and crawl faster to reach it, hoping that it will show me a way out, or at least, give me respite from the endless parade of the showering, murdering me. After a long time I reach the junction. It's an intersection leading away to both my right and left as well as continuing straight ahead. I look down the tunnel to my left; it fades into darkness and I can feel a waft of dry hot air coming from the dark. I can hear faint noises, perhaps of machinery. This tunnel does not appeal. To my right the tunnel rises slightly and turns out of view around a right angle. It's light at least, and there's no sense of foreboding emanating from that direction. Ahead it's more of the same and behind me, nothing. I realise whichever direction I take is an irreversible decision – there's no going back. I squat, what to do? I'm not going left that's for sure, and I can't bear to go forward. It has to be the right hand tunnel. I turn and start crawling up the incline. My legs and arm ache. The tunnel's roof is lower and crawling is difficult. I can smell something ahead, a sort of rich meaty smell, like cooking. I salivate. I'm hungry.

Ahead there is a large grate through which the smell is seeping and there are noises and voices. By the time I reach it I'm flat on my tummy. I peer through the grate, it's at floor level and I can see feet and hear voices speaking in a language I don't understand; the smell of cooking is intense. Is it Chinese food? I push the grate. It shifts just slightly in the top right hand corner. I thump it as hard as I can. It shifts a touch more. I repeat the thumping, concentrating on the corner where it's giving way. The grate moves and I can grasp the edge and I heave. It bends and then snaps off. I push it away and wriggle through the gap, it's tight but I slide through, the sweat on my body helping me to slip out onto a tiled floor. I have emerged, naked beside a large refrigerator in the corner. The floor is greasy and the kitchen is hot. No one has noticed me. Can they not see a naked cripple crouching in the corner of their kitchen?

I stand, they still pay not the slightest attention. I'm in the basement kitchen of a Chinese restaurant. Three grimy cooks are rushing about in front of a large range managing a million woks and shouting at the assistants who are busy chopping meat and vegetables with sharp cleavers and knives.

"Hey you!" I shout.

Nothing.

I walk around the range standing in the middle of the kitchen, still nothing.

They can't see or hear me.

I walk out of the kitchen down a narrow passageway and upstairs into the restaurant. It's about three quarters full and nobody shows any interest in me. I walk out into the street. It's evening and the road is busy. People, traffic, noisy buses, the clattering of endless bicycles, and me, naked in the street.

Nothing.

I recognise my location. I'm not far from my house. I start to walk. The noises and smells of the Angel assault my senses. I look across the road and see Yuko. She's standing, the mutilated mannequin oozing blood, and staring at me with one reproachful eye. I walk along the street and she keeps pace along the opposite side of the road. Nobody notices her or me. I dash down a side street and she is no longer visible. I am relieved. I look in a shop window. As I pass I have a reflection: it's of Yuko, not me, but it's my reflection. The sight makes me nauseous and I stagger away and vomit on some steps. I need to return home – this all feels too real. I break out into a run for the last 500 yards to my door. I see the green door to my house. The door is open. I go straight in, down the stairs and open the door to my room. Inside it is dark and the smell of musk tickles the back of my throat. In the light from the hallway I can see my body in the bed, sleeping. I feel sick and frightened. I let the door close and crouch in the corner, watching the faint outline of my sleeping form in the bed. I crouch, tighter and tighter into a ball, in the corner of the room.

Blackness.

My eyes open. I'm lying in bed under the duvet. I look over at the corner, no sign of me. I feel both relief and apprehension. This dream was so realistic it was indistinguishable from reality. I don't want these dreams to be real. I want them to stop. Is this how my mind is going to continue to deal with the events of my life? I have killed a woman and so can't be surprised by the fact that I am finding it hard to process this event. The shower beckons me. The hot water never fails to refresh and punish me simultaneously. I spend a long time letting the water fall over my body. By the time I finish the room is stuffed with a hot fog. I tumble out of the wet-room and into my clothes.

I have to see Martha. I find that I'm looking forward to seeing her which makes alarm bells ring in my mind. I've spent some considerable time building a wall around my soul that no person can penetrate. Has Martha snuck in through the tiniest of gaps? This thought discomforts me. I must eliminate the feeling of anticipation as it inevitably precedes the feeling of disappointment.

I find I've dressed myself on automatic. There are so many things I do on automatic; the mind only seems to come to life if something interferes with the normal routine of things, like the time I found a rat in my shoe, or a dead prostitute in my bathroom.

I'm tired.

Sleep is not regenerating me. Age and life are breaking me into ever-smaller pieces.

I muse my way to Martha's apartment. She's one of those who put in the hours when younger and made the right connections. She seems to think life is good and worth living. Her attitude both fascinates and repels me. I reach the entrance to her block and ring the entry phone. It buzzes and I walk in past the unmanned concierge desk.

She answers the door in a pretty floral dress, a vintage number; she's done her hair and makeup. She's also wearing a large smile. I check behind me wondering who it's for before I realise that she's smiling at me. She has three pairs of elegant high heel shoes and a pair of black Converse All Star baseball boots set neatly against the wall by the door. She'd like me to take off my tattered old brown brogues but I don't. I see a fast frown pass over her face and then it's gone, replaced by a smile. A smile too large for the occasion – I wonder what it means? I walk into the living room and slump onto the sofa still wearing my coat.

There's the sound of a cup breaking on the floor behind me. I realise it's her laughter.

"I thought perhaps we could have lunch here instead of going out."

"Ok, suits me. I'm tired, not been sleeping very well."

"I've made some nice fish and grilled vegetables."

I fucking hate fish and grilled vegetables.

"Great, I'm starving".

There's that clouded look again.

"Are you being sarcastic?"

What? She can't know I hate fish. If she does then she's done it on purpose. I want to hurl her through the window, to watch her body hit the pavement below, broken bones on broken bond.

"No, why'd you think that? Let's eat, I'm really famished."

"Oh good."

We eat the food. It's disgusting. After lunch we do what she had really called me for. I'm detached throughout. I notice that when I talk dirty, telling her that she likes the feel of my big fat cock in her cunt, that kind of thing, she gets wildly turned on. She writhes, and I pump. As I fuck her, I see Yuko standing on the balcony watching.

"Fucking hell."

"What?" Martha jerks and stops writhing. "What is it"? I have stopped thrusting and am staring at the balcony, at Yuko's mangled form, which is leaning against the balcony wall watching me. You would think that whatever power it is that can reconstruct her and bring her back from the dead could at least make her look presentable.

"Look on the balcony. What can you see?"

"My bicycle. Why, what can you see?"

"Nothing. It must've been a trick of the light."

"Good, now please make me come..." she demands in a less than playful tone. My cock is still hard so I finish my duty and spray my own life force over her breasts. Though I do so with one eye fixed on the balcony and Yuko, who is just standing watching.

After sex we chat a bit, well, Martha chats and I don't listen. I shower. On coming out of the shower I see that Yuko has gone.

Martha seems unbothered about anything, going about her business in a cheery haze induced by all the sex hormones racing around her body. I leave.

I walk back thorough the foyer, less than three hours after I arrived. I'm surprised to see a man at the concierge's desk, a wrinkly old black man in an outsize uniform, he gives me a sharp look as I pass. I ignore him.

Back in my room, I open the shower room door and there she is: Yuko – I mean she's most likely not there, but I can see her composite body standing in the corner looking at me. I shut the door and close my eyes.

"I'm going fucking mad."

I open them and the door again.

No sign of Yuko.

I'm relieved and take a piss. These appearances are disconcerting. She's dead, I know, I killed her. I don't believe in the Afterlife or any supernatural crap. I know she must be a product of my own mind. I'm not sure what to do about it. I can't go to the doctor's and say I'm having visions of a prostitute I brutally murdered and eviscerated, do you think I'm psychotic? I suspect the doctor would say yes and then I'd be locked up. Though perhaps that might be a good thing. Life in a secure mental hospital has to be superior to my life now. I'd be visible and I wouldn't have to kill people in order to feel real. Except they'd decide I wasn't mad, just a criminal, and then I'd spend the rest of my days in prison and that don't sound so good. I'll put up with the visions and perhaps, after I have killed someone else Yuko will go away. I open a tin of sardines in chilli oil. and eat them straight from the tin. For once they taste good.

Chapter 16: **Later**

Months have passed since I killed Yuko, and she's become an almost constant companion. I see her standing at traffic lights or on London's bridges as I go on my walks around town. Sometimes she is at the end of my bed when I wake. She never does anything, not since the incident with the knife. She only stands or walks along parallel with me and always on the other side of the road. I sometimes think about killing her again but I'm not sure you can kill an hallucination or ghost or whatever she is, and anyway I can't deal with the whole chopping her up all over again and there's no guarantee she won't just reappear. There was never any sign of her disappearance in the press or on the radio. It seems I was right about nobody caring about a vanished prostitute.

The London air has the scent of winter. It's a melancholy stink that pervades the city. The trees have lost their leaves and the river is a darker shade of sludge. The pavements are often coated in a delicate frost as I walk across them in the mornings. The days are short and dark and I am as invisible as ever. At least Yuko is companionship of a sort, though she never talks. And since Yuko's arrival my dreams have all but gone and I sleep better. I stand on the east side of London Bridge in the middle, watching the reflection of the marzipan Tower Bridge. Yuko stands a little way off from me. She watches me and I watch the bridge. I walk quickly toward her. She stands and waits. I reach her and grip her wrists forcing her to the edge of the balustrade, and then reach between her legs and hoist her onto the edge. She says nothing and does not resist. I flick her off the bridge and watch her tumble through the air and flop into the water. She sinks from view. It's not new: I have done this a few times before and it never makes a difference. She'll turn up again at some point.

I walk my beloved pavements home, underneath abstract Christmas lights that have been strung across the streets of the City where, officially, we don't celebrate the religious festival anymore. But the commercial one is bigger and brasher than ever, the lights celebrating the victory of the fiscal over the mystical. I walk up St John Street to the Angel and down Packington Street, looking into all the lit-up living rooms of houses and basement apartments, getting tantalising glimpses into the lives of the happy. I stop at the basement apartment of number 78. These people aggravate me beyond reason. They leave the shutters to their living room open so you can see right inside. As if they are flaunting their lifestyle, like it's a show and people are invited to stand, admire, envy or identify with them as they sit side by side on a long leather sofa, Apple laptops on their knees, tap-a-tap-tapping the keyboards. What are they doing? Emailing each other about how fucking great they are? They're an attractive couple, maybe in their late 20's and the room has wood floors, big chairs and modern minimalist objects. I notice that they've placed a Christmas tree near the fireplace. It looks incongruous in the room. They are always sitting laptopping and drinking red wine. Something about them makes my blood boil as I stand in the cold watching them and their perfect fucking life. I can see two expensive bikes chained to the bottom of the metal stairs leading down to the front door. I have watched this couple for weeks now and although I can see into other basement apartments along this street, it is these two and their smug self-righteous lives that have piqued my ire.

Occasionally Yuko will stand with me as I stare, but not tonight because I have thrown her in the river and there's no telling when she will reappear. I watch them for perhaps twenty minutes They have no need to look out of the window though perhaps they should. The girl always sits nearest to the window. She is willow thin, with long fair hair, big eyes and a flashing smile like a road-crossing beacon. He's tall, muscular and handsome in an interchangeable mountain biking kind of way. I hate them.

I walk away, seething. I should sleep: tomorrow I have to see the mental health nurse for my assessment. I reach home and walk into my room, kicking aside some empty sardine tins and cartons of soya milk. One of them still has milk inside, and as it flies across the room it arcs a trail of its fetid sour contents across the wall and carpet. I ignore it, and the smell. My room is littered with the wreckage of my paltry consumption. I haven't cleaned up for weeks. I strip off and throw my clothes on the bed, picking my way across the floor. I grab a greying towel off the table and head into the shower. The floor of the wet-room is grimy and slippery. I bang on the water and get wet thinking about the young couple just up the road and their ideal home. The water curls down the grating and disappears. Where to? Another world? Not really – more like a slimier extension of the one I live in. Five hundred yards from the ideal home and bright shiny perfection of number 78 is my world of slime, and I hate them even more for that knowledge. After a long time I slap off the tap and the flow of water stops. Drips descend like demented diamonds from the showerhead catching the light from the remaining working bulb as they fall. The towel has been sitting in the sink and is damp and clammy. I rub the moisture on me, the towel failing in its attempt to dry my body. A body I hate almost as much as I hate the residents of 78. Opening the door I step into the garbage in my room and drop the towel. My bed calls. I slip under the filthy cover and turn off the light, but it's not late and I don't fall asleep. I lie in bed, my mind replaying the scene in the basement at 78 and then merging it with throwing Yuko off the bridge. In my head I am throwing the winsome girl off the bridge and then her man. He is more trouble, but over he goes. I am happy to see that when he hits the water he does not even try to help her, but is only concerned with saving himself. He gives a good account of himself, but this is my fantasy and he must drown. I let him get to within striking distance of the shore before I make a strong undercurrent catch him and drag him under. I can feel myself smile in the dark. I wonder when Yuko will make her next appearance. She's never gone long, not these days. In a slow meandering of thought I [eventually] pass into sleep.

I am outside, naked in the frosted streetlight. I am not cold. In the street squats a spider. It's large, perhaps 6 inches across. It's the only thing in the road and is thrown into stark relief on the white frost covering the tarmac, its black body still as stone. I can see it in detail even though I am fifteen or so feet away. It's as if my vision has jumped to a higher level of acuity. The spider stares at me, its eight eyes catching the streetlight. The two largest eyes in the centre of its thorax seem to bore into my skin. It is covered in disgusting black hairs and I can see other tiny parasitic insects crawling amongst them. It has two huge fangs that drip venom,. like a nightmare creature from a horror movie and yet it is also perfect. A creature that has evolved into the exact requirements of its function, It's no kluge this spider, not like a human being. A rat scampers along the gutter between the spider and me. In a sudden pounce, the spider arcs into the air and lands on the rat's back. The rat rears up on its hind feet and twists, but it's too late – the spider is pumping its paralysing venom into the rodent's body. I watch the light of life dim in the rat's eyes as the spider drags it with surprising speed across the road and down an open manhole cover hesitating only to look back at me before it and the rat drop from sight. I know I have to follow them. I walk across the frost- covered road and peer down the hole. It must be an entrance to the sewers. I can see a greasy set of brackets diving into the dark. I shudder, though not through the cold, and start to climb down. It takes a lot longer than I feel it should. The bottom should have appeared under my feet a while back and the ladder is hard to negotiate with only one working arm. At last my feet hit the bottom, stepping into liquid that's flowing along at speed. The stink is a sweet sickly smell of shit combined with the acrid smell of urine so intense I can taste it. It's not entirely dark. There are festoon lights at long intervals along the tunnel, electric light bulbs hanging from thick yellow plastic-covered cable. There is one about twenty feet behind me and another off in the distance and another beyond that. I can see the small pools of light they give off. I turn and look at the one nearest me. My vision is still acute and I can see the spider with the rat on a ledge at my eye level. Several other spiders have joined it for a live rat feast. The spider is ignoring me. I turn away and decide to walk toward the distant lights. The sewer tunnel is about ten feet high and arched to a base that's about fifteen feet across. There's a raised walkway along the far wall and rats scurry back and forth. I'm standing in a river of crap, large lumps of shit passing between and around my legs. The river flows quickly and I decide to walk in the direction of the flow. I have no idea where I am going. I just walk. Every so often a discharge of shit, piss and water will fall from vents in the sides and roof of the tunnel. Sometimes I'm caught by one. I don't care. I pass light bulb after light bulb until I come to an intersection. Another tunnel flows into this one; it has an incline up and away from me. I take that tunnel and see a dead cat float past. Good, I hate cats and the idea that it may have drowned in human excrement is pleasing to me. I make my way up the inclined tunnel. Some of the time I have to crawl on my hands and knees. I stop.

Now I know why I am here. I am near number 78. Will their shit smell sweeter? Will it have a moral undertone to its aroma? I see a narrow tunnel leading off to the left. I will have to crawl but it doesn't bother me. I slither along the tunnel lubricated by the shit of the humans above, I slide with grace to the end of the tunnel. It ends in a vertical shaft with the same kind of bracket ladder as the one I came down earlier. There are smaller pipes spewing water and effluent over me as I climb. At the top is a cover. This one is closed and I can't let go with my one working arm to push it, so I drop my head and hunch my back and push at it with my shoulders. It moves a little. The skin on my shoulders tears as I push. I feel no pain. One more shove and it topples away from the hole, and I can climb out.

I'm at the bottom of the metal stairs of number 78 Packington Street. I have no idea how long I have been in the tunnel. It must have been hours though it's not that far. I step out from the shadow of the steps and see that the light is off in their living room. I walk to the door and try the handle. It turns and the door opens. I step through. It's dark, they must be asleep. I pad barefoot along the hall leaving footprints of shit on the wood. At the end of the hall is a door that must lead to the living room and its disgusting Christmas tree, and another door to my right. It's this door I push open. Good, it's their bedroom and they are in bed asleep. He has his back to her and she is trying to snuggle up to him. I stare. I leave and go into the living room and over to the kitchen area looking for a knife. I hear a slight cough and whirl around. It's the old man from the backstage of the theatre.

"You can't do anything here." he says.

He's sitting on their sofa playing with one of the laptops.

"You can cut these beautiful ones, but not here in this world, only in yours."

"Why are you here?"

"Why are you?" he replies.

I hesitate.

"Am I here?"

"It doesn't matter. Go and take another look at them," he wanders over to the Christmas tree. He removes a chocolate Santa and eats it

"Go on."

I go back to the bedroom. They are sprawled across the bed deep in sleep. The woman stirs and opens her eyes. She looks straight at me with a blank expression and turns over to resume sleeping. I can see the pores in her skin and the fabric of her underwear in great detail and his hair and eyebrows as if they were under a microscope. I return to the living room. The old man has gone, there's just silver and red chocolate Santa wrappings scattered on the floor, the same colour as her slippers.

I turn and leave the apartment. I don't bother closing the door behind me. I climb the metal steps into the street. The dawn is breaking but as it's winter the street is already busy with people rushing to work and children sliding to the gigantic academy on the corner. I walk along and no one notices me, naked and covered in shit. I spot more of the large spiders on window ledges and lampposts and in the trees. They see me and I see them. I make it back to my room. The bed is empty and I crawl into it shit and all.

I wake, confused. There is blood on the filthy sheet and the wall; my shoulders are cut and torn. I must have forced myself against the wall during the dream. I feel pain. Ignoring it, I lie in the bed and consider my dream. I have not had one of these vivid ones for a long time, not since Yuko's appearance. Perhaps the fact that I chucked her into the Thames had something to do with it. I feel disorientated by the experience. The manifestation of the old theatre guy was unpleasant in the extreme. I don't like him or his leering manner. I sit up and turn on the lamp. Today I have to go and see the primary healthcare mental nurse for an assessment. This happens every 6 months and I have to go or it affects my benefits, which are paltry enough as it is, and I can't risk them being cut. So I go and answer a load of inane questions.

Outside the last remnant of a frost is thawing under a weak winter sun. The road is bare and there is no enormous spider. There's a manhole over in the street but the cover is firmly in place. I'm relieved. Any sign that what I dreamt was true, and I might have to ask the nurse to section me voluntarily. I walk toward the health centre. The trip takes me past 78. I stop and peer down the steps. The mountain bikes aren't there – of course they bike to work, that's exactly the sort of self-important behaviour I would expect from them. I can't see into the corner under the metal stairs from the street so I descend the steps – there is a manhole cover tucked into the corner. How could I have known that? I couldn't possibly see it from the street. I walk back up the stairs, troubled. At the top I manage to avoid a collision with a passing pedestrian. I wander along the street. Then a thought occurs to me and I walk to the nearest basement and glance down. I can clearly see a manhole cover in the corner. That would explain it. I figure there is one in the corner of every basement in the street. A large grin spreads across my face. I just rationalised that there would be one at the bottom of the stairs at number 78. I continue on to my appointment.

At the health centre, the receptionist gives me a desultory look and nods at the stairs. At the top of the stairs I go through a thick dark brown fire-door, into a waiting room painted a painful shade of magnolia and containing seven grey plastic chairs and a dying pot plant. A notice board warns clients against abusing the staff alongside notices about sexually transmitted diseases and leaflets telling us losers how easy it is to get back into work once you've learnt to read. I have always wondered about the efficacy of leaflets about learning to read. I sit in one of the chairs, it doesn't matter which one. There is some classical music piped into the room – I think it's Grieg but I'm not sure. I'm early and wait for half an hour. I flick through an old knitting magazine; nobody else comes into the room. There are two small interview rooms off the waiting room. Halfway through the 'Amelia lace wrap' knitting pattern, the one without any purl stitches, one of the doors opens and a slight young woman calls my name. I stand. There's no one else here – why did she call my name as if the room was full? I say hello. She doesn't respond and I walk into the interview room. Inside are two chairs and a small table on which are laid out leaflets about stress, depression and anxiety. There's a large clock on the wall. It says 9. 50am. I sit, so does she. She's wearing a tight fitting blouse, grey trousers and a pink cardigan, machine knitted I note, but to a high quality. She has nice breasts, an aquiline face, thin lips and startling blue eyes; she's attractive. I am shabby, unshaven and decidedly unattractive but then this is not a date. She flicks through some notes in a thin buff folder and makes clicking noises with her tongue against the roof of her mouth.

"So, it's been over 6 months since we saw you last. How are you feeling?"

She doesn't wait for an answer.

"You were speaking of depression last time you were here. Has there been any change? Any improvement in your moods?"

She turns a page in my folder and does not look at me.

"Not really." I say. She still doesn't look at me.

"Did you read the literature we gave you last time?"

Is that what those leaflets are, were they written by Chekov?

"No."

"Why not?"

"Because I know what's in them and they can't help me. I know why I am like this and no leaflet is going to help."

"How do you know if you don't read them?"

Still she has not turned to look at me. I feel an anger rising inside me. "Are you going to spend the entire interview staring at those notes or are you actually going to talk to me?"

"What?"

"Look at me when you talk to me please."

She stares at the notes and then in small increments turns her face to look at me; her skin is white as ice. Is she scared? She's new to this and people like me scare her.

"Thank you." I say. "Now what do you want to know?"

"It says here that you were an engineer and that you stopped working some time ago – that you had an accident and that you are unfit to work. Is that still the case?"

"Is it still the case that I had an accident or that I am unfit to work?"

"Sorry?"

"Which are you asking?"

"Are you unfit to work?"

"That's the medical assessment and I'd say they were right."

"How does that make you feel, could that be contributing to your mental state?"

"Maybe?"

She stares at me in silence for just a little too long. I stare back.

"Have you had any suicidal thoughts?"

"It's always an option."

"What do you mean?"

"Death is always an option. But I think I have to serve the full life sentence. I am going to die. I don't need to hurry it but if you're offering a comfortable way out I'd consider it."

"No we aren't here to help…"

"I know."

"I meant we aren't here to help you commit suicide."

"Why not? It would be a useful service."

She shifts in her seat, I am making her uncomfortable and I probably smell, at least my clothes probably do.

"Mr Smith, is there anything we can do to help? Counselling perhaps?"

"Well there are two things that would help, a large bag of money or a pile of drugs and you can't give me either, perhaps a leaflet…"

"There's no need to be sarcastic."

"There isn't?"

Part of me was enjoying her discomfort and awkwardness. I have killed two people and she has no idea. Maybe I should tell her, that would be funny. I decide against it. I should recover the conversation.

"I'm sorry, look, my life is basically over. I have more of it to look back on than to look forward to and what I have got to look forward to is hardly a thrilling prospect. I am basically unemployable and I am too old and poor to get a partner. I can't sleep, my dreams are worse than staying awake and I am in pain constantly. So if I am crotchety I apologise. I have these interviews every 6 months or so and I know, as do you, that your brief is to establish if I can be forced to work in a fast food outlet or some such thing. As you can see customer service would not be the best way forward for me."

She relaxes a bit as I say this, taken in by my earnest manner. I could just strangle her and leave. It would be fun but foolish. I'd be caught straight away and that would interfere with my plans for the residents of 78 Packington Street. This is an odd thought. I didn't realise I had any plans for them. She is talking.

"…so, I think I will advise my manager that you need to be referred for therapy in the next few months. Perhaps we can help you break the cycle of desperation that you find yourself in."

Shit. I appear to have done too good a job. Play along.

"Ok I am prepared to try."

"Good."

"Will you write to me with the appointment?"

"Yes."

"Is that all?"

"Yes and thank you for coming."

"Pleasure."

I stand and she goes back to reading my notes. I grab my coat, hat, turn and leave. I don't shut the door on my way out. The waiting room is full of sad people: people who have lost their way in life and who haven't thought of killing or have dismissed the idea if they have, not realising that murder would help them to find their way back. Get out there and kill, that would be my advice. Start with the bitch in the interview room.

Chapter 17: **Show Me the Way to Go Home**

I had my interview with the counsellor some weeks ago. Then a letter arrived telling me to go and see the cognitive psychologist. I did that too, spouted a load of hogwash that she wanted to hear, was given a prescription for anti-depressants which I filled, and then after they had given me the tablets I threw them and their brightly coloured white blue and yellow box in the trash.

Yuko has not made a reappearance and my dreams are consistently disturbing. I wish she would come back so I could get some fucking sleep. I look around my room. Accumulated rubbish, food cans, milk cartons, empty porridge packets, unwashed clothes, towels, various shoes and pages of newspapers cover the entire floor. I squat on the bed. I haven't showered in a week. I don't want to go in the wet-room. I am concerned about what waits for me in there. I urinate in the sink and shit into plastic bags that I dispose of in litter-bins in the street. I know this sounds crazy but it's not, it's rational. If there is something in there waiting for me then it can't get out of the wet-room or it would have done so, therefore if I keep the door shut and don't open it then it – whatever it is – can't get me. There probably isn't anything but I cannot be sure, so I am taking precautionary measures just to be on the safe side.

I must have a beard, I can feel it, but as I have no mirror in my room and no reflection outside my room, I have not seen the result of my lack of shaving. The cellphone rang yesterday, I think it was Martha. She still calls occasionally but I never answer. The only thing in my life that I take care of these days are my knives; they are still as sharp as an icy morning, and lie on a tidy shelf in the cupboard. Next to them are the sharpening stones.

It's the morning and I decide to leave the house. I have

developed a craving of late for Nice biscuits. I picked up twenty packets at the market on Chapel Street a couple of weeks back. They were reduced, so I bought them. Everything in Chapel Market is reduced and cheap crap, and these biscuits are no exception. The last packet lies open next to the pile of unwashed plates. The garish turquoise packet with a red flag-like logo stating that 'Crawfords' who make the biscuits were established in 1813. NICE Coconut Flavoured Biscuits 200g. They are beige in colour and have a crenelated edge. On the top is imprinted the word NICE underneath a sprinkling of sugar. They in no way taste of coconut; they taste of flour and sugar and have the consistency of baby rusks. There is something reassuring about eating them. I munch away on the remaining few while reading the information on the pack, for the twentieth time. They contain no artificial colours or flavours, which probably explains why they don't taste of coconut. There is a little history:

"*The first Crawfords biscuits were baked by William Crawford in a small shop in Leith near Edinburgh in 1813. Ever since then the Crawford name has been trusted for quality everyday biscuits which are still made with the same skill and care at our bakeries*"

It doesn't clarify if the biscuits are any good or not, there's no measure of quality. The writing continues:

We take every care to ensure that these Crawfords biscuits reach you in perfect condition; if they fail to satisfy please return the entire package to our Customer Services Department at the address shown, saying when and where they were purchased.

Does anyone do that? Package up an unsatisfactory packet of biscuits and send them to the address stated. By the time the post had delivered them they would be dust. I can't imagine that anyone does that – perhaps I should, just to see what happens. More:

*Ingredients: Wheat Flour, Sugar, Vegetable Oil, Desiccated Coconut
(8%), Partially Inverted Sugar Syrup, Raising Agents (Ammonium
Bicarbonate, Sodium Bicarbonate), Salt. Contains Gluten.
Produced on a line handling milk.
No hydrogenated vegetable oil. Store in a cool dry place.*

No wonder I am addicted to them. They are pure sugar in a wheat
container. I finish the last one. I wonder what day it is. The month
is December, I'm pretty sure of that. I drag on clothes and kick
aside the mess on the floor until I find socks then shoes. I notice the
handle of Yuko's handbag poking through a jumble of empty
sardine cans and old plastic bags in the corner. I never did dispose
of it and had forgotten about it until now, as I stand half-dressed,
soiled socks in hand, staring at the handle. I pull on the other sock
and my grimy slick jeans, and then wade across the room to grab
the bag. I pull it out of its dirty hiding place and snap it open. There
are all her things still reproaching me from inside. I fling the bag on
the bed and look for my coat. I have to go out and get biscuits –
everything else can wait but I must have biscuits.

Outside it's a morose day. The grey pavement sulks under the
surly monochrome clouds. It threatens rain and every so often
there's a spit or two of water, but the welcome respite of a
downpour never comes. I scurry towards the market. As I come
onto Packington Street and pass 78, I notice the lights are on. I stop
and watch. I can see the couple wrapping presents and putting
them in a bag. Going away for Christmas? Into the welcome arms
of family and friends? I spit a large ball of saliva and phlegm at the
window. It misses.

I walk on up to the market. It's used for daily cheap goods,
mainly patronised by the poorer residents of the area, though every
so often they have a 'farmers market' for the affluent.

The stalls are noisy and the smell of frying onions attacks my
nostrils. The workers behind the stalls wear those stupid floppy red

hats that go to a point and are edged in fake white fur. Santa's helpers hats? Even the few Muslim traders that are still allowed to have stalls are wearing them. I pass fruit and veg stalls, cheap shoes, hats, crappy second-hand books, bootleg CDs and a fish van that I can smell long before I can see it. I find my stall. It sells all manner of food stuff in tins, packets and bags. It's usually cheaper than the supermarket, so for the last few months I have been getting most of my produce here. The stallholder nods at me and I nod back.

"What date is it?" I ask.

"Don't you know mate? It's the 23rd – day before Christmas Eve – better get your shopping done."

He turns to attend to a customer. I look at what's on offer and realise that I am sick of eating this processed shit. I am sick of eating food full stop. I step back and turn around. I am not eating anymore, not until I can decide what is the correct thing to eat. No more biscuits though, that's for sure. It's getting dark – must be around 4 pm. I have had a mood-shift and think I might be about to clean the room. It could do with it. Of course, the mood could have shifted again by the time I return home but I walk in a swift determined manner to get there before it does.

I remember Christmas. Jamillia would cook a huge meal filling the house with the smell of roasting meat. She and the boy would sing Christmas carols in the kitchen as they prepared food. Then she would infest the house with thousands of her Peruvian relatives and disagreeable friends all shouting, swigging and guzzling into the night.

"It's our tradition" she would shout.

She may have been a total cunt of a human being but she could cook. I pass 78. I see the loathsome couple sitting on the sofa laptopping again but I don't stop. I can sort them out later. As I walk past the building site that was social housing, I see some of those fluorescent orange safety vests lying in a pile on a stack of cellophane-wrapped paving slabs. I grab one as I walk past. It will come in useful in the morning. I reach my house and as I turn the key I can see that a manhole cover has been removed further down the road. It's marked by bright orange barriers and two workmen with breathing gear are climbing out of the dank hole in the ground. I smile and enter my world.

The room is disgusting. I stare at the detritus littering my space, decide that it is enough and set about cleaning it up. Grabbing a black plastic sack I start to fill it with cans and cartons and crap. Three bags later and I am nearly done with clearing the shit out of the room. That just leaves the floors and surfaces to clean and the clothes; they are stinking and filthy. I tie up the bags and hurl them outside onto the street. I run hot water in the sink and start on cleaning the dishes. It takes a while to get the encrusted food off the plates but I have time lots of time; it's about all I do have. A couple of hours later and I have cleaned up the room. I strip the bed and stuff the sheets and dirty clothes into my last black plastic sack and trudge to the Laundromat at the end of my street, pour my clothes into the washer and sit and think. As I watch the clothes churn around in the mechanical whirlpool I ruminate on my decision to put on the fluorescent safety vest early tomorrow morning, take my two best knives and kill the inhabitants of no 78. I have decided to go at about 6. 30am wearing the vest and bang on their door. They will have seen the workmen around, and through the frosted glass of their front door they'll assume the jacket and the early hour will mean it's a workman about something to do with the road and sewers. That, combined with the fact it's Christmas Eve and nothing bad has ever happened to them, will mean they will not suspect that a man has come to the door to murder them, to cut their throats and stand watching the blood drain out of them. I sit back and watch the clothes in the chaos of the washing machine. I feel happy.

Walking home with my black bag of fresh dry and folded washing still warm in the sack, I can feel a lift in my step, the pavement is pushing me towards my destiny. This is the first time since I killed

Yuko that I feel purposeful and it's a liberating feeling. I wonder where she has got to, it's been a while since I hurled her off the bridge. I check myself from this line of thought, *she* hasn't gone anywhere – *she* was a product of my mind, a phantasm, a fantasy; I didn't throw her off a bridge – I scattered her diced remains to the river and the city, but she didn't return to haunt me. The fact that I am not seeing her anymore means I am better. How the absence of the Yuko hallucination and the impending dispatch of the couple at 78 are linked I am not sure, but I think there must be some connection.

Back in my room, I turn out the clothes onto the bed and put them away. I have also placed Yuko's bag on the table. I open it and remove the bag of white powder. I tip the rest of the contents into a supermarket carrier bag, put some crumpled newspaper on top and I open a tin of pilchards in tomato sauce and pour it into the bag. I knot it and give it a good shake. The smell of fish and the slimy sauce should stop any curious fingers. I leave the house and walk down to the canal, find a bin and dump the plastic bag inside. I then pull Yuko's handbag out from under my jacket, find a rock or three and after putting them inside sink the purse into the canal. At last I have rid myself of the last vestiges of Yuko, what a curse that woman has been. I have kept the powder for number 78. I think it's cocaine and it might come in useful. Back in my room I start the knife-sharpening process. They are already sharp, but I do it to calm my nerves. The psychologist said that any activity that takes focus from the future into the present is good for me. Sharpening does that, so does murder, though I don't think that's what he had in mind. The sane and stable underestimate the industrious and creative abilities of the mentally challenged. The assumption is that the chaotic of mind can't achieve much. I would very much like to kill my psychologist so he could see the error of his diagnosis in person. I giggle at the idea that the last thing he would know was that he was wrong. In my lack of attention I deliver myself a cut on the finger from the boning knife, –nothing serious but it stings and is irritating. I go to the wet-room and find a Band Aid. I lie on the bed and read for a while, a book from the library called "The Crying of Lot 49", by Thomas Pynchon, a short novel about another world in another time, about people who are empty and yet full of hate and desolation. It's a good book. I like it. Maybe I'll read some of it to the lap-toppers as their life drips away. I decide it's time for sleep. I have an early start and a long day. Tomorrow is Christmas Eve. Sleep comes easily. It steals my consciousness as easily as a pickpocket could lift my wallet.

I'm outside an urban church in a wasteland of rubble and broken houses. There are towering blocks of apartments, the windows broken, taped up, and broken again; washing is draped from the windows and balconies, the ones that are not full of consumer junk, old mattresses, broken bikes, washing machines. They are vertical shantytowns, hovel stacked upon hovel. Poverty piled up high into the sky. I don't recognise the location, though it has a familiarity in that way dream geography possesses. The church looms up in front of me, barbed and sinister. The doors are open and a soft yellow light emanates through the inner frosted glass doors. The light flickers and waves, as enticing as the world around the church is repellent.

I cross and head to the church. I pass the gates and cross the graveyard. Each gravestone is a quarter the size of a normal headstone. The inscription on the nearest stone reads:

"In Memory Of our beloved Christian Died 2014 aged 1 year" The other stones are also all in memory of very young children aged up to 18 months. I know this even though I can't possibly read all the inscriptions and it makes me feel sick. I walk into the vestibule of the church past the huge black wooden doors and into the church. Only, it's no longer a church, it's some kind of factory or production facility. In the middle of the nave are two large stainless steel vats and along the transept are moulds, boxes and candles; hundreds and hundreds of candles, all a dark maroon in colour. I walk along the aisle toward the chancel and see the old man from the theatre and from the number 78 dream; he is in the sanctuary wearing a white surplice. He's busy,

chopping something on a large thick wooden chopping board set on the altar where a crucifix would normally be. His back is to me, so I can't make out what he's chopping but he's whistling a tune from the Disney cartoon Snow White and the Seven Dwarves as he works. I move to the side of the aisle and I can see that the front of his surplice is stained almost black with old, and wet from fresh, blood. He stops chopping and turns to face me: his hands are drenched in blood and his brow is covered in sweat, which he wipes away with the back of his hand, replacing the beads of sweat with a trail of blood. He looks even more ghoulish than usual. He fires a cadaverous grin at me, beckoning me over with the cleaver. I stumble on the three steps up to the sanctuary.

"Come, it's your turn to chop, I'll show you how."

He walks around the altar picking up something wriggling, the size of a large cat. I feel anxious. He unfolds his arms to reveal that he is carrying a baby. A clean, smooth, mewling, human child, a baby boy.

"This is the main ingredient for our candles."

I want to wretch.

The man wipes the wooden board clear of blood and places the baby on top, with tenderness. The child lets out a contented murmur. The man lifts the cleaver to shoulder height and grasps the baby's skull firmly in the other hand tipping the head back slightly. With a grin he brings the cleaver down sharply; it slices through the neck and spine in one fast cut. I hear the blade clunk into the wood: the man pulls the head away as blood jets out of the neck and into a silver chalice set at the end of the board. The man places the head on the stone surface of the altar and the child's eyes swivel around, still looking at things. Its mouth grimaces and then its eyes shut. The man grabs the body by the feet and holds it over the chalice, drains the blood, then walks into the nave and lobs the body into one of the steel vats.

"Rendering for fat, for the candles" he shouts.

He wanders back and picks up the head and drops it into a sack. He proceeds to pour the blood from the chalice into a large metal funnel, and I can see it is then pumped along a clear plastic tube to the other vat and dripped in through a filter.

"That goes into the wax for colour and purity, it makes the candle more holy and therefore closer to God" he says.

I turn back to the altar. I can feel bile rising in me.

"We'll get you one and you can have a go."

He walks behind the altar and I follow him. Behind the altar is a jagged hole in the wall exposing the rear of the altar to the outside world. Standing there is a young woman, holding a swaddled baby in her arms; it is wailing. The old man approaches her and takes the child: it calms immediately.

"I have a way with kids."

The woman backs away and then runs into the distance. The old man turns, holding the gurgling child, and smiling at me.

"This one's for you" he says.

"I don't want to" I reply.

"Why ever not? What's the difference between this little girl and the prostitute you killed?"

It is a good question. I cannot find a difference – if anything, the baby is less valuable and useful to society than Yuko was. I should have no problem in decapitating it but I do. Every fibre of my being rebels against killing the crying child. I know this is not logical, it's some evolutionary trick. I should kill it. It would be positive of me to overcome such an irrational response. Also, this is a dream, so I am not killing anything. I must behead the baby – I know beyond any shadow of a doubt that I have to slice up this small defenceless and dumb beast. I take the child and tuck it under my deformed arm and march back round to the chopping board. The old man follows, still grinning.

I unroll the baby girl from its blanket. It starts to cry. I lay it on its back on the wood and grab the cleaver, checking its edge for sharpness. I have no success in holding the child's head back with my deformed arm so I raise the cleaver and bring it down, just as the child turns its head: my strike takes off half the child's jaw and stops part way through the neck. I wrench the cleaver free and place it inside the baby's neck and push down. There is a satisfying crunch as I part the spinal cord and the head rolls away. Because of my inept strike most of the blood goes anywhere but in the chalice. The old man is by my side – he lifts the body and hurls it the 50 or so feet into the vat.

"They make the most delightful candles. So pure and they burn ever so slightly brighter for a few drops of baby blood. I think God is pleased by what I do."

I'm drenched in blood, but pleased that I no longer feel sick or repelled by what I've done. I feel as if I have crossed a barrier – as if I am free. This act of gross cruelty and death has freed me from the last of the redundant morality of a society that has no interest or use for me. I am ready.

I walk away from the altar and past the bubbling vats of baby fat and blood. I see lithe young women in white paper jumpsuits pouring wax into moulds. Outside the church, the lower part of the horizon is streaked with a maroon light from the dying sun; a light that looks like the dark blood that flows from a calf after its throat has been cut. I wonder which way to turn and decide it makes no difference, so I walk toward a tumbledown high-rise apartment block. The metal double doors are bent and thrown off their hinges as if some enormous dog has been chewing them. I step through the rent metal, and into the gloom-filled interior of the lobby. There are two elevators: one is standing open –obviously broken – the other is slowly descending, at least according to the illuminated numbers above the doors. 25, 24, 23, 22, 21, 20. The lift continues its downward journey. 19, 18, 17, 16, 15. I can hear the distant clanking and whirring of the lift machinery, 14, there's no 13th floor... 12, 11, 10. The light on 10 burns bright and then blinks out with a ffffffffft 9, 8, 7, 6, 5. A grinding sound accompanies the clanking 4, 3, 2, 1. The elevator is here. After what seems an age the grey steel doors begin to slide open, a light the colour of dark urine seeps out of the elevator and a smooth female voice announces:

"Doors opening, Ground floor."

Crouched at the back is a boy, about 8 years old, he's wearing grey shorts and a grey blazer like an old-fashioned school uniform from a black and white movie. He has his head down so his unkempt greasy hair obscures his face. He is wearing shiny black lace up shoes and white socks.

The boy makes no sound.

Neither do I.

Without any notice at all, the boy looks up at the roof of the elevator and then runs past me as fast as a whippet, away out through the tangled doors, disappearing from view. I walk into the elevator and stare up at the ceiling. If you can see nothing then I am staring at it. The roof of the elevator is a void, the absence of anything. Not darkness, for that has some kind of presence. This was absolute nothing. This was what existed before the universe. The feeling it engenders in me is one of detached fear, a reasoned terror. The doors close and the lift rises. The void above my head seems to press down on me; the lights indicating floors on the inside of the lift aren't working. I press the button for the fifteenth floor. There's no reason – it's just the easiest one to reach. The lift grinds on, up and up. At last it stops. The void above the lift is closer now and has started to drip down the sides of the lift. The doors open, and I leap out. I'm on a landing. There's no one to be seen, just four doors to four apartments and piles of trash outside each one. The floor of the landing is sticky and the walls drip with condensation. I stare at the doors reminded of a strange logic game I once read involving tigers, ladies behind doors and a prisoner that had to deduce whether it was a tiger or lady in a room from signs put on the doors – signs like "both rooms contain a tiger" and "at least one room contains a tiger," – there are no signs to indicate what might be behind any of these doors, but I have to choose one, as I am not getting back in that lift. The door on the far right is green and shabby like the door to my house and the trash outside is tidy and piled up in order, tins and bottles washed, indicating an occupant who is attempting to retain some dignity.

I walk to the door and turn the handle. Locked. I look for a doorbell, there is none, but there is a small fox-shaped doorknocker. I rap the door with it and wait. I hear a shuffling noise and the door clicks open, just a fraction. I push the door open but stay on the doorstep. I can see a dingy hallway. The carpet is dark brown, the colour of dried blood. There are boxes and packages stacked along the wall and no sign of any occupant. A musty smell leaks out of the doorway and behind it lingers an older scent – it's familiar but I can't place it – like flowers that have died long ago and left a trace of a once delicate perfume. I step inside the hallway and in a moment of politeness I call out to see if anyone's home. Somebody had to have opened the door, but there is no answer. I can see a door at the far end of the hall. It is ajar and from inside there's a flickering and shimmering of pale blue light and a quiet buzzing noise. It could be a TV with the sound down. I walk towards the door and push it open; there is indeed a TV set flickering in the corner – the pictures are indistinct but it looks like some kind of nature programme; animals are ripping each other apart. first a killer whale savaging seal pups, then hyenas pulling apart a gazelle. The images continue in no apparent order, just slaughter after slaughter. There is a high-backed armchair to the side of the TV and sitting in it is a small boy, perhaps six years old. He is staring at the TV, chewing on a carcass – perhaps that of a rat. He's dressed in ripped clothes; his hair is matted and dirty. He looks at me. I look at him. This time the child's face is not mine. I feel relief at this. The child jumps out of the chair with remarkable speed and dashes toward my legs. He wraps his arms around my right knee and sinks his teeth into my calf. The pain is excruciating.

My eyes open wide and I jump out of bed. It is pitch black in my room as I try and press my foot flat to the floor and walk, the pain causes me to cry out and jerk my foot up, but I know it has to be flat on the floor to kill this cramp. It's happened enough times before for me to know how to deal with it. I should have stretched this morning. The pain starts to subside and I'm left standing breathless and naked in the middle of my room.

Chapter 18: **Wishing You a Merry Christmas**

I check my phone for the time. It's 5.30 am. Perfect, I have enough time to shower, dress, and equip myself for the task ahead. Leaving the house, I slip the door shut behind me. I don't want anyone to notice that I have left early this morning. It's unlikely, but you can never tell. Frost crunches under my boots as I walk. The boots are generic work boots, two sizes too big. I bought them at the market in Petticoat Lane and I will dispose of them after this morning. Any footprints I leave will not be those of my size. I am folded inside a huge black donkey-jacket that I bought second-hand from the giant 'boot-sale' in the Lea valley and on top of this I have the bright orange safety jacket that I stole from the building site. I have changed the number on the back from 1066 to 90666. Just to confuse the CCTV if it gets me, which it will. The outfit is finished off with a peaked black 'beanie' hat pulled well down, black leather gloves and, underneath, blue overalls that I purchased from a DIY superstore chain. I have not shaved and have a healthy growth of beard to further confuse things. I estimate quite a furore in the media and from respectable society after this event After all, it will have happened to 'one of their own' and not some feckless losers or members of the subclass. Under my coat I have the two knives wrapped in newspaper and tucked into my belt. I carry a clipboard for further effect. I have long ago noted the position of the CCTV cameras, and the only ones I have to walk past on my way to 78 Packington Street are the ones around the Islington Academy. They mostly point inward to monitor the Academy's grounds and buildings in case anyone escapes the institution with an education, but there are some that look outward around the gates and entrances. It's on these that I will be able to be seen, but I am counting on them not being comprehensively checked during the holidays unless there's an incident involving the school, and even if they are, I will just be an unrecognisable workman in the background. The walk is a short one – four minutes and I'm at the corner of Packington Street. I march up the road until I am level with the gate leading to the flight of metal stairs that descend to the entrance of the apartment, an entrance that is conveniently hidden under the steps that go up to the main door of the house above. I look down at the window. It is dark but the shutters are open and the blind is not down. I am taken aback. Perhaps they are not home; maybe they left for the country earlier than planned. Obviously I have no idea if they are going somewhere. I just assumed that as a young childless couple they will be travelling to one or the other's parents and relatives on Christmas day. That they could have left early or gone elsewhere had just not occurred to me.

Well, I may as well carry on and knock; if they are not in then no harm's done. I descend the staircase being careful not to slip on the frost-laden metal steps. I try and keep my foot falls light, I don't want to risk waking them before I am ready. Time slows as I pad down the stairs, each movement of my foot feels as if it is in slow motion. My senses are acute, I see and hear a rat scratching under the stairs. At last I'm in the shelter of the covered doorway, I wedge the clipboard into my bad hand and prop it against my waist. I slide the long wide knife out of its place in my belt and remove the newspaper. The wide, long blade looks grey and dead under the orange streetlight. I push the doorbell with my gloved hand, the same hand that holds the knife. I then turn my clipboard side to the door and place the hand holding the knife out of sight, tucked just behind my hip and I ring the doorbell again. A light comes on in the hall and I hear footsteps coming to the door, and the outside light clicks on.

"Who is it?"

"Council, repairing the drains, need you to authorise access to the sewer from your premises."

"It's damn early …"

"Sorry sir have to do it before we can sort out the rest of the problems."

"OK. Well fine then...."

The light flicks off and I hear footsteps retreating from the door.

"Sorry sir, to bother you, but I need you to sign an authorisation form."

The footsteps stop and the light returns.

"What?"

"Need you to sign the form sir, can't start without it, I can show you ID sir, if you are anxious."

"No I am not anxious."

I hear the door being unlocked and the handle turns. The door cracks open. There he is – the cunt. Standing in a dressing gown staring at the clipboard.

"Well?"

"If you could just sign sir"

"Where?"

He cranes his neck forward to look at the form on the clipboard, exposing the left side of his neck. It's now or never. I swing my right arm out in a short fast arc. I inject the tip of the blade straight into the muscle in the side of his neck, in a further fraction of a second it slices through his windpipe stifling any attempt to cry out, not that he has the time. Once it's through the windpipe I make a short twist and reverse the cut severing his carotid artery, sending a fountain of blood and a gurgled last gasp into the air. The blood decorates the outside of the open front door – annoying – that'll need to be cleaned off before I leave. He sags to his knees; I push him into the hallway, he falls back, body twitching and blood spurting, his legs jerking around the floor like a slaughtered cow. I grab the clipboard from where I had dropped it on the floor, shut the door and flick off the outside light. I look at his body lying on the floor as the jerking subsides. I hear a muffled voice from behind a door in the hallway.

"Will, what's going on? Hurry back."

Will's not hurrying anywhere; a pool of dark blood has formed on the hardwood floor around his head, like a blackcurrant jus with his head as the centrepiece. His neck gapes open sporting a smiling gash; his eyes are wide open in surprise.

He's dead.

Now for that bitch.

I step around the body in its pool of sauce and drop my jacket and the vest in a corner by the door to the living room. He had left the light in the hallway off, off so as not to disturb his girlfriend, or whatever the fuck she is. I can see another door in the far wall of the hallway. It was from behind there that the voice had come. He had made only a small crumpled thump when he hit the floor. My closing the door had been noisier. Barely two minutes has passed and yet time has expanded to fill my senses and each second feels like a lifetime. I put down the long wide-bladed knife on the floor, patting it in thanks for its sterling performance. I pull the boning knife from my belt and remove its protective wrapping of paper. I like to use the Daily Mail: it seems the appropriate paper to use, feeding as it does on prejudice and ignorance. It was a tough choice – all newspapers have something to recommend them for the wrapping of murder weapons – but the Daily Mail came out ahead. In a perfect world I would be eviscerating a member of staff of that stalwart supporter of all that's holy and right about this country, but unfortunately I'm not, although I have no idea what these two do for a living – perhaps they *do* write for the Daily Mail. I smile at the thought. I grip the handle of the knife and slide over to the door. She will be half asleep and expecting her partner to be coming back to bed after dealing with the nuisance at the door. She is about to get a much bigger and more final Christmas surprise than she has bargained for. I turn the handle; I know I will only have a few seconds to take in the layout of the room. I push the door open with a slow tentative motion. I see a large double bed with an iron frame sticking up at both ends. I wonder if he has ever tied her to the frame and fucked her – too late now. I can see her lying under the duvet on the far side of the bed. On my side is a small table with a lamp, and along the wall, a set of built-in cupboards. I creep across the floor towards the bed. The figure shuffles a mite under the bedclothes. The room is lit by vague orange strips of light that have found their way past the venetian blind; they cross the roof and come part-way down the far wall. I reach the edge of the bed and grab the corner of the duvet in my hand. No point in killing her without her knowing. No point in that at all. I transfer the knife to my left hand. I can't stab with it but I can hold it while I rip back the duvet and then transfer the knife back to my right hand. She will be so confused that she won't have time to respond. She'll think I'm him.

I grasp the edge of the duvet and with a rising tide of adrenaline in my guts and a hard-on growing in my pants, I rip back the covers in one move. She's lying there in a small vest top and panties. I switch the knife to my good hand and jump onto the bed. She starts to come round and looks at me, confusion in her face. Her mouth opens to form a scream, but I stall the yell by puncturing one of her lungs with a jab from the long, thin, sharp boning knife. The breath leaves her. I pull the knife out and shaft it into her other lung. The air leaves her body with a small but defined rush. She falls back onto the bed, blood soaking the covers and mattress. People don't die quickly from a punctured lung that's why I choose it. The woman is gasping and frothing a mixture of blood and saliva from her mouth. I notice that her hands, instead of going to the wound in her chest, are cradling her abdomen – interesting – I click the lamp on. I see the fear and pain in her face. I grab her panties and cut them off then I straddle her body and work my way up, and in a gentle and tender way I let my weight down onto her chest for a moment. Her face distorts in agony. I climb off and place my shin on her throat and press down. As I do this I place the point of the knife into the dip where the jaw meets the ear and thrust the knife in. Time to finish her. I am not a monster, no need to make her suffer more than absolutely needed. I switch the knife back and sever the nerve. She slumps.

She's as dead as the mattress she's lying on.

I check their clock: 7 am. Only half-an-hour from start to finish. I'm impressed. I stand back and look at my handiwork. I have blood all over the crotch and legs of my work overalls, but nevertheless a job well done. I open the bedside drawers – there's nothing of interest to me there. I look through her purse – there's £20. I take that and return the purse to the bedside table.
I decide to have a look around.

I walk over to the wardrobes, nothing in them but clothes and shoes. I take a pair of his blue jeans, remove my work overalls and put his jeans on. They are an ok fit. I wander out into the hall and through into the living area. I walk over to the window and pull down the blind, then I put on the light. I see his jacket on a chair and go through the pockets – £40 and an 'oyster' card. I take both but nothing else. I see their laptops sitting on the sofa. I pick them up, open them and then I drop them one by one onto the floor and stamp on them until they are smashed beyond repair.

I go over to the Christmas tree and topple it, then I crush underfoot the presents on the floor. I notice a door in the far wall. I stroll over and throw the light switch. It's a small room and it's been converted into a nursery: a cot, children's clothes, a baby bath and other infant paraphernalia clutter the room. I hug a soft furry toy koala bear whilst I consider my discovery. Then I march back into the bedroom and plunge my knife into her belly just above the pubic bone. The sharp knife slices her open like a peach. I pull her lower abdomen open and root around with one hand. It's as I suspected: a foetus. It's a tiny alien-like creature. I have neatly severed it into two. Well, that's good. I have stopped another parasite from entering the world, an unplanned bonus. Today is starting well. I look again in the bedside drawer and pull out some papers. I wonder what their names are. I open a document. It's a marriage certificate dated only a month before. The cunts were man and wife, I laugh out loud. His name was William Crawford.

"*Hah! Hello biscuit boy.*"

Hers is Jenny Abercrombie. I crumple the document up and stuff it into the bloody aperture that was once her womb. I wipe my glove on the bed sheet and look through a door that leads to the bathroom., All white tiles and very clean and smart.

I glance in the mirror – is that hazy face me? The eyes glint murderous rage and the chin and lower part of the face are smeared in blood from performing cunnilingus on a dead woman. I gaze with more intent. I can't make out the features, the mirror seems distorted. I decide that it's not me, I don't look like that. I give the mirror a sharp hard tap with the bottom of an expensive-looking perfume bottle. Both shatter. Feeling less dissatisfied I take a piss in the toilet and flush it, then I return to the bedroom. Jenny is laying face-up, legs splayed on the bed. I smile at her. She does not return my grin. I return to the wardrobe and open the drawers inside. Nothing unusual in the top two: underwear, socks, that kind of thing. In the third drawer is a jewellery box, an old brown leather one like my mother used to have. I lift it out and place it on the bed, open it, and spread apart the cantilevered top compartments. Inside is a riot of Art Deco and other vintage jewellery, – lots of gold and stones. Inside the bottom compartment is a wad of notes – £50 notes – must be at least a thousand quid. I glower at my find. What should I do? Obviously I could use the money, but I know nothing about selling stolen jewellery and that would be a quick way to get caught. Also, if I take it then this will be nothing more than a cheap robbery and I am not a thief. I pull out the cash and count it – two thousand pounds – tempting. If they have this in cash then the chances are no-one knows they have it, so I could take the money – after all they don't need it – and leave the jewellery. That way, the police will not think it's a robbery and they'll be more puzzled and confused, which pleases me. I pocket the cash and replace the jewellery and the box, carefully closing the drawers and the wardrobe. I walk back to the hall. Will lies in his pool of blood., I turn on the light to get a better look. His dressing-gown has come untied and his cock is on display. It's erect – I find that odd – but it is a good size. Jenny must have liked it when he fucked her. His face wears an expression of dismay, normal in the circumstances. I flick the light off and go back into the living area. I have a look on the shelves at the book collection. It's impressive, with lots of hardback leather-bound volumes that look old. There are family photos in silver frames and, of course, their own wedding photo, fancy and smiling, at some posh church; personally I feel they look better now after my ministrations. I wander over to the kitchen area and open the cupboards. I'm hungry.

I look through the foodstuff. It's like a giant Harrod's Christmas hamper. There is: a Rannoch Smokery 'Scottish Roast Smoked Venison' and 'Smoked Duck'; a Waitrose 'Orange & Honey Roast Ham'; a Wensleydale Creamery 'Real Yorkshire Wensleydale & Cranberry' cheese; Edinburgh Preserves; Rosemary Dipping Crackers; Henshelwood's 'Chutney for Cheese' along with 'Chutney for Game Pies & Cold Meats'; 'Olives Et Al Sunshine Olives with Rosemary, Garlic & Tomatoes', 'Et Al Tapenade Morocaine from Olives'; Preserved Lemons, Capers & Garlic; Paxton & Whitfield 'Classic Port Pâté with Chicken Livers'; Shropshire Fine Herbs 'Thyme Oatmeal Biscuits'; Hickory Smoked Marcona Almonds; a Harrod's Christmas Cake.

I pull out a box of Dorset Cereals 'Fantastically Fruity Muesli'. I frown at the unnecessary adjective in the title, but I see a jar of Manuka honey, find natural yogurt in the fridge, and make a bowl of breakfast. Next I eat the olives. It all tastes magical.

I replace the yogurt in the fridge and see that they have no turkey or any joint of meat. It appears my new friends Will and Jenny were going away for the festivities without telling me. I leave the bowl on the table, but I wash the spoon and replace it by the side of the bowl. I think I am about ready to leave when one last touch occurs to me. I go over to the destroyed Christmas tree and pick up a round glass Santa decoration from the floor. It's still intact. I walk through to where Will is lying and stand the Santa upright in the wound across his neck. A nice Christmassy touch I think. I fold my work overalls, find a plastic carrier bag and put them into it. Time to go.

I pick up my jacket and put it on and remove the high-visibility vest, fold it and put it in the carrier bag. I have worn gloves the whole time so no fingerprints. No DNA. Perhaps a bit in the yogurt, but it will be too contaminated to be of use and they will be looking for a person known to the family first, as there's no forced entry and no sign of a robbery. The computers are destroyed so it's unlikely they will have recorded anything. Webcams? Didn't see any, but I wasn't looking, best have a good look. I carefully walk the apartment looking for a cam and find one in the baby's room but it's not hooked up; they were probably going to use it for monitoring the child. I can still be caught – no crime is perfect – but then again this isn't a crime, it's vengeance.

It's 8 am. I have been here an hour and it's beginning to get light. I must wipe the blood off the front door. I fetch a damp cloth and some kitchen spray. The blood has spattered down the door in an arc. I spray it with the bleach and wipe it off until it looks clean and then I do it again to make sure. I grab a bottle of mineral water from the fridge and as I leave I pour it over the door to wash off the bleach. It's raining hard, this is good – it will make the CCTV less useful. I close the door and climb the metal steps. At the top of the stairs I look back at the apartment. Lights are out, blind down, it all looks quiet and peaceful; from the outside you would never be able to tell that the apartment contained the slaughtered remains of a happy family. I stride off through the rain, up to Essex Road. I weave between people, taking a circuitous route back to my room. It's Christmas Eve. At least I have a little windfall now to help me through this appalling time of year. I will take the overalls to the Laundromat, then I must get rid of them, the boots and the jacket. The clothes recycling bin at Old Street will be appropriate, I will dump these borrowed jeans in there as well. There is absolutely nothing to connect me to Jenny and Will, nothing at all. The police in their infinite stupidity will spend days, if not weeks, chasing around the wrong woods barking up the wrong trees. I let slip a small cold smile as I rush alongside the other people out and about, going to work or off to do Christmas shopping. I cut down Greenman Street, Popham Road and into Coleman Fields; there are no CCTV cameras covering the parts of the streets I walk down and I make it to my door unobserved.

Back in my room I open a tin of pear quarters and consume them, – I'm ravenous. I strip off and bundle my clothes into a black plastic rubbish sack ready to take to the Laundromat. I extract the large bundle of banknotes from the pocket of the jacket and throw them on the bed alongside the two knives and their paper wrapping. I feel calm and content, I have rid myself of an annoying irritant, a stone in my shoe. I can relax and enjoy the festive break without having to be burdened by the existence of Will and Jenny. I suspect they will be found either tomorrow or Boxing Day. There are no papers on Christmas Day but on Boxing Day a good gory murder of a couple of stalwart middle-class citizens should be just the thing for the tabloid front pages. If not, well, that's ok too, but my theory is that they occupy the kind of space in society that cannot be ignored: the murder of those particular people will not go unnoticed in the same way as the brutal disassembling of a prostitute, because they are 'proper' people.

Fuck them. Fuck them all. I feel a rage and I want to return to the apartment and cut those fuckers up into little bits. I calm myself, – I cannot return – it would be to guarantee my capture and I am not yet ready for capture.

Under the hot water of the shower I close my eyes and replay the scene from earlier. I enjoy it and wash away the smell of dead woman and child from my body. I dress and grab the bag of clothes. I stash the cash taking one £50 note with me and leave for the Laundromat. It's 11 am. I sit in the Laundromat watching the clothes tumble in the large IPSO commercial washing machine, an

18lb front-loader, these are recent machines. The owner had a refit in the last few years and dumped most of the old American 'Washcomat' machines (apart from a few of the really large ones) and installed the newer but also American, IPSO machines distributed out of Halifax USA,. The advantage being that they have a twenty-seven minute cycle. He has also installed the 45lb stack dryers, which dry faster and cost more. I suspect that running a Laundromat is a profitable business. The walls are littered with various signs about service washes "not available on Xmas Eve", opening and closing times "8 am – 9 pm Mon – Sat 9 am – 7 pm Sun all year inc Xmas day", and a load of other rules and regulations: "no alcohol, no hot food, no animals allowed, would patrons kindly refrain from spitting". There is a slate-grey washing powder machine that dispenses a cup of 'Wonder Powder', according to the sticker on the front of the metal cabinet, for 20p. I decide to throw the boots in with the other stuff, better sure than sorry. Time spins around in synch with the machine. It's set on the hottest wash – might as well try and boil away my sins. I wonder for a moment about what Jamillia the Cunt and my son are doing this Christmas. I expect I have this thought every year at this time, though I can't recall that I have ever had it before. I shake it off, it's unwelcome, and stare harder at the spinning black jacket through the damp porthole that shows the inside of the washing machine. I may have placed too much washing powder in the machine as the smears and lather of white liquid are thick and glutinous. I couldn't care less. The thought has gone. The machine enters its spin cycle and shakes and quivers like jelly at a children's party.

I transfer the washing to the line of large yellow dryers and feed it with coins. I can see the CCTV in the corner of the Laundromat. I think, although I have no real reason to, that the owner is too cheap to fit real cameras, or at least re-uses the cards each day to save money. Anyway I am doing some washing – the only strange thing would be that I threw in a pair of work boots, and if asked, I gave the clothes to charity. How would I feel if I was arrested? I wouldn't care; they would be hard-pressed to prove anything and I don't have anything to lose, so fuck them,. They are so fucking stupid that they couldn't catch me – even if I confessed. They will waste a lot of time trying to figure out which of the many people that Will and Jenny knew could have had a motive for killing them. I have no motive, at least not any that they would understand. Complete alienation from society and a visceral hatred of people who have the things I desire but am unequipped to get is not something your average plod could fathom. The drying fabric and leather turn, the boots make a rhythmic clunking as they tumble about in the dryer. It's a reassuring noise, like the clickety click of rail carriages at night on a long journey. The idea of spending the rest of my life in a warm jail with regular meals and educational and recreational facilities is not abhorrent to me. I would miss the walking through the London streets, but then again, that is only me retracing the steps of a failed past. Jail would represent a new start for me, but they have to catch me first and they don't even know that I have killed anyone.

The dryer stops turning and I open the large circular glass door. A gust of heated and lint-laden air hits me in the face. The coat is still damp, but the overalls and the jeans and boots are dry enough. I remove them and shut the door, feed in a few more coins, and the drum starts up again. I stuff the dry clothes and boots into the bag and sit and watch the coat turn and bash against the door. It reminds me of a drowning man hammering at a porthole trying to get out of a water-filled tunnel as I watch him drown. The rest of the world recedes as I watch the drowning man clutching at nothing, spinning around and over and over. I see Will's face in the coat and then the machine stops and the coat flops to the bottom of the machine.

Dead.

I sit for a minute or so before standing and retrieving the coat from the dryer, placing it in the bag. I put on my own coat and hat and leave the Laundromat. The walk to the recycling bins is not a long one, perhaps twenty minutes. The large black wheelie bins lurk in a recess of the New North Road at the Old Street end. I push the clothes inside the clothing bin, and the boots into the shoe bin. I scrunch the plastic bag into my pocket and walk away. I am entertained by the idea that my clothes will soon grace the bodies of the homeless or some other good cause. Smiling, I walk home, stopping at the Co-op supermarket wedged under the Gainsborough Studios, a very plush apartment block, part of which overlooks the canal. By the time I get to my room I am thankful to be out of the cold. I eat and lie down for a rest – it has been a long morning and I am starting to feel tired. I close my eyes for a moment and sleep takes me to the other place.

Chapter 19: **I Wish You a Merry Christmas**

I stand in my room and although it's in complete darkness I can see everything in detail. My own sleeping body lying under the duvet, one foot sticking out from under the edge like an abandoned toy. I see the top of my head poking out of the top of the covers, my face pushed down into the pillow, skin sagging and bent under the pressure, my hair grey and greasy, my face half obscured.

Am I standing outside my body looking around? Or am I inside my body and my dreaming mind has constructed this image? There's nothing I can do that can confirm the position I now find myself in. I think I will just accept the situation. I look around. There is Yuko's handbag – didn't I throw it away? I haven't seen her since I threw her off the bridge before bringing Will and Jenny's self-satisfied existence to an end. I am glad I did, it was a worthwhile action, a little vengeance from the underside. I see my sharp knives resting in the sink and my clothes lying on the floor. I turn and walk out of the door across the hall to the empty room. I spot a trail of peanut shells lying across the floor and disappearing up the stairs; it seems the bawling landlady has been shouting her way around the house, I must cut off that cockroach's head before I leave... am I leaving? Strange. I have no plans to go anywhere but she is a cunt and deserves to have her throat cut, although that would disturb the musical symmetry of my murder quartet and have me heading toward a symphony. I am not yet ready for a symphony of death.

Soon, but not yet.

I try the door to the always-empty room; it doesn't move; I shove against it with my shoulder and it shifts slowly as if there is something on the other side obstructing it. The room is empty. I walk across to the other door, the one that leads out to the lightwell, and twist the handle. A light mist spills through, like smoke from an autumn bonfire; it curls and shifts and fills the room with remarkable speed enveloping me and making the room vanish. Under my feet is the familiar smooth and perfect Portland Stone pavement, leading away straight as a girder into the featureless distance, a flat calm mirror-ocean to my right. The pavement is warm under my feet, the air is cold around my body.

I walk.

I walk naked along the straight pavement. I walk and the towers of black rock start to appear around me. I can see a figure ahead in the distance; I can't make out who it is, but he or she seems to be dressed in red. It walks towards me.

To my amusement I see that it's the man from the theatre wearing a Santa outfit and holding the hand of the little girl he was fisting in the alpine chalet. Why do I feel reassured by seeing this monstrous creature? He lets out a lascivious toothless grin and waves his free hand in welcome. I stand and let him approach.

"Merry Christmas to you," he says.

I say nothing, just look at him.

"We are pleased to see that you are getting better.".

"Yes, you are nearly ready," says the little girl, her voice chiming out in the silence.

She then drops her dress and runs naked into a mirror-like sea and starts to swim away. I watch.

"One more thing and you will be ready to join [us]."

"I don't want to join you."

"Yes you do. The other place has no use for you, nor you for it. Here is where you must come."

With that, he too walks to the water's edge and swims away. I return to walking along the pavement. After a short while I see another figure sitting on a block of stone next to the pavement. It is Yuko. I stomp past unable to look at her, but I feel her eyes on my back as I walk away.

"Why did you kill me?"

I walk on, ignoring the question. Ahead, the pavement seems to run straight into one of those huge intimidating blocks of rock. I walk on, unperturbed by the imminent ending of the pavement. There is no obvious entrance or doorway or anything other than a wall of impenetrable rough solid rock rising up high in front of me. I consider my options. To go back is probably impossible, but I turn and take a look; sure enough, after a few metres everything fades into nothing. – Imagine being in a pitch black room where you can see nothing, not even your hand, in front of your face; now take away the darkness and leave nothing. It's sort of like that.

I decide to scout around the edge of the block, perhaps the pavement comes out on the other side. I turn the corner to be greeted with a continued wall of featureless rock and no pavement emerging from underneath. Instead there is a small stunted tree set about five metres away from the wall of rock. In amongst the leaves I can see what appears to be a small frog. I stare at the small green creature and it stares back, the bulbous eyes on either side of its head fixed on me. It starts to grow and I can see in its eyes a replay of my most recent murder. There is me knocking on the door and thrusting my knife into Will's throat. I'm smiling. I didn't realise that I was smiling as I carried out these things, but I am. As I shove the knife into Jenny I have a broad grin. I see myself trash the Christmas tree and I see myself fixing breakfast and behind me, as I eat, I also see the theatre man. I step back and the frog shrinks back to its normal tiny self. I look around and see that an entrance is now visible in the wall of rock. I shrug and walk inside. The light seeping in from outside soon wanes and is replaced by a low, gloomy radiance. If misery had been converted into light this is what it would be like. It provides enough illumination to see the floor and a few feet ahead, but it's the most reluctant light that ever existed. I am standing in a long narrow tunnel with a curved roof and flat floor, made of thousands of tiny deep blue tiles. I walk down the blue pathway., I see there are small alcoves set back in the side of the tunnel. In the first one there are three bats hanging upside down: they are silver-grey in colour and sleeping. They remind me of the bats that lived in the attic of my childhood house. The ones my father smoked out and then shot. I walk on – another alcove – inside this is a crushed and broken child's bicycle, the one that was run over by the ice cream van when I was six. The third alcove is in the opposite wall and contains a small metal unicorn and a large metal cube; I don't know the meaning of these objects. I decide to ignore any future alcoves, no matter how interesting they may seem. Ahead of me I see a low arched wooden door. For all its look of age and stiffness the door swings freely and opens wide. I step through into a cavern; the walls and floor are covered in a soft green moss and some kind of roots criss-cross the floor, converging around a large old and ornate writing desk. It is the Bureau du Roi – an 18th century cylinder desk also called "Bureau Kaunitz".

I see an open wooden trapdoor with a set of rickety wooden stairs leading down. The staircase curls down around itself into a beautiful sunlit room. It's a remarkable surprise to find this healthy, revitalising force in this dark world., it's something that has been missing in both my worlds for many years. Sunlight, not the weak, brittle light of winter and of London, more the warm, round, heavy sunlight of the tropics, the sunlight of California, the sunshine of growth and abundance. How odd to find a room full of it in my subconscious.

I reach the bottom of the steps. There's a wall of ramshackle windows to my right and old skylights to my left. The light streams in through both. I feel delighted to be here. I want to look out through the window, but I realise I must not – though I have no idea why. I notice a door in the far wall of the room more of a hatchway, like those you see in the bowels of ocean-going ships. I don't want to leave the sun-filled room, but I have no choice. I push the hatch, it's heavy but moves with ease. I step over the metal lip and into a gloomy chamber. I have been here before: it's the room in the ship's hold. In front of me is the table, and sitting on it are the three tumblers, two of which are empty. This time there is no trussed up naked woman hanging above the table and no drooling dog under it either. There is just the table and the one tumbler of dark brown spicy liquid. My mouth waters at the prospect of drinking it. I walk to the table and up-end the glass into my mouth swallowing.

Everything dissolves into darkness. I hang inside the dark, suspended like a fly in a dark web, I like the feeling, there's no up nor down, no sound and no sight, nothing is demanded of me. My consciousness fades.

My eyes open. I'm surprised there was no violence in this dream. I feel refreshed rather than depleted by this sleep.

Christmas Day. I wish myself a very merry Christmas and smile – what a stupid fucking concept. I masturbate to mental images of Will and Jenny fucking each other then I shower. I sit on my bed and stare at my twisted feet for an hour or two. Time hangs in the air of my room, each second is palpable – they don't so much pass as expire –dying one after the other and falling to the floor, littering the threadbare carpet. Thousands upon thousands of these dead little husks of time lie shadowlike on the floor, the bed, everywhere. I amuse myself by imagining that I am killing each second in person, throttling this one and stabbing that one. Can I wait a minute and massacre 60 in one go? I'm bored of this game and wade through the corpses of dead seconds to open a tin of sardines. Christmas day, what a fucking waste of time, the day that the Son of God, who's not the Son of God wasn't born. The only good thing about this day is that the streets are quiet and everything is closed, well, except the Asian shops and the Turkish restaurants and shops over in Stoke Newington. Good thing – because that's where I am going to get my Christmas day kebab. I wonder if they have discovered Will and Jenny and baby Crawford yet? I shall walk past and take a look. There's that murderer-revisiting-the-scene-of-the-crime thing happening again. I reach for my clothes, only to find that I have no clean underwear; I took all the killing garments to the Laundromat but forgot to take any of my daily dirty laundry.

"*Shit.*"

I pick up a pair that has been in the laundry bag for a week or so; they should have aired out by now. I pull on the rest of my clothes, shoes and coat, and grab another £50 note from the pile. I pick up my phone: there's a text message from Martha wishing me a merry Christmas. It's been there since last night, I just hadn't noticed. I think I can deal with seeing Martha again. I don't like her but she's marginally better than nothing. I think this as I tramp along the hall., I open the door and stand stock still in shock. I had not calculated for this.

Snow.

Chapter 20: **Slay Ride**

Thick white snow covers everything. It descends like a slow motion shroud, wrapping everything in its cold clammy folds. Nothing is omitted. It falls with a relentless certainty that only natural phenomena possess. I stare. The snow has removed perspective from the world. I gaze out at an infinity curve of purposeless grace. I shut the door and return downstairs to my room. This surprise requires new attire. I rummage around under the bed until I find an old pair of walking boots, they have lain there forgotten for at least ten years, of course, the advantage of getting old is that your feet stay the same size. I recover my hat and scarf from under a pile of trash and find mismatching gloves. Now I can leave the building knowing a different, more uniform world has replaced the one I know, and that ordinary things will be unrecognisable. I feel a shiver of pleasure at the prospect that the world I loathe has, for a short duration, been obliterated and replaced with a newer, more sympathetic landscape.

The snow is falling thicker and with an urgency that makes the idea of walking to Stoke Newington even more appealing. I step into the virgin snow and shut the door. The crunch of my foot as it sinks, an inch or more, into the feather-like layer of flakes is like the sound of money to a banker. I walk down the steps and into a blizzard. There's no wind and the snow falls straight down, but in the haphazard way that other sky-borne water doesn't possess. The sky is dark grey and seems to start only a few feet above my head. I can see only a dozen or so metres in any direction. I laugh.

"This is fucking great."

I set off for Packington Street to see what is happening at number 78. It takes only a few seconds for the front of my jacket, hat and scarf to be covered in a layer of snow, and I've left only a slit open between hat and scarf for my eyes. Even so, snowflakes settle on my eye lashes, creating small, out-of-focus drops of water as they melt under the heat of my body. Every so often I brush the snow off, and then after the third or so time I stop. Why bother? I will become a walking snowman. The journey to Packington Street takes about double the normal time, and at the bottom I look up toward 78. It has become so dark the streetlights have come on and I can see the bright orange snowflakes rushing past and around the light like frenetic moths. A car trundles past, moving in a slow, careful way as if unsure what this new environment might contain. I cross the road and walk up Packington Street on the same side as the apartment. I see no blue flashing lights as I draw up alongside the gate, no police tape nor signs of life. They have not been found yet and the snow will remove any traces of my outside presence. I smile a quiet smile although perhaps a little disappointed that my handiwork remains undiscovered. I trudge up onto the Essex Road. All the shops are shut and the road deserted. I like this feeling of being the only living thing on the planet; the effect is spoiled when an Islington fox scampers out from Britannia Row and across the road. My walk along Essex Road and over onto Newington Green Road is quiet as a grave. The snow has removed the pavements though I can feel their strength lying under the soft white covering. Some of the Turkish shops along Newington Green Road are open and there are a few people in the street, lumbering along like textile snowmen. No one acknowledges each other. I walk past the darkened Weavers Arms and notice that the Turkish tyre shop opposite is open. Strange. I turn left into Barretts Grove, a long residential street of houses, many of which sport unpleasant flashing Christmas decorations in the windows, garish outlines of reindeer and Santa in his sleigh and all manner of other shapes, all made, no doubt, in some sweat-drenched basement by Chinese children. I heave myself along the street. I am fascinated by the fact that no one is out in the snow, playing. Soon I will arrive on Stokey High Street and from there it is only a short distance to the Turkish restaurant where I have decided to eat my Christmas day meal. Testi was made famous a few years back for a gunfight that took place there. Two rival drug gangs' war spilled over into the normal world when one gang took it upon itself to attack the leader of the other gang as he was eating dinner with his family. Seven people were killed – mostly innocent diners and staff – it made the papers and TV. The restaurant recovered and now has a fine reputation. This will be my first visit to the establishment.

I hit Stoke Newington High Street about a quarter of a mile downstream from Testi. A river of snow has washed the road away. The last pathetic daylight dies, a wind has started up, the shop and streetlights flicker through the dense curtain of snowflakes that whirl in incomprehensible patterns to the ground, and then, as if defying gravity, some of them lift back up into the air to dart to the left or right as if not satisfied with the places they came to rest.

I turn left and work my way up the High Street. It's hard going, the wind is driving snow into my face and piling it up around my boots. I am enjoying the sensation; the flakes melt on my face as I march toward Testi. This part of the High Street defies the usual Christmas day shutdown that hits London. The shops, restaurants and barbers salons are open and the lights burst through the thick snow. There are not many people about but there are a few braving the weather for a pint of milk or a haircut. I reach Testi: its umber light glows out onto the street turning the snow from white to a puerile orange inviting me inside as I stare in through the window. The long charcoal grill smokes alongside the glass cabinet displaying meats on skewers and trays of liver and sheep's testicles. There are only a few people inside, and the man tasked with minding the grill pokes at the coals in an absent-minded way as a few lumps of meat on long flat metal skewers sizzle over them. The walls inside are painted a dark shade of orange and are covered in trinkets, the tables are wooden and the floor tiled. I stand under the green awning taking in the menu; the snow is less intense here in the shelter of the shop front. The food looks good and thanks to the reluctant generosity of Will and Jenny I can afford to eat here.

I push open the door and am greeted by a blast of warmth and the smoky tang of grilled meat. I stamp the snow off my boots and wipe down my jacket. A small Turkish man with a grin like a mantrap rushes over to welcome me, telling me to sit anywhere I want. The place isn't busy; there's a family group in the far corner: a man and a woman with their backs to me and opposite them a young girl and a boy, perhaps about seven, and five years old. The children look vaguely familiar, but then all children look the same. There is a table near the grill that has several Turkish-looking women sat around it; I assume they are relatives of the staff and owner, they talk amongst themselves drinking small glasses of Turkish tea. Other than that and a solitary couple in the corner, whose faces I cannot see, the place is empty. I choose the table behind the family group, hang my coat on the back of the chair and grab the menu. I'm famished. I look outside: the snow is falling with more intensity, as if yearning to escape from the sky. I see occasional headlights glide past, and the indistinct shape of a large yellow municipal snowplough lumbers past spraying snow up onto the already groaning pavement. I turn back to the menu. 'Pizola', that's my choice: lamb chops charcoal-grilled, served with rice and salad, accompanied by 'Pide' or Turkish bread, and to drink, a glass or two of Turkish tea. I glance around for a waiter and find the small man with the grin that could kill standing by my shoulder. I suppose he has nothing much to do, but I am disconcerted by his stealth. I order.

The children at the table near me seem more familiar. I try to get a better look at them but every time I try to fix them in my line of vision they move, or turn their heads, and I can never look at them for long enough. I find it exasperating and turn to watch the other diners. No one pays me the slightest attention. I may as well not be there except for the fact that the small grinning man is watching me with a hawkish look. I turn away and read the notes attached to the menu. Testi, it turns out, is the Turkish word for jug;

marinated lamb's testicles are on the menu, along with an impressive variety of grilled offal. The offal brings back a memory of Yuko – I shrug it off, that event feels like a million years away – from another world. My tea arrives in a small wide-lipped glass with a metal holder. It has fresh mint leaves inside the amber liquid, curls of steam drift off the top. It tastes strong and earthy. The Pizola arrives shortly after the tea, along with plates of assorted salad including roasted onions in a pomegranate pickle, and a wooden bowl of flatbread. The chops are roasted to perfection with a thick black crust on the outside and pink flesh on the inside; the rice is pert and fluffy.

I focus on the food. Biting into the chop is an intense experience and I allow my mouth to savour the flavour of something other than soy milk porridge and tinned sardines. It's been a long time since I have eaten food this good, Access to fine tasting food is not something that should depend on money. My soul shivers with a sensual delight at this contact, as if waking up from a long bad dream. My mouth waters and I drool some saliva onto my plate. I glance around, quickly wiping my mouth with the napkin – of course nobody has noticed. I start on the second of the four chops. Again, I feel a shudder in my body as the taste explodes in my mouth. I shovel forkfuls of rice into my mouth. I must look like a starved man with his first plate of food; in a way I suppose I am. It all tastes so superb, the way a condemned man's last meal should taste, though I think the knowledge of impending doom might blunt the taste buds somewhat. Whereas the fact that I have had to kill to get this meal makes me like some primeval hunter and has heightened my senses. I'm halfway through the third lamb chop and have made short work of the onion and bread, when I glance up from my work on the food to see the young girl at the table in front looking straight at me. I realise where I have seen her before. She is the girl in the chalet with the man from the theatre, the one he was fist-fucking in my dream. I halt all my movement, the dripping lamb chop motionless, held by my hand on its way to my mouth. The girl lets out a small demure knowing smile and returns to her food. It can't be her – she's not real – my mind is tricking me. I move only my eyes to look at the boy sitting next to her. He's wearing a tidy tweed jacket and white shirt buttoned up tight at the neck.

"Fuck." I mutter under my breath. It's me – me at five years old in the house on the fiord. The boy is subdued, head down eating slowly. I place my lamb chop back on the plate. I'm wary and anxious; the rational part of my mind is whirring, trying to work out what is going on. Perhaps I have seen these children before – on the street somewhere –registered them subconsciously and then used them in my dreams in some way? They can't be from my dreams, that's not possible.

"They are, they are." Screams the other part of my mind, the part that is telling me to get the fuck out of the restaurant and get out right now. I force myself to stay in my seat and turn my head just enough to look at the rest of the room. I don't want to give any indication that I have seen anything untoward. I notice the couple are talking intently – I still can't see their faces and the Turkish women have fallen silent: they are staring at the grinning man who is not grinning anymore. They are all staring at the man tending the grill as he picks up a long pointed skewer and walks towards the couple. His feet make no sound on the tiled floor; they should but they don't. He paces up behind the woman, the skewer gripped in his hand, knuckles white with tension. I look back at the table where the children sit. The boy is looking up: he sports a livid black eye. I turn back to the couple. The grill cook has reached the back of the woman. He stands silent and still behind her, waiting – waiting for what? I feel an urge to shout out a warning but no sound will exit from my throat. I hear chair legs grating on the floor as they are moved.

The adults with the children have stood up and now I can see them. The man from the theatre and the woman from the house by the sea: my heart shrinks and my stomach turns a double flip inside my body. They are transfixed, watching the unfolding scenario of the couple and the grill cook, – he has grabbed the woman's hair and thrusts the skewer into her just where the jaw joins the neck. Blood spurts and she slumps forward – the man with her pays no attention – he looks up and I recognise William Crawford. I push my chair back and get to my feet. My legs feel weak. I ignore my coat, and whirl and run to the door, followed only by the hushed eyes of the silent Turkish women. I reach the door and yank it open. Snow whirls in accompanied by an icy cold burst of air. The snow curls around me like cold fingers and pulls me out into the street.

Outside I can see nothing, just a sheet of white. I hear sirens and a thundering sound. I dash across the street, the thundering rumble getting closer, there's flashing yellow lights above me and I see a snowplough bearing down out of control, and then, in a moment I am flying, in slow motion, through the air. I can see the driver of the snowplough, fear etched across his face. I smile as I make contact with the windscreen. It cracks and then I'm saying hello to a row of flashing yellow lights on the top of the cab and then it is gone. Higher and higher I sail. I see the snowplough from above, its beetle-like yellow shape with the silver jaws at the front, hurtling across the road. The creature mounts the pavement and leaps into the front of Testi clearing the snow from the pavement as it thunders in through the plate glass of the window, there is a tremendous grating and high pitched tinkling sound overlaid with human screeches and groans. I feel suspended in the air observing the broken bond of the pavement at the same time as seeing the truck disappear into the restaurant. The truck comes to a rest, the yellow amber of its flashing lights rotate out of the shattered restaurant façade and through the falling snow.

Time stops.

I see smoke coming out of the building. It caresses the snow in a strange dance of opposites, twisting up in rhythms that match the snow's descent. A column of smoke weaves through the thick but discreet sheet of flakes, followed by a sheet of roiling flame spilling out of the wrecked window and up the front of the building, evaporating the snow and filling my eyes with orange heat. I make brutal contact with the road: the panorama before me vanishes as does time.

I am in darkness, not the kind of dark caused by turning off a light, not the type of dark where you know there is something hidden in the absence of light. This is the dark in which nothing ever was, is, or will be. I am suspended or surrounded or immersed in nothing, this is the absolute absence of anything. I am here, wherever 'here' is. I have no feeling, no body, just a pinprick of thought in Nothing. No up no down, no anywhere, no direction. Am I dead? Is this death just a micron of thought inside an infinity of nothingness? It doesn't feel like anything, there's no time. I can think I suppose, though I don't care to; any life I may have had is irrelevant to me here, though there is no 'here' for anything to be relevant to in any case. I like this place but it's not a place – perhaps it is an instance of nothing – is this what it was like or is like before the universe existed? Nothing. I like Nothing, it's undemanding. I feel something in this vastness of empty void.? A pinprick of grey in the corner of my thought: it spreads. The nothing retreats under the onslaught of something. Dammit, I want the nothing back but the grey has taken over and I can feel again. I have a body and it is still and flat, my sense of feeling is returning. Something is stuck in my throat and I can feel air being forced into my lungs; I can't feel my arms or legs, maybe I no longer have arms or legs. I can feel my head resting on something soft. Is this one of my dreams? My eyes are firmly shut and through the eyelids I can sense light of some kind. I hear voices:

"We're not sure of his condition. There is intermittent brain function but as you can see he's unable to breath unassisted, has 1st degree burns to his face and upper body."

" Will he come out of this coma?"

"Impossible to tell. Do you know what happened and who he is?"

"All we know is that the vehicle crashed into the restaurant ruptured a main gas pipe and the hot coals from the grill ignited it causing the explosion. Everyone in the restaurant died in the resulting fire. We've no idea who he is, no ID, his fingerprints aren't on file and the universal DNA register said he's a 43 year old mother of three."

"Yeah that software has been a billion pound problem for years"

So he's a bit of a mystery."

"Well, regulations state that after two weeks we have to turn off the machines."

"I know"

He should be on DNA register, everyone is.

"Well he isn't. Anyway once you turn him off, it's not our problem."

I hear the door shut as the talkers leave. I am in a hospital. That's boring. I fade into the nothing again.

The fog opens to the rocky flat landscape. The pavement is there, so flat, warm and welcoming. I can see the mirror-calm ocean and the towers of black rock in the distance. It all rushes away to be replaced by the sound of footsteps.

I hear a door open. People are standing by my bed. I can hear them talking about me, about my coma. I could open my eyes if I wanted to. I just don't.

In the back of my mind I can see the pavement.
I hear it calling me, warm and welcoming.
There's nothing for me in this world.
The pavement calls and I answer.